A
Killer Clue

Also by Victoria Gilbert

The Hunter and Clewe Mysteries
A Cryptic Clue
The Book Lover's B&B Mysteries
A Fatal Booking
Reserved for Murder
Booked for Death
The Blue Ridge Library Mysteries
Murder Checks Out
Death in the Margins
Renewed for Murder
A Deadly Edition
Bound for Murder
Past Due for Murder
Shelved Under Murder
A Murder for the Books
The Mirror of Immortality Series
Scepter of Fire
Crown of Ice

A
Killer Clue

A HUNTER AND CLEWE MYSTERY

Victoria Gilbert

CROOKED
LANE

NEW YORK

Copyright © 2024 by Vicki L. Weavil

Published in the United States by Crooked Lane Books, an imprint of The Quick Brown Fox & Company LLC.

Crooked Lane Books and its logo are trademarks of The Quick Brown Fox & Company LLC.

Library of Congress Catalog-in-Publication data available upon request.

ISBN (hardcover): 978-1-63910-643-1
ISBN (ebook): 978-1-63910-644-8

Cover design by Alan Ayers

Printed in the United States.

www.crookedlanebooks.com

Crooked Lane Books
34 West 27th St., 10th Floor
New York, NY 10001

First Edition: September 2024

10 9 8 7 6 5 4 3 2 1

Dedicated, with thanks, to my editor,
Faith Black Ross—
who makes all my books so much better.

Chapter One

I've often been told that one shouldn't live in the past. Which is good advice, but ignores one crucial fact—the past lives in us.

Although he was only in his thirties, I knew his past weighed heavily on my boss, Cameron Clewe. Slumped against a bookshelf in the library of Aircroft, the elegant estate he'd inherited from his wealthy stepfather, Cam appeared defeated.

"So the latest private investigation came up empty, just like all the others?" I asked, rolling my chair away from the large antique desk I used as a work space. I studied Cam for a moment. Dressed in tailored ivory linen pants and a pale jade polo shirt, the tall, slender young man looked like he'd stepped out of an advertisement in an upscale men's magazine.

"Unfortunately. It seems my father remains a ghost." Cam shrugged. "Perhaps because that's what he is. We don't even know if he's still alive."

The polished walnut of the bookcase made the perfect backdrop for Cam's shaggy auburn hair. He had the lean build of a runner or swimmer; sports he'd told me he enjoyed. Although knowing what a loner he was, I doubted he'd ever been part of a team. He was definitely handsome, but his good looks were somewhat dampened by the anxiety haunting his sea-green eyes.

"Maybe," I said, "but it's just as likely he's simply disappeared. I'm guessing he'd be somewhere in his mid-sixties, so there's no reason to think he's dead."

A faint smile curved Cam's thin lips. "True. That isn't extremely old."

I crossed my arms over my chest. "I'm not just saying that because I'm sixty-one."

"I'd never imagine you would." Cam strolled over to the desk and picked up a hardbound book before peering at the screen of my laptop. "I'm always fascinated by this, Jane. All the information you have to enter, in a specific order, and with just the right punctuation. It's almost like a code."

"No mystery, just cataloging," I said.

Cam flipped open the book. "*Dance of Death* by Helen McCloy. Her first novel, if I remember correctly."

"Yes, published in 1938. You know, she lived to be ninety, and was still having books published in her late seventies." I leaned back in my chair and met Cam's amused gaze.

"Point taken." Cam's expression sobered. "But even if my dad is still alive, it seems he doesn't want to be found. Not that it should surprise me. He's never tried to contact me."

"To be fair, your stepfather told him you'd died only a few months after your mom passed away."

"Good old Albert Clewe. He definitely didn't want me to know he wasn't my biological father." Cam laid the book back on the desk. "He could've told me, you know. It wouldn't have made that much difference. We weren't terribly close anyway."

"I think maybe it was more about pride than anything else," I said.

"He certainly had plenty of that." Cam looked over at the open door of the library. "I hear Lauren."

The staccato beat of high heels tapping against wood floors grew louder. *That's definitely Lauren. The new housekeeper, Jenna Brown, wears flat shoes, like me, and we're the only other women on the estate.*

Lauren Walker stepped into the library. An attractive young woman, she always dressed the part of a personal assistant to a wealthy boss. Today her shantung silk dress discreetly displayed her lovely figure, its peach shade a perfect complement to her dark complexion.

"There you are, Cam. I've been looking all over for you." Lauren swept a hand through her black curls. Her stern expression softened as she examined the two of us. "Of course, I should've known you'd be in here if you weren't in your office."

"Cam was just sharing some news with me," I said.

Lauren's dark eyes narrowed. "About the ongoing search for your father, I suppose." She shared a sympathetic glance with me. "I know you've been preoccupied with that lately, Cam, but you still need to keep track of meetings and other business dealings. Did you forget you have an appointment today?"

"Refresh my memory—who's coming?" Cam's tone was tinged with wariness. He wasn't fond of people visiting Aircroft unless they were friends or, at the very least, acquaintances he knew well.

"That woman who runs the bookshop in Chapel Hill. Eloise something. She's delivering a book you requested." Lauren glanced at the delicate gold watch encircling her slender wrist. "She'll probably be here any minute. Do you want me to bring her here, or would you rather meet in your office?"

Cam thrust his hands into his pockets. "Here is fine, and it's Eloise Anderson. She runs Last Chapter Bookshop. I'm sure you've seen that name on invoices."

"Oh, right." Lauren fixed Cam with an inquiring stare. "Why is she driving an hour and a half to deliver a book? She's always shipped everything before."

"I think she may have another agenda." Cam rocked back on his heels. "At least, that's my educated guess."

"And what might that be?" Lauren asked.

"Not to tap me for money, if that's what you're worried about." Cam straightened and slipped his hands from his pockets. "I'd rather not say more, if you don't mind. It would be a shame to share her personal information if I'm wrong."

The doorbell chimed. "Well, I'd better go and welcome her." Lauren turned and tip-tapped her way down the corridor that led to the front entry hall.

I stood. "If you have a meeting, I should probably disappear for a bit. Honestly, I don't mind the break. Cataloging your book collections is interesting, but sometimes I need to get up and walk so my knees don't stiffen up." I shot Cam a grin. "You know, since I'm so old."

"You're not, and I'd like you to stay," Cam said as footsteps rang out again from the hall. "If Eloise is here for the reason I suspect, her business may involve you."

"Really? Why would that be?" I circled around the desk to stand next to him.

"You'll see. If I'm right, that is." Cam brushed a lock of hair away from his forehead as Lauren reappeared in the doorway, accompanied by a short, curvaceous, young woman. She wore emerald-green glasses and her round face was framed by a sleek bob of dark blonde hair.

"Cam, Jane—this is Eloise Anderson." Lauren waved a hand toward us. "And this is Cameron Clewe, along with Jane Hunter, who's a librarian hired to catalog Cam's book and ephemera collections."

The young woman offered a tentative smile. Her eyes—clear blue as a summer sky—shone brightly behind the lenses of her glasses. "Very nice to meet you both," she said. "Of course, I know Cam, if only through the emails and texts we've shared over the last few years."

"Right, well, I'll leave you to your meeting." Lauren took a few steps before turning around in the doorway. "Sorry, I should've asked if you'd like something to drink, Ms. Anderson. I'm happy to get some water or tea or whatever you might want."

"No, no, I'm fine." Eloise clutched the wrapped package she was holding closer to her chest. "But thanks so much, Ms. Walker."

"Just Lauren is fine." Flashing a bright smile, Lauren disappeared into the hall.

"Is that the book you brought?" I asked, pointing toward the package. "It must be quite valuable for you to want to hand-deliver it."

"Oh no, that isn't it. I mean, the book is something you wanted, Cam. That first edition of *The Cape Cod Mystery* by Phoebe Atwood Taylor. But I could've sent it to you, only . . ."

Cam's fingers beat a tattoo against the top edge of the desk. "Only that's not why you decided to come in person, was it, Eloise? The book was an excuse."

"Okay, now you really need to explain," I said, allowing exasperation to color my tone. Sometimes Cam's directness registered as rudeness.

"Eloise is actually here because she wants my help." Cam lifted his hands. "And yours, Jane, since you're my partner in our amateur sleuthing operation."

"What do you mean?" I turned to Eloise. "I thought you were a book dealer."

"I am," she said, meeting my inquiring gaze. "But your boss is right—I'm also here to ask a favor." She squared her shoulders and shifted her focus to Cam. "I want you to help me prove my mother was not a murderer."

Chapter Two

"A little late, isn't it? From what I've read, she was convicted after a lengthy trial and spent many years in prison." Cam's gaze remained laser-focused on Eloise, despite my attempt to get his attention.

Eloise lifted her chin and met Cam's intense stare with a defiant glare of her own. "It's true that my mother was in jail for fifteen years. She died recently, still in prison, but I suppose you already know that."

Standing your ground. Good for you. I turned to Eloise and waved a hand toward one of the wingback chairs placed on either side of a small cherry table. "Have a seat, Eloise."

"Oh right, I forgot that." The color rose in Cam's face, throwing his smattering of freckles into high relief. "Please sit down."

Eloise sank down into the upholstered chair, setting her package and purse on the table beside her. From the appreciative gaze she cast around the room, I could tell that she was as impressed by the library as I'd been when I'd first seen it.

Cam shot me a sheepish look before grabbing the task chair at the desk and rolling it over to face the two armchairs. "You take the other comfortable chair, Jane. I'll use this."

"Thank you." I cast him a smile. I made it a point to acknowledge Cam's attempts to be more socially aware.

As I sat down, I observed Cam sneaking speculative looks at Eloise. *He's finally realized how cute she is,* I thought. Eloise fortunately didn't notice his scrutiny. She was too busy examining every inch of the library.

I could understand her interest—while the library didn't possess the grandeur of many other spaces at Aircroft, it was still beautiful, and certainly a room any book lover would appreciate. A stone fireplace dominated the far wall, but wooden bookcases polished to an ebony sheen flanked the fireplace and covered all the other walls. Beneath some of the bookcases were cabinets in the same dark wood, their brass hardware dulled by years of use. Gold and silver flourishes tooled into the leather spines of the older book volumes glinted under soft white lighting hidden beneath the shelves.

"What a magical library," Eloise said, her face glowing with appreciation.

This elicited a rare unforced smile from Cam. "Definitely one of my favorite rooms in the house. You'll have to examine the collection more closely before you leave."

Eloise smiled in return. "I'd love to."

I cleared my throat, hoping to get the conversation back on track. "You two have only spoken via email until today?"

"Some texts as well." Cam settled into the task chair, stretching his long legs out in front of him. "But it's been just a business relationship up to this point, continuing an arrangement started by my father long before I was born."

"We've worked with Cam for a few years. I mean, I have." Eloise dropped her gaze to her hands, which were tightly clasped in her lap. "My parents used to track down books for Cam's father, Albert, and I did too, up until he died. It's just me and a few part-time salespeople now. Our one long-term business partner retired a few years ago."

"You seem young to have taken all that on," I said. "But obviously you've handled it well, since you're still in business."

"I'm thirty-three." Eloise shrugged. "I know I don't look it, which everyone tells me is a good thing."

"It is. You'll be happy to look five to ten years younger than your actual age when you're as old as me," I said.

"Now Jane, I thought we'd established that you weren't that ancient," Cam said with a wry smile. He swiveled the task chair to face Eloise more directly. "Getting back to the reason for your visit, I confess I suspected it was the motive for this in-person delivery. When you said you were coming, I remembered reading up on your mother's case several years ago. It's a fascinating mystery. Supposedly solved, but in my opinion, as well as some other investigators', there are more than a few loose ends."

Eloise sat back. "And that's why I'm here. I discovered a lot of online chatter about how you'd gotten involved in some cold cases and uncovered the information needed to solve them. Which gave me hope. I thought maybe you'd be willing to help clear my mother's name."

"Most of those cases didn't involve murder, though." I frowned. The one murder case Cam and I had investigated had involved more danger than I was comfortable with.

"Only the first one, which wasn't exactly a cold case, although criminal actions from the past did play a part. Still, you have to admit, Jane, that the process is the same, murder or no murder." Cam leaned forward, gripping his knees with both hands. "Tell me, Eloise, why are you so sure your mother is innocent?"

"You mean beyond the fact that I loved her and know she wasn't capable of killing anyone, much less my dad?" Eloise's feathery brows drew together over her pert nose. "It's a lot of things. Evidence that didn't add up and the lack of a real motive, as well as her inability to kill an insect, much less a man. Over the years I pleaded with her to allow me to fight to reopen the case, but she always begged me not to. Then, a few months ago, she died suddenly." A tremor rippled through Eloise's voice. "When I saw the brief, but damning, news reports written about her after she passed, I knew I had to at least try to clear her name."

"I'm so sorry. What happened? She couldn't have been very old," I said.

"She had a bad heart. No one knew it, though, because she didn't share her symptoms with the prison health facility." Eloise lifted her free hand and wiped a tear from her cheek. "She was only fifty-seven."

"Younger than me," I said under my breath before adding, "Why do you think she was opposed to a reexamination of her case? That doesn't sound logical, especially if she was innocent."

Eloise shook her head. "I don't know. Maybe she didn't want to put me through the horrors of another trial."

"Or she was protecting someone." Cam's knee bounced as he tapped his heel against the floor. He stilled his leg when he caught my warning look. "Is it possible your mother suspected that someone she cared about, like a family member or close friend, had killed your father?"

Eloise straightened and fixed Cam with a sharp stare. "I can't imagine who that could've been. She wouldn't have hesitated to expose anyone if she truly thought they'd murdered Dad."

Cam settled back in his chair, his eyes as bright as his jade shirt as he intently studied Eloise. "Even you?"

Chapter Three

E loise leapt to her feet. "What are you suggesting?"

"Only that the one person your mother was most likely to protect was her daughter, even if that meant she ended up in jail instead of you." Cam clasped his hands in his lap.

To keep from anxiously gripping the chair arms, I thought as I turned to Eloise. "It's one possible reason your mom wouldn't let you reopen the case."

"You think she suspected me?" Eloise's voice rose to a squeak on the last word.

"Hard to say," Cam replied, pressing his palms against his thighs. "But to be clear, I don't think you're a murderer, Eloise. Nothing I've uncovered has made me question your innocence."

"You've already conducted some significant research on the case?" I asked.

"Several years ago. I might not remember it that clearly." Ignoring my snort, Cam gazed speculatively at Eloise. "Do you mind if I share the story, as I understand it?"

Slumping back down in her chair, Eloise murmured her assent.

Cam leaned back, cradling the back of his head in his linked fingers. "Eloise's mother was Abigail Anderson, called Abby by everyone who knew her. Her dad was Kenneth, better known as Ken. They owned Last Chapter Bookshop in Chapel Hill, North Carolina, along with a partner . . ." He looked toward Eloise.

"Neil Knight," she said.

"Right. Anyway, the shop specialized in vintage and rare books, which is why my father, who was nothing if not a collector, used their services."

Stepfather, I thought, but didn't correct Cam. That fact wasn't exactly public knowledge.

"By all accounts, Abby and Ken had a happy marriage, although like most small businesses they often faced financial challenges. They had one child, a daughter." As Cam lowered his arms, he indicated Eloise with a flourish of his fine-boned right hand.

"Mom was only twenty-three when I was born," Eloise said. "She took on a lot of responsibility pretty young."

"But so did you. I think you were still a teenager at the time of the murder, right?" Cam's expression softened, giving him a more boyish appearance.

Eloise nodded. "I'd just turned eighteen. Which was lucky, as it turned out."

"Because you weren't forced into the foster care system? Yes, that was fortunate." Cam continued his recitation of facts in a more dispassionate tone. "The family lived in an apartment above the shop. That was important to the case, because when the police arrived at the murder scene, they found all the entrances to the store locked."

"Or so they said," Eloise interjected. "Who knows if that's actually true?"

The gleam in Cam's eyes betrayed his increasing interest in Eloise, who was, I admitted, cannier than I'd initially thought. "Ken Anderson was discovered behind the bookshop counter, stabbed to death. The murder weapon, an ordinary knife that Abby confessed was kept at the counter to cut strings on packages, was later found in a far corner of the bookstacks. There were no prints on the knife, so the authorities assumed that the perpetrator had worn gloves." He shot me a glance. "It came out during the trial that Abby Anderson regularly wore gloves to bed because she had severely chapped hands and used a thick lotion she didn't want to get on the sheets. Those gloves were never found."

Eloise sliced the air with one hand. "Now wait, before you jump to conclusions, my mom said she threw them away because they were covered in blood. Not because she'd stabbed my dad, but from her attempts to save his life after she found him lying on the floor of the shop. He was already dead, but she was in shock and wanted to do anything she could to save him, so she pressed her hands over the wound. She tossed the gloves in the bin outside, which was emptied when the trash was collected later that morning."

I scooted forward in my chair. "I suppose the authorities checked the dump site?"

"They did, but the gloves were never found." Eloise bit her lower lip. "That was one of the things that convinced the jury that my mom's story was a lie."

"That and the fact that there was no evidence that anyone else was ever in the building that night or morning," Cam said. "Including you, I believe."

Color flushed Eloise's cheeks. "I was visiting my friend Lisa overnight."

"Something your mother supposedly insisted upon, according to that friend's parents." Cam tapped his fingers against his knees.

"She planned for you to be away, which also didn't look good after the fact."

"It wasn't like that. My mom suggested I stay overnight with Lisa because she'd just gotten a rejection from her top choice university and was despondent. That's what I was told, anyway. Mom and Lisa's mother were good friends. She said that's how she knew about the rejection letter. Only . . ." Eloise turned to me, biting her lower lip.

"Only Lisa's mother told the authorities that wasn't the truth," Cam said. "It was one more lie to add to the tally against Abby Anderson."

"I suppose it made it look like your mom wanted you out of the way." I cast Eloise a sympathetic glance. "Which would've created doubt about premeditation in the jurors' minds."

Eloise shifted in her chair. "I did think it was odd, especially when Lisa was totally surprised by my sympathy over her rejection. Of course I asked Mom about it later. She said she did want me out of the apartment, but only because she hoped to speak to my dad in private about some financial matters. Things she didn't want me to worry about."

"Did your parents often argue about money?" I asked, remembering my own quarrels with my ex-husband over his exorbitant spending. *There were certainly times when I'd restrained myself from slapping him, so I can imagine a more violent reaction if Abby Anderson was pushed too far . . .*

Eloise looked down at her hands, which were clenched in her lap. "No."

"Listen, Eloise, if you want our help, you need to be honest," Cam said.

"Alright, maybe sometimes." Eloise lifted her head to meet Cam's cool gaze. "But like I've said, my mom wasn't violent. Maybe she yelled at Dad from time to time. And maybe he yelled back. But that doesn't mean Mom killed him."

"Of course not," I said. "Still, if they were having financial problems, we can't ignore that fact. If only because it means there could be other people involved, like your parents' partner, or a lender, or someone like that."

"Was there any evidence that your father was borrowing money from less than reputable sources?" Cam asked.

"Not that I know of," Eloise said quickly. *A little too quickly*, I thought. "But honestly, I really knew nothing about the financial side of the bookshop. My parents trained me in book acquisition and sales, but they didn't involve me in the finances. I mean, they taught me how to run a store, but they didn't let me see the actual books for Last Chapter."

"That's interesting. I'd have thought they would want you to be immersed in all aspects of the business, since I assume they meant you to take charge after they retired or whatever," I said.

Eloise slipped off her glasses and dabbed at her eyes with a tissue she'd pulled from her purse. "It was a mess when I did have to take over. Some of the bookkeeping seemed . . . off. But at that point Neil was still a partner in the business and he helped me sort it out."

"Did he?" Cam arched his brows. "Alright then, what do you say, Jane? Should we take on this case?"

"I don't mind," I said, after a moment's hesitation. "Although you must understand, Eloise—we can't promise to deliver the results you desire."

Eloise bobbed her head. "I know. But having someone try to help . . . well, that's worth a lot to me. Oh, and there is one more thing." She popped on her glasses and fished through her purse, pulling out a folded piece of paper. "I found this among the personal effects the prison sent me after Mom died. I think it could be new evidence, or at least a good lead." She stood and crossed to Cam.

He took the paper from Eloise's outstretched hand and read it as she stood in front of him.

"It's a curious note," he said, looking up at Eloise. "May I keep it? I'd like to investigate the implications of this further."

"Of course," she said. Turning to me, she pressed her hand to her heart. "Thank you, both of you, for agreeing to take a closer look at my mom's case. I hope you'll find the evidence that will finally exonerate her."

"We'll do our best." I stood to clasp her proffered hand.

Cam, rising to his feet as well, looked at me over Eloise's shoulder. "Now we have some book-related stuff to talk about, so if you don't mind, Jane . . ."

"Of course," I said, fighting the urge to demand that Cam divulge what was in the letter Eloise had handed him. *Not to worry, he'll tell me later,* I reminded myself. "I was hoping to take a walk in the gardens anyway." I gave Eloise a nod. "Very nice to meet you. Safe travels home."

Eloise offered me her thanks, while Cam, not unexpectedly, said nothing. Instead, he launched into a conversation with Eloise about other books he wished to acquire.

I left the library before I allowed myself to roll my eyes.

Chapter Four

As I walked through the expansive gardens, it was my turn to be overtaken by the past.

The sweet and spicy scent of roses transported me back to another time and another garden. A smaller, less manicured garden, true, but the silken rose petals I recalled from the garden in my memory were a perfect match to Aircroft's blossoms. As was the breeze offsetting the humidity of North Carolina in May, although in my recollection, the wind was stronger, blowing a lock of my brown hair into my eyes and blurring my vision. That momentary veil was the reason I hadn't realized what was happening until I'd brushed back my hair and noticed my then-boyfriend kneeling in front of me.

Back in the present, I grimaced, remembering how thrilled I'd been when Gary had asked me to marry him. My response had been an immediate and enthusiastic *yes*. At the time, I'd declared it the best day of my life.

If only I'd known . . . Sadly, our marriage had turned out to be a disaster, ending in divorce when our daughter, Bailey, was still an infant. But of course, not having the ability to see into the future, I'd accepted Gary's proposal. Perhaps it was just as well. Despite Gary's drinking, infidelities, and verbal abuse, I knew I wouldn't change my original choice, not when it had given me my daughter.

I shook my head, erasing such thoughts. I couldn't change my past, but I could banish negative memories and focus on all the positive aspects of my current life. Which included Bailey as well as my new job, not to mention the opportunity to enjoy the glamour of Aircroft and its splendid gardens. I took a deep, cleansing breath as I stared down a long flagstone path bordered on one side by carefully cultivated flower beds and on the other by a rectangle of manicured grass. A matching path lined the other side of the garden. Both walkways ended at a marble-columned, open-sided building with a timber roof. In front of this pavilion, a fountain spewed sparkling water that tumbled down a stepped water feature into a koi pond.

Strolling over to the small pond, I considered the implications of taking on the Anderson case. Cam had raised my salary when we'd started our private investigation of cold cases, acknowledging it would add additional hours to my original cataloging job, so I wasn't concerned about the workload. It was the murder aspect that made my stomach churn. When we'd agreed, after helping to solve a case involving the death of Cam's ex-girlfriend, to discreetly take on some cold cases, Cam had assured me that we'd focus on less deadly crimes. Which had been true, up to now. So far our cases had centered on lost or stolen valuables, missing relatives, or illegally obtained inheritances, not murder.

I stared down into the koi pond, where the fish swam in lazy circles, their iridescent scales reflecting the light like the tiny mirrors sewn into the hippie-style tunics I'd worn in my youth. Eloise's plea for help had moved me, but I wasn't sure I wanted to investigate another murder. I knew from experience that such a case could make anyone digging into the crime a target.

Footsteps made me turn to face the back of the house.

"Good, I hoped to catch you before you went back inside," Cam said as he approached me. "We need to talk."

I raised my eyebrows. "Has Eloise left already?"

"No, Lauren is giving her a tour of the house." As Cam brushed his hair away from his forehead, sunlight tipped the flyaway strands red as fire. "Anyway, I wanted to make sure we were on the same page regarding Eloise's request for our help. You seemed a little hesitant."

I looked him up and down, noticing how he was shifting from foot to foot. *Excitement? Or simply nervous energy?* "From what you said regarding the circumstances of the murder, it seems like such an open and shut case. Are you sure we can do any good?"

"I think there are still threads to tug," Cam said.

"Like that paper Eloise handed to you?" I tipped my head and fixed him with an inquisitive stare. "What did it say, anyway?"

"It was an anonymous note, passed to Abby in a book. According to Eloise, Abby had no idea who had sent it, or how they'd smuggled it into the prison and slipped it inside a library book. But yes, it's an interesting clue."

I placed my fists on my hips. "And are you going to tell me what it says, or are you going to force me to guess?"

"Oh, right. Sorry, I was lost in thought. Considering a few possible lines of inquiry." Cam offered me an apologetic smile. "The note was a little cryptic, as one might expect with an anonymous message, but the writer mentioned something about *special information* that could be the key to solving Abby's problems."

"Information that could obtain her release? If that were true, why wouldn't Abby share it?"

Cam shook his head. "I'm not sure. Eloise says she wondered if it was something her mother knew, even if she didn't realize its importance, that could help reopen her case and clear her name."

"Which is what Eloise wanted," I said thoughtfully. "Do you think she could've sent it? She admitted to pushing her mom to allow a reopening of the case."

"The thought did cross my mind." Cam's expression conveyed his approval of my question. "But that's something we could find out, don't you think?"

"You really want to take this on, don't you?" I asked. "Even if there's little hope that we can prove Abby's innocence."

"I would very much like to try. Not just because I'd be doing a favor for a business associate, but also because . . ."

"You're bored and want a new challenge," I said, dropping my arms to my sides.

"That too," Cam agreed, staring at a spot over my head.

Which made me question if there was another reason. *Like a sudden, more personal, interest in his book dealer.*

"So if we're in agreement," Cam continued, still not meeting my eyes, "I'll let Eloise know, and then start our investigation by looking into Detective Parker. Hopefully he's still alive. If so, I want to discover where he lives, if he's still on the force or retired, and figure out how to talk to him."

"How to convince him to talk to us, you mean. But I'm sure you'll concoct some devious way to do so." I cast him a sardonic smile.

"Not devious. Slightly disguised, perhaps." Cam shrugged. "It helps to be rich. I can always lure him in with promises to discuss a donation to one of his favorite charities, or something along those lines."

"Like I said, devious." I adjusted my features into a more professional expression. "So boss, what do you want me to do?"

"Visit Eloise at the bookshop. Soon, like tomorrow. Don't worry, I'll arrange it with her."

"What am I supposed to be doing there? Other than asking Eloise a few more questions, I mean."

"I want you to take some photos. If we're going to try to understand this murder, we need a clear idea of the layout of the store, the number and placement of doors and windows, how the apartment upstairs connects with the shop, and so on."

"That makes sense. Okay, I'll drive to Chapel Hill. Only . . ." I looked up into Cam's angular face with a little smile. "I'm afraid I have this problem whenever I enter a bookstore . . ."

Cam's eyebrows arched over his sparkling eyes. "I have an open account with Last Chapter. If you feel the irrepressible urge to buy a few books, you can charge them to me."

"Why thank you," I said, with sincere gratitude. "Maybe you should come along? I'm sure Eloise stocks many books that might interest you."

The brightness in Cam's eyes dimmed. "No, I don't think so. I have too much to do. Video business meetings and other things. You understand."

"Of course," I said.

I did understand. But it wasn't business—it was Cam's reluctance to leave the safety, or, more precisely, the emotional security, of his estate. I wouldn't say anything about that, though. I'd realized soon after starting my new job that it was better to allow Cam to set his own limits. He'd visited my apartment a few times in the seven months since I'd started working at Aircroft, and had stopped by the adjacent bungalow to talk to my landlord, Vincent Fisher, once or twice. We'd even gone out to dinner a couple of times at a quiet local restaurant, and visited artist Brendan Sloan's gallery once. That was progress. Convincing him to travel farther afield would take more time.

And patience, I reminded myself.

"So 'once more unto the breach'?" I said.

"Just don't forget—there's a 'dear friends' in that quote," he replied, laying a hand on my shoulder.

"So there is." I offered him a warm smile. "So there is."

Chapter Five

The drive to Chapel Hill didn't take too long, especially with the new bypass around Greensboro cutting out most of that city's traffic. It took about an hour and twenty minutes—just long enough to listen to a few chapters of my latest audiobook.

Of course, the closer I got to the campus of UNC-Chapel Hill, the more traffic I encountered. Having traveled to the area for library meetings when I'd worked for one of the campuses in the UNC system, I knew to remain vigilant. Students crossing the streets were often too preoccupied with rushing to class, or too focused on their cell phones, to pay attention to vehicles.

My GPS directed me to the Franklin-Rosemary Historic District, which was on the northeastern edge of the campus. This area of oak-lined streets primarily featured elegant nineteenth-century homes, but there were a few businesses located on the outskirts of the residential zone. I pulled into an alley that led to a small parking lot behind two unpretentious brick buildings.

Circling around to the front of the buildings, I located Last Chapter by its charming carved wooden sign and large plate glass window filled with displays of books. I glanced at my phone to check the time. My internet search had confirmed that the store opened at ten and it was already ten-thirty. Taking a deep breath, I pocketed my phone and opened the heavy oak door.

I was immediately struck with the familiar scents of old leather and aged paper, overlaid with a whiff of dust. Last Chapter was, I was delighted to see, an homage to the bookshops of years past. Its walls were covered with wooden shelves so jammed with books that some were precariously piled on the top of the full row of volumes beneath them. The lighting, avoiding the cold glare of fluorescent fixtures, shed a golden glow over the bookcases that filled the center of the shop. There were no racks of toys, postcards, or any of the other miscellaneous items found at larger, more modern shops. The only materials on display were books, books, and more books.

I followed one of the aisles to reach the back of the bookstore, looking straight ahead to avoid the distractions of all the enticing spines. But I couldn't help but glimpse a few titles that I'd have to examine more closely once I'd gotten a good sense of the store layout and had taken the photos Cam had requested.

Reaching the sales desk, I was surprised to see no one at the counter. "Hello?" I called out. "Anyone here?"

It was possible the sales clerk was somewhere in the back of the store. Behind the desk was a door with a sign that read *Employees Only*. I assumed this was the stockroom, where books were stored and packaged up for delivery. Since I knew Last Chapter conducted searches for specific books requested by clients, they would need space to store acquisitions that would never be shelved in the public areas of the shop.

I tapped the old-fashioned bell on the desk and a loud ding resounded throughout the store. But no one appeared.

"That's strange," I said aloud, confused about the shop being left unattended. I looked up at the open rafters of the wooden ceiling, searching for security cameras, but found only one, positioned to look down upon the service desk. *Not particularly helpful*, I thought, pulling my cell phone from my pocket. I took a few photos of the desk and surrounding area to show to Cam. Due to the maze of bookshelves, it would be difficult to get pictures of the entire store.

That might provide some evidence to support Eloise's claim, I thought. *Someone definitely could've snuck in and killed Ken Anderson and fled without being seen.*

I moved away from the desk area, checking out any possible entrances and exits. While the only windows, at the front and back of the building, were sealed shut, I discovered two doors around a corner from the desk. One obviously led to the apartment above the shop, since my quick peek when I cracked the door revealed a staircase. The other had a hazy window in the top half. Standing on tiptoe, I peered out and realized this door led to a loading dock. The door had a dead bolt that appeared newer than the simple twist lock at the center of its doorknob.

But the dead bolt wasn't latched. I stared at the door for a moment, wondering if Eloise or her staff left it unbolted when the store was open. As I took a photo of both doors, a loud thump from around the corner made me jog back to the service counter.

The noise had to have come from whatever is behind that Employees Only *door*, I thought, weighing my options. While I didn't want to trespass, I was worried that someone working in the back could've fallen. *No doubt they have some tall shelving units that require ladders.*

I stepped behind the service desk and gave the knob on the staff door a little twist. It obviously wasn't locked, and I slowly pushed the door ajar and peeked into the room.

It appeared to be an office. There were no windows and the lights were off, so all I could really see were rough shapes and shadows. What looked like a large wooden desk flanked by file cabinets filled one side of the room, while bookshelves covered the other three walls. There was another door directly across the room that I assumed led to a larger storeroom.

Lowering my gaze, I noticed a bulky shape lying in the middle of the floor. A sob drew my attention to another figure, a few feet away. Seated in front of one of the bookcases, the figure was curled in on itself in a fetal position.

"Eloise?" I asked. "Is that you?" I slid my fingers over the chipped plaster wall just inside the door, searching for a switch. Flicking it on, I blinked as the overhead lights flared.

It *was* Eloise seated by the bookcase, her arms wrapped around her bent legs and her head lowered, hiding her face. She rocked back and forth as another sob escaped her throat.

But the object on the floor wasn't a fallen pile of books or a rumpled tarp. It was a man, lying face down, with a knife protruding from his neck. A dark liquid pooled around his head and shoulders.

Blood, I realized, as my mind glitched, not immediately comprehending the scene. *He's lying in blood and there's a knife and Eloise is the only one here.*

I automatically pulled my cell phone from my pocket and tapped in 911. When the dispatcher answered, I couldn't remember the street address and just stammered out something about Last Chapter Bookshop in Chapel Hill. "Someone's been stabbed," I said, when prompted to explain the emergency.

The dispatcher asked if the victim was still breathing. "Not sure," I replied, glancing over at Eloise. She looked up, her bone-white face covered in a sheen of tears. "Is he breathing?" I asked her, modulating my voice to a calm monotone.

As she shook her head, I noticed crimson streaks in the hair plastered to her forehead and cheek. Her glasses were missing. Without them, her eyes appeared wider and more luminous. She stared directly at me, but it was as if she didn't see me at all. Her gaze pierced through me, focused on something over my shoulder.

"You checked?" I asked. Another nod. I told the dispatcher what I knew, which was little enough, before crossing to kneel beside the prone figure. "No, I won't touch anything," I said, laying down my phone and sitting back on my heels. Turning to Eloise, I asked if she knew the man.

"I do," she said, her voice coming out as a croak. "It's Detective Bruce Parker."

I stared at the man's crumpled body. "The man who was in charge of your mother's case?"

"Yes." Eloise unfolded her arms and legs and used a sturdy shelf for balance as she rose to her feet. "He contacted me. Said he had something he wanted to share about my mom. Something he'd just found out and wanted me to know. That he would stop by today to talk."

Sirens wailed. Eloise spun on her heel and stared through the open staff door, into the shop. "They're coming."

"Where were you?" I asked. "When he was stabbed, were you in the room?"

She swayed slightly. Gripping the edge of a shelf to steady herself, she met my concerned gaze with a little lift of her chin. "In the storeroom. Back there," she said, motioning toward the door in the far wall. "He asked me about something, you see. A book."

"What do you mean?" I stood up as the wail of sirens grew louder. "He wanted you to find a book in your storeroom?"

"I didn't understand either. He said he would explain once I showed it to him. Told me he'd keep an eye out for any customers if I'd go and look for that book. But then I couldn't find it, even though I knew our inventory ledgers included that range of numbers." Eloise lifted her hands, which were stained with blood. "So after a bit I came back to the office to explain and that's when . . ." Eloise blinked away tears. "That's when I found him, like this."

"You didn't hear anything?"

"No. I was in the far corner of the storeroom and focused on my search, and this is an old building, with thick walls."

The slam of the front doors and thunder of heavy-soled shoes pummeling the wood floors of the shop stopped me from asking anything more. I stood aside as both law enforcement and emergency personnel rushed into the office.

I was herded out into the sales area of the bookshop by two officers, one who barraged me with questions while the other looked me over, obviously checking for any traces of blood or other evidence. Finally satisfied that I hadn't arrived on the scene until after Detective Parker was dead, the investigators took my official statement and contact information and told me I'd need to make myself available to answer any additional questions. "Basically, anytime," the officer said, when I asked about a time frame. "Best if you don't leave the state for a while."

"There goes my trip to Bora Bora," I replied, earning a glare instead of the chuckle I was going for. As one of the police officers escorted me to my car—using the back door to avoid the press, who'd already shown up—I mentioned the fact that the dead bolt on that door had not been latched when I arrived. "Someone could've gotten in and out that way, as well as the front door," I said. "I think the doorknob lock is one of those you can set before you exit. You know, it's already set to lock once you pull the door closed behind you."

"Is that so?" The officer, a lanky young woman who towered over me, gave me the side-eye.

"I just wanted you to know that someone could've gotten away easily enough before Ms. Anderson re-entered the office. And of course the front door was open, so they could've just strolled in."

The officer just made a noncommittal noise and stood with her arms crossed over her chest until I got in my car and took off.

I drove a short distance before pulling into an empty church parking lot. After taking some deep breaths to calm my nerves, I called Cam to tell him what had happened.

"You're sure Eloise was there with the body when you walked into the office?" he asked.

"Definitely. Sitting in the dark, which is a little strange, now that I think of it." I gazed out my side window at a crepe myrtle, which had leafed out but not yet bloomed. "I don't know why the lights were off. Eloise said she left Parker in the office when she went into the storeroom to find a book. And no, I didn't find out what book it was."

"Too bad. That would've been helpful." I could hear Cam's fingers drumming against his desk. "As for the lights, that might help Eloise's case. She had no reason to turn off the lights if she was planning to return with that book. But a case could be made that the actual killer turned them off without thinking. To cover their crime, so to speak."

"Are we going to be taking on this murder as well as the cold case one?" I asked, already knowing the answer.

"We have to do whatever we can to help Eloise. You know she'll be the prime suspect."

"With good reason, you must admit."

"Must I?" Cam's light tone didn't fool me. I could tell he was already planning to provide Eloise with all the assistance he, and his considerable wealth, could offer.

"The victim was the detective who helped convict her mother," I said. "And she was the only person I saw in or near the building, not to mention she had blood on her hands and clothes, and even in her hair."

"Circumstantial evidence," Cam replied. "She probably tried to save the guy. You could get a lot of blood transfer from checking for a pulse or attempting to stanch the wound or whatever."

"True." I slumped down in my seat. "Okay, you have the gist. We can discuss this another time. Right now I want to head back to my apartment and chill. It's been quite a day."

"It's still only mid-afternoon. You could stop by Aircroft on your way home."

"I could, but I won't. Goodbye, Cam. Talk to you tomorrow," I said, ending the call.

Chapter Six

After my brief conversation with Cam, I drove home from Chapel Hill dreaming about a large glass of wine and a chunky book. I was definitely ready to kick off my shoes and relax on my well-worn sofa with some light jazz playing in the background.

But as soon as I parked in front of his brick bungalow, my landlord, Vince, opened his front door and strolled out. "Hello, Jane," he said, leaning over the balustrade of the covered porch's white railing. "Do you have a minute?"

Knowing Vince's minutes tended to stretch into hours, I swallowed a sigh and plastered on a smile. "Sure. I have some news to share, anyway," I said. As I crossed the small gravel parking lot, I fought the urge to cast a longing look toward the stairs that led to my small apartment over Vince's garage.

Vince and I were both in our sixties, although he was five years my senior. He was attractive in a rough-hewn sort of way, his hazel eyes bright behind the lenses of his wire-framed glasses. Only slightly taller than me, he had a stocky build and a full head of steel-gray hair.

Also like me, Vince was supposedly retired. But after a career as a reporter and editor for a local newspaper, he'd turned his investigative skills to other uses, like working on a historical account of the Airley family, who'd originally built Aircroft. He'd also offered some invaluable assistance to Cam and me. It didn't hurt to have a reporter helping us dig into cold cases, especially someone who still had connections to several news organizations.

"Have you already heard about a murder in Chapel Hill?" I asked, shifting the strap of my purse from one shoulder to the other.

"No, but I haven't checked any news today. A murder, you say?" Vince looked me up and down. "Didn't you go there today to visit that bookshop where another murder took place years ago? That's what you told me when we ran into each other before you drove off this morning."

"I did. And stumbled over another dead body, I'm afraid." I swayed slightly. Saying those words brought back a vision of the murder scene.

"What? Well, for heaven's sake, come inside and sit down." Vince strode across the porch to reach his front door. "My news seems pretty insignificant compared to that," he added as he gripped the doorknob, "but I do have some information that might be of interest, in terms of another cold case."

"The death of Calvin Airley?" I asked, noting the barely repressed excitement in Vince's eyes. The fate of the lost heir to Aircroft was one of Vince's obsessions. Calvin, the only child of the wealthy couple who'd built Aircroft in the 1920s, had died young, in what officials had called an accident. Many people disagreed with this finding, suspecting that Calvin had committed suicide, but Vince was convinced he'd been murdered.

"No, this is the one involving the mystery woman you've been trying to trace."

"Really?" This information wiped away any regrets over my wine and book. The *mystery woman*, as we called her, had appeared in an old picture I'd found in the attic at Aircroft. Although we knew she must've had some connection to the Airleys, since her photo was included in their family collection, no one seemed to know who she was. The fact that a sketch of the same woman, considerably older, drawn by Cam's late mother, Patricia Clewe, had turned up in Patricia's art studio had only deepened the mystery.

"It's actually Donna's info, if I'm honest." Vince smiled. "You know what a clever sleuth she can be when she puts her mind to it."

"Is Donna here?" I asked, hoping that Vince's girlfriend was visiting. I hadn't seen Donna in a few weeks and would be happy to catch up with her. "She must've parked in the garage."

"Yeah, she did. Thought it would keep the car cooler. Come on in if you have time. You can tell us all about this new murder and Donna can share her news while we split a bottle of wine." Vince held open the front door, allowing me to walk in ahead of him.

I stepped into the airy, open space, marveling as I always did at the disconnect between the exterior and interior of Vince's home. Other than painting the shutters forest green, he hadn't changed the outside of his traditional 1920s brick bungalow, but inside he'd removed walls and altered almost everything to fit a Scandinavian aesthetic. The open great room, connected to a sleek and bright kitchen by an expansive island, had off-white walls accented by blond wood trim and floors. On one wall a large flatscreen television was surrounded by austere wood cabinets and bookshelves, facing a low-backed ivory sofa that was anchored by a shaggy blue rug.

Seated in a sculptural wood chair across from the sofa, Donna Valenti looked up as Vince and I entered. She was a short, plump woman whose vitality made her seem younger than her sixty-four years. "Jane! So good to see you. I was hoping you'd drop by." As she sat forward, her pewter-gray braid, still threaded with a few dark-brown strands, fell over her shoulder.

"I know. We haven't talked in far too long," I said. "Of course, you and Vince were out of town for a while on one of your exciting trips. Hawaii of all places. I have to admit I'm envious."

"It was lovely," Donna said. "But it's always good to be back home."

"So they tell me." I cast her a smile. "Not that I would know anything about taking a trip anywhere these days. It seems I'm indispensable at work."

"And how is Cam?" Vince asked, as he headed over to the kitchen island.

I laughed. "You think I'm indispensable to Cam?"

"I think you're doing two jobs at once because your boss needs a partner in his new avocation," Vince said.

Donna's scarlet sandals swept a trail through the pile of the rug in front of her chair. "Now Vince, you know Jane is equally obsessed with these cold cases. Right, Jane?"

"I'm afraid you're correct," I replied as I sat down on the sofa across from her.

"So, white or red?" Vince held up a bottle of wine. "I have this pinot noir, but there's a nice Australian chardonnay chilling in the fridge."

"I think I'd prefer the white. If only because I'm sitting on this lovely but very pale sofa," I replied.

Vince set down the bottle and turned to open the refrigerator. "Good point. White it is." Returning to the kitchen island with the chardonnay, he pointed the corkscrew at his girlfriend. "Donna, before you spill your very interesting info, Jane needs to tell us about her day. It was apparently a not-so-great one." He shook his head as he drew out the wine cork. "She encountered another murder scene."

"Oh dear, how did that happen?" Donna asked, her deep brown eyes widening.

I leaned back against the sofa cushions and launched into a recitation of the day's events, keeping my tone as neutral as possible. But when I reached the part where I'd almost fallen over Bruce Parker's prone body, my voice cracked.

"Here, you definitely need this," Vince said, handing me a large glass of wine.

I took a long swallow before responding. "It wasn't pleasant, that's for sure. And then there were all the questions from the police."

Vince returned with two more glasses of wine, one of which he gave Donna before he sat at the other end of the sofa.

"What a horrible experience," Donna said, with a little shudder. "And when you were trying to clear that young woman's mother's name, too."

"Yes, it doesn't look good for Eloise. She was the only one in the store when I found the body." I frowned. "It's starting to seem like a repetition of her mom's case."

"The Anderson murder. I definitely remember all the news reports on that case. Tons of coverage at the time." Vince's expression grew thoughtful. "Same MO—a stabbing, and only one person in the building at the time."

"That we know of," I said. "The back door was locked, but the dead bolt was not engaged. It was only the doorknob, which could've been set to lock after someone shut it from the outside. I told the police about that, of course."

Vince motioned toward me with his wineglass. "Excellent sleuthing."

"The ironic thing is that I was going to ask you about the original murder," I said, turning sideways to face Vince. "I figured you might've done some reporting on it back in the day, or know someone who did."

Vince set his wineglass on a glass-topped side table. "It was about fifteen years ago, wasn't it?"

"Must've been," Donna said. "I remember hearing about it when I was still the secondary secretary at the high school. Before I got promoted to lead," she added, with a glance toward me.

"Correct. Eloise Anderson was only eighteen when her mom was accused of stabbing her dad. Everyone said it was an open-and-shut case, but Eloise never believed that her mom was guilty," I said.

Vince raised his bushy eyebrows. "She's asked you and Cam to help prove her mother's innocence?"

"Guessed it in one. So I'd already planned to pick your brain about what you remember about the case. If you have any contacts, or any notes related to it, that would be a bonus."

"Sure thing. It was a bit puzzling." Taking off his glasses, Vince absently polished the lenses with the hem of his loose cotton shirt. "The evidence definitely pointed to Abby Anderson as the killer, but the motive always seemed murky to me." He popped his glasses back on. "Let me dig up my notes and I'll be happy to share them with you. And Cam as well, if you want. Who knows, it may even be pertinent to this new murder."

"You still have materials from that far back?" I asked.

Donna rolled her eyes. "Oh, honey, he still has his notebooks from college. You should see the basement. Boxes upon boxes."

"All very well organized," Vince said.

"Then I approve." I gave Donna a conspiratorial smile. "I mean, how could I not? I'm a librarian, after all."

Donna groaned. "I should've known I wouldn't get any support from you in my fight to get him to ditch some of that stuff."

"Well, dear, if it helps clear Abby Anderson's name, keeping everything might be a stroke of good fortune." Vince turned to me, the lines bracketing his mouth deepening. "But it won't be any use in terms of today's tragedy. Tell me, Jane, do you think the daughter is guilty?"

I considered his question for a moment. "It certainly appears that way. But I've learned that not everything is what it looks like at first glance. Anyway, I think Cam and I should still investigate the cold case concerning Eloise's mother." I shrugged. "It might have relevance, who knows? After all, Bruce Parker was the lead detective on the Ken Anderson murder."

Donna took a sip of wine before meeting my gaze. "Which is just another strike against the poor girl."

"I know," I said with a sigh. "It gives Eloise Anderson a motive."

Chapter Seven

Vince, obviously sensing my distress, sat up straighter. "Changing the subject—Donna, why don't you tell Jane what you found out about our mystery woman."

"I didn't exactly find out anything," Donna said, with an apologetic smile. "But I did discover someone who might've known her."

"A person who lives in this area?" I finished off my wine and set the glass on the end table beside me.

Donna nodded. "Yes, right here in town. It was the funniest thing, really. I wasn't trying to ferret out any information. I was simply talking with a friend at one of my book clubs."

"She attends three." Vince lifted his glass in a little salute. "Never let it be said that my gal wastes a minute of her day."

Donna sniffed. "I just love to read, and my groups cover different genres. I'm sure Jane understands. She's a librarian, after all."

I smiled, biting back any comment. The truth was, as much as I liked to read, I didn't do nearly the amount of it as I had before I'd become a librarian. Sometimes, after cataloging all day, my brain was too fried to allow me to concentrate on reading a book for pleasure.

"Just kidding around." Vince took a long swallow of his wine.

"I know, dear." Donna cast him an indulgent look. "Anyway, I can see Jane is itching for me to get back to the main subject." Placing her wineglass on the side table next to her chair, she slid forward in her seat. "I have this friend, you see. Just a little older than me . . ."

Vince snorted. "That woman has a good twelve years on you."

"She's seventy-seven, so more like thirteen, but that's not really relevant." Donna pursed her lips. "No, maybe it is, because she's old enough to have been alive when the Airley family was still living at Aircroft."

"She knew them?" I asked, excitement raising the pitch of my voice.

Donna's dark eyes sparkled with matching enthusiasm. "Better than that—she actually lived on the estate for several years."

"Seriously?" I leaned forward, pressing my palms against my knees.

"Her mother was the housekeeper for the Airleys in the fifties, so Ruth—that's her name, Ruth Young—lived there as well. Her dad had passed away soon after Ruth was born. Her mom being a single parent made landing a live-in position at Aircroft a real coup."

"Free room and board," Vince said. "A good deal, for sure."

"Did Ruth know Calvin Airley?" I asked, my thoughts whirling. "That could help your research too, Vince."

Vince's sigh filled the space between us. "She did, but unfortunately neither she nor her mother was at the estate when Calvin died. They'd taken a leave of absence to travel to Pennsylvania because Ruth's grandmother passed away and they had to attend the funeral."

"Ruth was only eleven when Calvin had his accident. Or whatever it was," Donna added, with a swift glance toward Vince. "Her mother left Aircroft not long after that."

"Because Samuel and Bridget Airley closed up the estate for a while after Calvin's death. They did return, of course, but by then Ruth's mother had found another position," Vince said.

"So what insights might Ruth have on our mystery woman?" I asked.

"I honestly don't know. But she was living at the estate, and was old enough to notice things, like someone taking photos of young women on the grounds." Donna shrugged. "I didn't have the picture with me, so I didn't bother to press her on that point. I mean, it was a while ago, long before Cam's dad, Albert, purchased the estate. I figured when the Airley family was living there, which would be the time Ruth remembers, there had to be lots of girls visiting Aircroft, especially when Calvin was in his late twenties."

"I've told Donna about Samuel and Bridget's plan to marry Calvin off to a society girl, and how they invited families with eligible misses to the estate for parties and such," Vince said.

"More than once." Donna rolled her eyes.

Vince ignored this. "So, as Donna said, Ruth probably observed many young women visiting Aircroft."

"But we have the photo," I said. "We can ask her about that specific girl."

"Right, but I thought it best if you did that, Jane." Color flushed Donna's cheeks. "I may have told a tiny white lie, like how you were doing some research to help Cameron Clewe compile a history of the estate. I thought that might make Ruth more willing to share her memories. I asked her if she'd be willing to speak with you, and she said yes. I'd introduce you, of course."

"You didn't think she'd willing to talk to Vince?" I asked, giving him a sidelong look.

Vince cleared his throat. "Well, you see, the thing is . . ."

"The last time he spoke with Ruth on the subject of Aircroft and the Airley family, he kind of fell back into his tough reporter persona." Donna gave a little shake of her head. "Pushed her too hard. Now she refuses to talk to him again."

"I see." I met Vince's abashed expression with a smile. "Well, of course I'm happy to speak to her. I can show her the photo and drawing, or at least my copies of the originals, and see if she recognizes the woman."

"Thanks. I'd like to solve that mystery, even if it doesn't help me find any proof about what actually happened to Calvin." Vince rose to his feet. "More wine?"

"No thanks, I'd better head up to the apartment while I can still climb the stairs." I stood, slinging my purse strap back over my shoulder, and headed for the door. "Thank you for the information, Donna, and the future introduction to Ruth Young, and for agreeing to look through your notes on the Anderson case, Vince. And thank you both for listening to me. I think it's easier to process a traumatic experience when you talk to someone about it."

"We're here, if you find you need to talk some more," Donna said.

Standing at the front door, I offered them both a smile. "I know, and that will definitely help me sleep better tonight."

Chapter Eight

Checking my phone before heading into work on Friday morning, I noticed I'd received recent messages from Donna and Bailey. Always worried my daughter might be contacting me due to some emergency, I read Bailey's text first.

"Oh, that might not be good," I said aloud. Bailey said her stint with a national touring company of *Les Misérables* was ending in a few weeks and she hoped she could stay with me while she lined up some auditions in New York.

I frowned. It wasn't that I didn't want to see my daughter; it was the likelihood that she would want to help me investigate the Anderson case, which might not only place her in danger, but would also put her in close contact with Cam. Knowing Bailey's taste in men, I was afraid she might find Cam irresistible. Handsome, intelligent, and carrying a lot of baggage? Right up her alley.

But of course I responded with an open invitation to stay at my apartment. *It's small*, I texted back, *and there's only one bedroom and one bathroom. So as long as you don't mind a folding cot, you're welcome to crash with me for as long as you need.*

Thanks, Mom. Will send details later.

I sighed and told myself that since I was due some vacation days, I could always try to keep my boss and my daughter apart. "Oh, who are you kidding? You know Bailey will insist on seeing Aircroft." I sighed. There was nothing I could do about it now. I'd tuck away any worries about her charming Cam—which she could do without breaking a sweat—to deal with later.

The message from Donna was a request to meet her, and Ruth Young, at her condo Saturday afternoon. I agreed to this plan with enthusiasm.

When I arrived at work, Lauren met me in the grand entrance hall.

"Cam asked that you join him in the main sitting room as soon as you got in today," she said. "Do you know which room that is?"

"The one with all of Albert Clewe's travel mementos?" I asked, looking past her to the grand staircase, with its double sweep of polished wood steps and intricately carved balustrades. A marble fireplace that I'd never seen lit was nestled in the arch formed by the stairs.

"That's it." Lauren glanced up into the high ceiling, which was crisscrossed by a geometric arrangement of wooden rafters. "Another bulb burned out," she said, shaking her head. "I thought it seemed rather dark in here."

"Who replaces those?" I asked, following her gaze upward. The ceiling rose at least twenty feet above the polished floor of the entry hall. I didn't envy anyone who had to replace a lightbulb in one of the black iron chandeliers. "Not you, I hope."

"Oh no, definitely not. We have a handyman on retainer for those sorts of things." Lauren flashed me a smile. "If it came down to me, there'd be no light in here at all, except what comes in through the windows. You certainly wouldn't catch me climbing a ladder tall enough to change those bulbs."

"I'd hope not." I looked her over, admiring her tailored lemon-yellow jacket and matching pencil skirt. "How is Cam this morning? Should I be prepared for mild, moderate, or extreme grumpiness?"

Lauren laughed. "Actually, none of those. He seems strangely . . . energized."

"It's probably the Anderson case. Especially now that there's another murder in the mix."

"Most likely," Lauren said, her expression sobering. "He asked me to contact a couple of high-powered defense lawyers yesterday afternoon."

"He's going to hire one of them to defend Eloise Anderson, I suppose." I tapped my foot against the parquet floor. "That could be a risky venture, at least in terms of public opinion."

"I doubt Cam cares about that," Lauren said dryly. "He's determined to help that young woman however he can."

From her concerned expression, I suspected Lauren thought our boss was harboring more than a professional interest in Eloise. "Which is very commendable, don't you think?"

"Of course, of course," Lauren said, with a wave of her hand. "Ms. Anderson might be stuck with an overworked public defender, otherwise. And regardless of her guilt or innocence, she deserves good representation."

"Well, let me go and see what Cam wants. I have a backlog of cataloging at this point, so the sooner I hear him out, the faster I can get back to my actual job."

"I'll leave you to it, then. I too must get back to work." Lauren offered me another smile before turning and heading down the hall that led to the kitchen.

I set off in the opposite direction, down the corridor that led to the main sitting room and the music room, among other spaces.

Reaching the sitting room, I rapped the thick wooden door and waited for Cam to call out, "Come in," before I entered.

Like the library, the sitting room featured dark wood finishes, but it was filled with leather armchairs, round side tables, and several glass-fronted display cases instead of bookshelves. Above the ebony paneling, the plaster walls were painted moss green, which made the room appear dark, despite the fact that the heavy drapes were typically pulled back from the tall windows.

Cam was seated in his favorite wingback chair. Although the maroon-tinted leather clashed with his bright auburn hair, it provided the perfect background for his white cotton shirt and light-blue pants. "Jane, here you are at last," he said, carefully placing a bookmark inside the book he'd been reading.

He's trying to present a calm façade, I thought as I crossed to the chair facing him, *but the nervous jiggling of his leg gives him away*. I sat down, balancing my soft-sided briefcase and my purse in my lap. "Lauren said you wanted to speak with me?"

Cam's sea-green gaze sparkled. "I want to hear all about yesterday's events. How everything appeared, before and after you discovered the body."

"Cheerful morning conversation, in other words," I said.

Cam set his book on the side table and leaned forward, gripping his knees. "It is important, especially if we want to prove Eloise's innocence."

"Do we want to do that?" I studied his face, noting the crimson flush highlighting his high cheekbones.

"Of course." Cam leapt to his feet and strode over to one of the display cases. "I know Eloise and I only officially met the other day, but we've corresponded for some time. Knowing her reserved personality, it seems highly unlikely that she would ever viciously stab someone."

I examined him for a moment, noticing how his slender shoulders were bent back, like bird wings. *Tension*, I thought. "Still waters can run deep, or so they say."

Cam toyed with a ceramic figurine sitting on top of the cabinet for a minute before offering any response. "I suppose. But I still find it hard to believe."

"You'd better hear me out before you make any decision." I launched into a detailed description of my visit to Last Chapter. "There wasn't anyone else around when I arrived, I'm almost positive of that," I said, after I concluded my story. "The only living person there, besides me, was Eloise, and like I told you yesterday, she was splattered with blood and huddled a short distance from the body of the detective who'd helped convict her mother."

Cam turned his head and stared out one of the windows. "It does look bad for her. Which is one reason I want to provide her with the best possible counsel."

I set my briefcase and purse on the floor and stood up. Strolling over to where he was standing, I crossed my arms over my chest. "Listen, I know you want to help. If only to preserve a business you depend on for many of your book acquisitions . . ." I dropped my arms as Cam spun around and faced me, his lips drawn into a tight line. "But Eloise had both motive and opportunity. She told me she knew ahead of time that Detective Parker might stop by the bookshop, so she could've easily planned to kill him. Or perhaps it wasn't premeditated. Maybe she simply snapped."

"On the other hand, she could be innocent." Cam crossed his arms over his chest.

"Yes, but we have to consider all the alternatives if we want to prove that," I said, keeping my tone mild. "That's my point; not that

I absolutely think she's guilty. I don't. But if we don't look at all the possible angles, we'll miss something important."

Cam's taut lips relaxed into a faint smile. "Ah, so you're playing devil's advocate."

"What I'm trying to do is to get you to see that we can't assume anything. I know you like Eloise." I held up my hand, palm out. "Don't get bent out of shape over that comment. It's perfectly understandable. I like her too. But we won't be helping her if we don't dig deeper and uncover the truth behind this murder."

"Both murders," Cam said.

I raised my eyebrows. "You think they're connected?"

"I believe they could be." Cam strode back to his chair and sat down.

I followed, settling in the facing chair again. "What makes you think there's any connection?"

"The victim, of course." With his elbows on the chair arms, Cam rested his chin on his clasped hands. "Detective Parker suddenly wanted to speak to Eloise. Why would that be, after all these years?"

"He was finally ready to admit that he'd made mistakes during the original investigation?"

Cam dropped his arms and slid back in his chair. "Or he'd always had questions, even if he wouldn't admit it, and had continued to quietly investigate the case."

"And found new evidence that might exonerate Abby Anderson," I said, with a snap of my fingers. "That certainly could've been the case. And if the actual killer somehow found out that Parker was going to share this information with Eloise, they may have decided to silence him."

"Exactly." Cam's smile expressed his approval of my reasoning. "Following that logic, I want to look into a business that used to compete with the Andersons in acquiring rare books. Benton House, owned by Gloria Benton and her family. They're based in High Point."

"That makes sense," I said. High Point was well known for its furniture stores and the annual Furniture Mart, and selling antiques and other collectibles would tie in with that.

"Art and antiques are their focus," Cam said, "but they sometimes dabble in rare books. Apparently, there were some contentious bidding wars that took place between the Andersons and the Bentons."

"Contentious enough to lead to murder?" I asked, not bothering to mask the skepticism in my tone.

Cam shrugged. "Who knows. Anyway, they're still in business, so I asked Lauren to set up a meeting with Gloria's son, David."

"To do what?" I met Cam's intent gaze with a little shake of my head. "Question them about the Anderson case?"

"Not directly. I simply want to get a sense of how they do business."

"Which means David Benton will come to this meeting assuming you want them to acquire antiques or rare books for you?" Grabbing my briefcase and purse off the floor, I slung both straps over my shoulder. "Are you going to inquire about a book he might have to find on the black market, just to observe how he reacts?"

Cam lifted his hands. "You see, this is why we work so well together. We think alike."

"I don't know about that," I said, rising to my feet. "Maybe I've just learned how your mind works."

Cam stood to face me. "Good. Perhaps someday you can explain it to me."

Chapter Nine

I drove to Donna's condo on Saturday, hopeful that my visit would provide the opportunity to uncover more details about Calvin Airley as well as the mystery woman in the photo and drawing.

Donna lived in a wooded condo complex not far from Old Salem, a village that preserved the history of the Moravians who'd settled the area in the mid-eighteenth century. Like Williamsburg, Old Salem included private homes as well as restored and reconstructed buildings owned by the Old Salem corporation. The public areas were staffed by living-history interpreters, who provided visitors a taste of Moravian life in the eighteenth and nineteenth centuries. The area also encompassed some independent institutions, like Salem Academy and College and Home Moravian Church. Near the church, which was founded in 1771, was an expansive Moravian cemetery called God's Acre, where an Easter sunrise service was held each year, complete with traditional brass bands.

Since she lived close enough to walk to the site, I'd taken several strolls with Donna and Vince in Old Salem. It was a charming place, its brick sidewalks shaded by old-growth trees. We particularly enjoyed walking outside of the tourist area, where there were no crowds and plenty of lovely vintage homes and gardens. I doubted that we'd do any walking today, though. Donna had told me that Ruth, who was in her late seventies, was not in the best of health.

Parking in front of Donna's ground-level condo, I peeked in my rearview mirror to make sure my short hair was tidy and that I didn't have any lipstick on my teeth. Satisfied that I looked acceptable, I walked up to Donna's front door and rang the bell.

She greeted me with a bright smile and ushered me into her unit, which she'd decorated in a style that evoked a country cottage. White kitchen cabinets, window curtains, and trim provided a bright backdrop to various shades of blue as well as yellow decorative accents.

Donna introduced me to Ruth Young, who was seated in a sapphire-fabric armchair facing the sky-blue sofa.

"Hello," I said, sitting down on the sofa. "I'm delighted to meet you."

Ruth's black eyes sparkled in her lined face. Her white hair, cropped close to her scalp, provided a vivid contrast to her dark skin. She was a petite woman who appeared to be slightly hunched over in her chair.

"Excuse me if I don't jump up to greet you. Rheumatoid arthritis," she said, holding up her gnarled hands. "Dreadful disease. They've made some progress on new drugs, but not until after my joints were already in bad shape."

"Sorry to hear that," I said.

"Well, nothing to be done." Ruth placed her hands in her lap. "At least I can still get around with a cane. The worst of it is my hands."

"Which is a real shame," Donna said, giving me a sidelong glance as she sat at the other end of the sofa. "Ruth was an extremely talented quilter when she was a bit younger. That's how we met, at the quilting circle at church."

Ruth nodded. "I do miss that. Sometimes I go to the meetings just for the companionship, but of course I'm no use with a needle these days."

"But she still contributes. We make the quilts for shelters, you see. Ruth might not be sewing with us now, but she supplies us with some lovely fabric scraps from time to time," Donna said.

"Least I can do." Ruth turned her bright gaze on me. "Now Jane, I understand you're interested in the years I spent at Aircroft, when my mama was the housekeeper there."

I leaned forward. "Very interested. My boss, Cameron Clewe, wants to eventually develop some sort of history of the estate. He's thinking something that could be posted online, on a website featuring Aircroft." This white lie was not so far from possibility that I had any trouble delivering it.

Donna cleared her throat. "Anyway, we're interested in any of your recollections. As you know, Vince has been working on a book about the Airley family for some time."

"I do indeed," Ruth said with an audible sniff. "He's bound and determined to prove poor Calvin Airley was murdered, isn't he?" She shook her head. "Now I don't know what really happened, but dredging up that tragedy after all these years just seems hurtful to me."

"All that aside, I think Jane is really more interested in your impressions of the family and what it was like to live at Aircroft back in the fifties. That is when you and your mom were there, right?"

"Yes, 1950 to 1957." Ruth lowered her lashes over her eyes, as if focusing inward, on her memories. "But you have to remember I was just a child. When we arrived at Aircroft I was four, and I was only eleven when we left."

"Why did you leave?" I asked, ignoring the sharp glance Donna threw my way. "Was there any trouble between your mom and the Airleys?"

"Oh no, nothing like that," Ruth said, with a dismissive wave of her hand. "You may have heard that Mr. and Mrs. Airley closed down the estate for a spell after Calvin died. During that time Mama got another job offer. It was at a prominent doctor's home situated close to our extended family. Mama needed the money—she couldn't wait out the Airleys indefinitely—and she also thought it would be good for me to spend more time around my cousins and other relatives."

"I see. And when was that, exactly?" I asked.

"Not long after Calvin died, so in 1957. We heard about it, of course, and rushed back from my grandma's funeral, just so we could attend Calvin's service." Ruth looked up, sorrow shadowing her eyes. "It was a terribly sad affair."

"I imagine so. Those poor parents—to lose their only child must've been so tragic," Donna said, her voice brimming with sympathy.

"Calvin was a nice boy," Ruth said. "Always pleasant to me, anyway. Mr. and Mrs. Airley were very distant. They sort of looked over my head without seeing me, if you know what I mean. But Calvin would stop and talk to me, especially when I was out playing in the gardens. He was an amateur naturalist, you know."

"Really? I didn't realize that," I said.

"Oh yes. He was always outside, studying plants and butterflies and things like that." Ruth grimaced. "That's how they think he slipped off that ledge."

"Where did that happen? I don't think I've ever seen the actual spot."

"Behind the wilder part of the gardens and across a meadow. There's an old quarry back there. Something that had been dug out to access building stone before the Airleys bought the land. It was partially filled in when I was a child, but I still remember all of Mama's warnings." Ruth smiled, obviously recalling her mom. "She said she'd whup me good if I ever did so much as cross that meadow."

"So did you?" Donna gave Ruth a wink.

Ruth grinned. "Of course. I was something of a hellion back then. But only once. Calvin caught me messing around the edge of the cliff and read me the riot act. Told me it was a good way to get killed; that he'd done some climbing in the area but you had to know what you were doing and use ropes and such. He was very firm with me, and I could see how serious he was. Said he wouldn't tell Mama, though. And he didn't, bless his heart."

"But he went out in the rain, when the ground was muddy, and slipped off the edge," I said, more to myself than the others.

Ruth fixed me with a fierce stare. "So they say."

"You don't believe it?" I asked, widening my eyes.

"Not sure what happened." Ruth sat back in her chair. "I wasn't there and don't care to speculate."

"I understand. And really, I wouldn't expect you to know that. But there is something else, totally unrelated, that you may be able to help me with." I grabbed my purse from the floor and set it in my lap. "The thing is, when I was doing some research for Mr. Clewe, I discovered an unlabeled photo of a young woman tucked in among the Airley family photographs. I've shown it around, and even Vince with all his research"—I cast Donna a sidelong glance—"doesn't know who it is. She's a mystery to everyone."

"There were many young ladies coming and going when I lived at Aircroft." Ruth narrowed her eyes. "Lots of parties and that sort of thing. It used to make tons of work for Mama, especially after they all left. Far too much clean-up after those young people."

"Vince claims the Airleys wanted Calvin to marry well," Donna said, as I pulled the copied photo of the younger version of our mystery woman from my purse.

"Oh yes. Calvin's parents were hell-bent on introducing him to the daughters of their business acquaintances and other fine young misses. But he was having none of it." Ruth's lips twisted into a sardonic smile. "He was always looking to escape those events. Used to hide out in the kitchen storeroom or other places the guests wouldn't look. I found him a couple of times, but he always swore me to secrecy." Ruth lifted her chin. "I never betrayed him. I could tell he didn't much like those parties, or the girls who were chasing him. He said they just wanted his money, which was probably mostly true."

"What about this young woman?" Rising to my feet, I crossed to Ruth's chair and handed her the copy of the photo. "Do you remember ever seeing her at Aircroft?"

Ruth's hands shook slightly as she held the picture closer to her face. "Oh my goodness, I didn't know such a thing existed." As she looked up at me, her fingers lost their grip and she dropped the photo into her lap. "Yes, I recognize her. That's Calvin's girl. That's Lily."

Chapter Ten

My face flushing with excitement, I stepped closer to Ruth's chair. "Lily who?"

"I'm afraid I don't know. I never heard her surname spoken," Ruth said, pressing her back into the chair cushions.

I stepped back. "But you're sure her first name was Lily?"

"Absolutely. I was actually introduced to her by Calvin. He trusted me, you see, just like I trusted him. He knew I wouldn't tell his parents, or even my mama, about his many rendezvous with Lily."

"They were meeting in secret? Such a romantic story." Donna's audible sigh made me smile.

But only for a moment. "Yes, but this story didn't end well," I said, thinking of Calvin's death and the disappearance of his true love.

"No, it certainly didn't." Ruth held up the picture. "I was so upset when I heard about Calvin's death. It seemed so senseless. I did try to find out where Lily went, but I could never get anyone in the general area to admit to knowing her."

"But surely she would've had to live around here, wouldn't she? How would Calvin have met her, otherwise?" I asked as I took the copied photo from her.

"I don't know where they met, or how, but I suspect Lily was working somewhere in the area. Restaurant or retail store or something like that. She once mentioned she had family living around here, but said she wasn't in touch with them much and that she lived on her own. Then again, she wasn't so very young. More like late twenties, close to Calvin's age," Ruth said.

As I crossed back to the sofa to extract the second copied photo from my purse, Donna stood up. "Heavens, I've been the worst hostess. Would either of you like coffee or tea or anything?"

Ruth cast her a warm smile. "No harm done. I knew you were both anxious to question me about the past. But a little water would be good."

"Nothing for me," I said, as Donna walked into her open kitchen. Carrying the second picture back to Ruth's chair, I held it out so she could see it. "I found this tucked into one of Patricia Clewe's old sketchbooks. It looks like the same woman, only quite a bit older."

Ruth leaned forward to peer at the paper. "It does look like Lily. Did Patricia Clewe draw this?"

"Yes. She even signed it," I said, pointing to the lower right corner.

"Well, I'll be." Ruth straightened and gazed up at me, her eyebrows drawn in over her nose. "Now why would Lily have returned to Aircroft as an older woman? Calvin was long gone and the Airleys hadn't lived there for years."

"Maybe Patricia Clewe didn't draw this sketch at the estate. She could've been working at a studio somewhere, and Lily whoever was just an available model," Donna said as she hurried over with a glass of water. She set it on a small table next to Ruth's chair before returning to her own seat on the sofa.

Ruth shook her head. "Doubtful. I never met Pat Clewe, but I know she didn't get out much. Her health wasn't too good, or so I heard."

"That's true." I folded the copy of the picture as I strolled back to the sofa.

"Did you notice the date?" Ruth asked. "Scribbled under the signature. Looked like just a flourish at first, but I think it's a year."

I plopped down on the sofa and examined my copy of the drawing. Sure enough, under the artist's name was another scribble. I squinted at it, finally making out what it was. "1989," I said. "Funny how I never saw that before."

"You were concentrating on her face, I bet." Donna tapped her chin with one finger. "If I'm remembering things correctly, that was the year Cameron Clewe was born."

I calculated back from Cam's age in my head. "That would be right."

"Stuff rubs off from Vince talking about his research. And talking, and talking . . ." Donna flashed a grin.

"Is there anything else you can recall about Lily?" I asked, turning back to Ruth.

Holding her glass with both hands, Ruth took a few sips of water. "Just that she was very nice to me. Didn't talk down, even though I was a kid. And I could tell that Calvin was madly in love with her. I might've only been ten or eleven, but I could tell." Ruth set her water glass down with a frown. "She didn't attend Calvin's funeral. Leastwise, I didn't see her there."

"Was Calvin buried at Aircroft?" Donna asked. "I know some of those big estates have their own family plots."

"No, at the local Episcopal church cemetery," Ruth said. "His mother and father were eventually buried there too. Fancy gravestone with an angel statue. You can't miss it."

"I'll have to check that out," I said. As I slipped the folded picture back into my purse, my cell phone vibrated against my hand. I pulled it out and checked the screen. "Uh-oh, that's Cam. I'd better take this."

Donna motioned toward her sliding patio doors. "Feel free to step outside if you want a little privacy."

I nodded my thanks, answering the call while I pushed open the doors wide enough to slip out onto the small flagstone patio. "Hello, Cam. What's up?" I asked, over the squeal of the doors as I pulled them shut.

"Eloise has been arrested," he said.

"That's unfortunate."

"Very." I could hear Cam's fingers tapping the side of his phone. "She's to be arraigned Monday. The lawyer I asked to represent her thinks she may make bail, but it will be a significant amount."

I touched my fingertip to the velvety pink petal of one of the potted roses that flanked the patio. "Are you paying for this lawyer?"

"Yes." Cam cleared his throat. "I told Eloise she could eventually repay me, but I don't plan to press for the money. A few rare books will settle the account."

"That sounds fair." I leaned forward to breathe in the spicy-sweet scent of the roses. "And are you paying her bail, regardless of how expensive it is?"

"Yes." I could hear the determination in Cam's voice. "I also intend to ask her to stay at Aircroft while she awaits trial. The lawyer told me she can't leave the state, but just traveling to the Winston-Salem area wouldn't be a problem. Especially if I vouch for her."

"Now that sounds tricky. Very nice of you, but possibly dangerous. What if she flees Aircroft and goes on the lam? That could make trouble for you."

"Nothing I can't handle," Cam said shortly. "Besides, Eloise won't go on the run. She owns a family business. She isn't going to abandon the bookshop."

"I don't know. All this kind of makes it look like . . ."

"Like what?" Cam's tone grew frosty.

"That maybe you two are more than just friends. Which might not really help her case, if you plan to be a character witness."

"That's ridiculous. I want to help someone I respect, and who I believe to be innocent. That's all."

"If you say so," I replied, realizing switching the subject might be a smart move. "By the way, I'm at Donna Valenti's home, speaking with an older friend of hers who lived at Aircroft back when Calvin Airley was still alive. She's actually told us the first name of our mystery woman."

"And that is?" Inquisitiveness replaced the ice in Cam's voice.

"Lily. Ring any bells?"

"No. Never heard Al mention that name, although she must've visited at least once since my mother drew her portrait. Of course, he was often away, traveling for business."

I noticed that Cam was using Albert Clewe's first name rather than calling him "Dad," but knew better than to comment. "It's somewhere to start, I suppose. A first name is better than what we had before, which was nothing."

"It should be quite helpful. Lily isn't the most common of names."

"That's what I thought," I said, as another phone rang at Cam's end. "Do you need to get that?"

"Yes, business call. Have to go." Cam hung up before I could slip in a goodbye.

I rejoined Donna and Ruth in the living room of the condo, tapping the phone against my palm.

"Oh, you missed it. Ruth was telling me about the grand parties they used to have at Aircroft." Donna sighed. "Things were still very glamorous back in the fifties. I was just a baby in 1959, so I'm more of a sixties kid. That was a whole different thing."

"Yeah, the counter-culture and all that," I said. "Not so glamorous, although fun in its own way."

"Definitely fun. I was a bit young to really get caught up in the hippie movement, but I did enjoy a few local festivals."

"Well now, this is something I've never heard about." Ruth clutched the cane leaning against her chair and pointed it at Donna. "Spill all the details, missy."

"Goodness, look at the time." Donna held up her hand, displaying her silver wristwatch. "I probably should be getting you back home, Ruth. I know you said your son was stopping by to visit and bring you dinner around five."

Ruth tapped the face of her own watch. "It's only just now four. We have time. You're simply trying to weasel out of telling us the stories of your wild youth."

"Guilty," Donna said with a broad smile. "But really, my past isn't all that interesting."

"Why do I doubt that?" I asked, sharing a knowing look with Ruth. "Alright, you're off the hook for now, but we won't forget."

"No, we certainly will not. Now, if someone will lend me their arm, I'll get up and you can drive me home, Donna."

I hurried over and helped Ruth to her feet. As I stepped back, I offered her a warm smile. "Thanks so much for agreeing to speak with us today, Ruth. I really appreciate it, and I know my boss will too."

"It was no bother." Ruth, leaning on the cane, met my gaze with a searching look. "All I ask is that if you do find Lily, you let her know I'd love to see her again, okay?"

"I'll be happy to do that. But you know, she might've already passed. She'd probably be in her mid-nineties by now, if she was in her later twenties when you were ten and eleven," I said.

Ruth waved one hand from side to side. "That's not so old these days. I plan to be around when I reach that age. Maybe in a wheel-chair or whatever, but I wouldn't count out someone just because they're in their nineties."

"Well, I certainly wouldn't count *you* out," I told her.

Ruth glanced over at Donna. "You weren't wrong. She is pretty smart, isn't she?"

"No question about that," Donna said. "And almost as tenacious as Vince."

I laughed and wished both women a good day before making my exit. Sitting in my car for a moment before driving off, I pulled out both pieces of paper and studied the copies of the photo and drawing again. "Now I know why your photograph turned up in the Airley family photos, Lily," I said aloud. "Calvin must've taken it. His parents probably found it among his things and just shoved it in with their other photographs. But what were you doing at Aircroft in 1989, and why would Patricia Clewe draw your portrait?"

The picture offered no answer to this part of the mystery, and obviously Ruth didn't know anything about Lily's later visit to Air-croft. That was still a tangle I'd have to unravel.

Chapter Eleven

The first two work days of the next week were uneventful, but on Wednesday I knew that Eloise had arrived at Aircroft as soon as I topped the hill of the country road leading from town to the estate. Vehicles were lined up along the sides of the road, including small vans with dishes on top. They turned the two-lane road into one very narrow lane, and I had to drive with great caution to avoid sideswiping a couple of the larger trucks.

Sitting on the road, with a mob of people wielding microphones swarming my car, I wasn't sure how I was going to turn onto the estate's private lane and pass through the security gates without either running over a reporter or allowing part of the crowd to drive or dash through behind me. I was just about to text Lauren when a young woman wearing a uniform approached my car.

I noticed her badge said Leland Private Security. So, not the police. I assumed Cam had hired the security firm to protect Aircroft from unwanted visitors.

"Hi, I'm Jane Hunter," I said, as the young woman leaned into my partially opened side window. "I actually work on the estate."

After consulting something on her phone, the security officer asked for my driver's license, which I handed over to her.

"Yes, you're on the list," she said, as she returned my license. "Just let us clear a path for you and you can go through."

She waved over two other security guards, and together they forced the reporters and other media personnel to step back from the driveway. I drove past the crowd, shouts filling my ears as the reporters lobbed questions at me. Which I ignored, of course. When I had to lower my driver's side window again in order to punch in the gate code, the guards stood shoulder to shoulder alongside my car to prevent anyone from slipping through or seeing the sequence of numbers I entered into the keypad. One of the guards barked out a command to stay back or face criminal trespassing charges as I passed through the open gates.

I was happy to leave the commotion behind as I drove farther down the long lane that led to the main house. I parked near the detached garage and hurried along the paved path to the mansion, looking over my shoulder and from side to side to make sure no one had slipped through the perimeter established by the security team.

Lauren met me right outside the double front doors. "So sorry you have to run the gauntlet just to come to work," she said, as she ushered me inside.

"It's okay. As long as Cam keeps some security out front, that is."

"Don't worry, he will. At least until all this furor dies down." Lauren tugged down the hem of her gold-and-black-print tunic top, which she was wearing over a pair of black skinny jeans. "I know, I know. Not my usual work outfit," she said as she caught my gaze. "But I decided to stay here at Aircroft rather than travel back and forth to my apartment because of all those vultures at the gate. It was a last-minute decision and I just threw stuff into a suitcase without much thought."

"You look perfectly lovely, as always," I said. "So I assume Eloise Anderson is here somewhere?"

"She arrived very early this morning." Lauren's maroon-tinted lips tightened. "Cam had a driver bring her. He tried to set it up so that the press wouldn't realize where she'd gone, but as you could see, that didn't work."

"Someone was probably watching her every move, from the police station back to the bookshop, once she was released on bail." Following Lauren across the entry hall, I gave her a sidelong glance. "Was it a lot of money, the bail?"

"Not inconsiderable," she replied, her expression giving away her feelings on the matter. "But Cam didn't hesitate to pay it."

"Very nice of him," I said dryly.

Lauren stopped walking and faced me with an appraising look. "You think it's possible she *is* guilty, don't you?"

"It's possible," I said. "But you know what they say—everyone should be considered innocent until proven guilty."

Lauren pursed her lips and stared at me for a moment before her icy expression melted. "I thought I'd head to the kitchen for some coffee. Cam's on an overseas call, which means I'm not needed at the moment. Care to join me?"

"Sure, why not. I could use some coffee before I dive back into cataloging," I said.

When we reached the kitchen, we both greeted Mateo Marin, Cam's live-in chef.

"Coffee's ready," he said. "And there are some muffins in the bread box. Please help yourselves. I have to run out to the kitchen garden to gather some vegetables for today's meals." He pulled a large wicker basket from a shelf near one of the back doors and headed outside.

Lauren filled a white ceramic mug with coffee. "There should be cream in the fridge," she said, pointing to the smaller of two industrial-sized stainless-steel refrigerators. "I remember you don't drink it black."

After I filled my own mug and grabbed the cream, I sat down on a stool across the kitchen worktable from Lauren. "Not to be nosy, but I can tell you aren't thrilled with having Eloise Anderson as a guest. I can see why, after encountering that mess at the front gates."

"That's one reason." Lauren took a sip of her coffee. "There's also the money for the twenty-four seven security detail, as well as the lawyers and the bail. I mean, Cam has plenty, but not all of it is readily available at a moment's notice."

"Then there's Cam's obvious interest in Eloise," I said, keeping my gaze focused on the spoon I was casually swirling in my coffee.

"Then there's that," Lauren said gloomily.

I looked up to meet her troubled gaze. "You've mentioned that Cam usually lets the women do the chasing, and then sometimes allows them to catch him. For a brief time, anyway. But this seems a little different."

"It is." Lauren tapped the rim of her mug with one polished fingernail. "Eloise is honestly not showing any particular interest in Cam, other than as a friend and benefactor. But I'm afraid Cam seems . . ."

"Besotted?" I blew on my coffee before taking a long swallow.

Lauren shook her head. "Not quite that extreme. But he definitely seems interested in her as more than a friend. It probably wouldn't be obvious to most people, but I can see it."

"Does he have a tell?" I asked.

"Maybe. His expression when he looks at her is one giveaway. He also talks about her a lot more than necessary." Lauren took another sip of coffee. "It's not like he's falling all over her or anything. Of course, Cam never shows that much emotion."

"Hmmm," I mumbled, not wanting to betray Cam by mentioning the times I'd definitely seen him express his feelings.

"Not that it's any of business who Cam likes, but I just worry that he's diving in again without checking the depth of the pool." Lauren dabbed her lips, leaving traces of her lipstick on the napkin. "If it turns out that Eloise really did kill that detective, Cam will be crushed."

And you care about that, I thought, taking another swig of coffee. *Not just because he's your boss, but because you care about him.* But I refused to say such a thing out loud. I'd never want to embarrass Lauren, who was as proud as she was beautiful and intelligent.

"I wouldn't worry too much," I said, with a sympathetic smile. "I'm sure he'll manage to get over anything, in time."

"Oh, well, of course." Lauren hopped off her stool. "I suppose I'd better get to work. I need to tackle some paperwork for a few charities Cam sponsors." She stretched out one hand. "Are you done? I can carry both mugs over to the dishwasher if you want."

"Thanks, but I actually think I'll grab another cup to take to the library," I said. As Lauren crossed the room, her mug dangling from her fingers, I added, "It's nice of you to worry about your boss so much."

"As if you don't?" After placing her mug in the dishwasher, Lauren turned to face me. She gripped the edge of the adjacent counter with both hands as if to steady herself. "You worry about him too."

"Oh, I admit I do," I said. "Well, maybe not worry so much as care about his wellbeing."

"Same." Wariness edged Lauren's voice. "But that's just being a decent human being, don't you think?"

"Absolutely," I said, sliding off my stool and grabbing my empty mug. As I strolled over to the counter that held the coffee maker, Lauren offered me a quick goodbye and left the kitchen, her heels tapping a rapid staccato beat.

Carrying my filled coffee mug to the library, I inwardly mused about how foolish people could be. *If only Lauren could bring herself to say something . . .* But I understood her reluctance. It could jeopardize her job, for one thing. Not to mention that there was no promise she'd receive a positive response, which could endanger her dignity as well as her heart. *Relationships*, I thought, *are such a gamble. And despite what books and movies would have us believe, there's never any guarantee that everyone will find their true love.* I snorted at my own sentimentality. *Whatever that is.*

The morning passed swiftly as soon as I settled into cataloging. I was absorbed by my work on the Helen McCloy books and papers when footsteps alerted me that someone was entering the library.

Expecting to see Cam or Lauren, I was taken aback when Eloise approached my desk.

"Sorry, I didn't mean to startle you," she said, clutching the front edge of the thin white sweater she wore over a royal blue sundress. "Cam told me you'd be working in the library, and I just wanted to come and thank you."

"Thank me?" I raised my eyebrows. "Whatever for?"

"For not freaking out when you found me the other day. I know it must've been a horrible shock."

"No need to thank me," I said, rolling my chair back from the desk. "I simply alerted the authorities, like anyone would've done."

"Yes, but . . ." Eloise twisted a button on her sweater. "You didn't immediately jump to the conclusion that I'd killed anyone. I mean, that's what I've heard from my lawyers. You even told the police that the back door dead bolt wasn't latched, which might help my defense."

"I just stated the facts." I looked her over, noting the paleness of her face and the redness rimming her wide blue eyes. "The lights were off in the office too, which I mentioned because I thought that was another odd thing. I didn't think you'd meet Detective Parker in a dark office."

Eloise's lashes fluttered behind the lenses of her glasses. "You're right, I didn't. I told the police that the lights were on when I left the office to go search for that book in the storeroom."

"What book was that, exactly?" I asked. "I mean, it seems strange that Parker asked you to find a book. What possible connection could that have to your mom's case?"

"I don't know." Eloise must've read the disbelief in my face because she threw up her hands. "I realize that sounds ridiculous, but the truth is that the books kept in the storeroom are shelved by inventory numbers. Detective Parker just gave me the number."

"How in the world would he know something like that?" I asked, motioning toward one of the armchairs. "Please, sit down. You look done in."

"I am exhausted." Eloise hurried over to the closer armchair and sank into its soft cushions. "To your question, I have no idea where he got that number, or why. He said he'd explain it to me once I brought him the book."

"But the book wasn't there?"

Eloise shook her head. "No. We store the books in acid-free cardboard cases, marked with their inventory number. There was nothing with that number. Not where it was supposed to be, or anywhere around that area. And when I checked the ledgers where we record all the titles and their numbers, it wasn't there either."

I rolled my chair around to the side of the desk so I could face Eloise more directly. "Wait—you're saying the item wasn't listed in the inventory? But before you said that range of numbers was in the ledgers."

"It was, but the page it should've been listed on was missing. Torn out, actually. I could see bits of paper still clinging to the gutter."

"I'm surprised that no one noticed that before," I said.

"It's not as odd as you think. Those records were for older acquisitions, including stock my parents bought when they purchased the store. My dad didn't like to toss books, so he just kept that stuff, even though it wasn't anything he's was particularly interested in."

"So, for some reason, Detective Parker learned of a book that should've been in your shop, but ended up going missing, along with its inventory record?" Pressing my elbow against the chair arm, I rested my chin on my fist. "Which means that book might be the key to why Parker was murdered."

"Not just Parker," said Cam from the doorway, "but also Eloise's father."

Chapter Twelve

"Your new theory?" I asked, as Cam strolled into the library. "One of them," he replied, sitting in the other armchair. "Sorry, Eloise. I should've mentioned this idea to you before I blurted it out," he added, stretching an arm over the small cherry table separating the chairs.

He couldn't quite touch her arm, and Eloise made no effort to reach for his hand. "It's okay," she said, casting him a brief smile. "The same thought had already occurred to me."

Dropping his hand onto the padded arm of his chair, Cam turned his gaze on me. "By the way, David Benton just rang and told Lauren he was in the area and wondered if he could stop by this afternoon. She said yes, of course. He should be here any minute."

"From Benton House?" Eloise jumped up out of her chair. "He's coming here?"

"Yes, it's an area of investigation . . ." Cam said, before Eloise cut him off by holding up one hand, palm out.

"I don't want to see him," she said, turning away. "Those people were nothing but ugly to my mother during her trial. Gloria Benton even got on the stand and implied all sorts of things about my parents stealing from clients." She yanked the open front of her sweater together, balling up a wad of material in her fist, and strode over to the open door. "If you'll excuse me, I'm going to retreat to my room."

"Well, that touched a nerve," I said after Eloise left.

Cam stared at the empty doorway. "So there was bad blood between the Bentons and the Andersons. I thought as much, but Eloise's reaction solidifies it."

"I'm sure she didn't mean to be rude," I said, noticing Cam's pensive expression. "Her nerves are probably frayed as old electrical wire right now."

"Of course," he said, with a glance at his watch. "I suppose it will take a little extra time for Benton to make his way past all those hyenas at the gates, but I think I'll just wait here, if that's alright with you."

"Okay, I don't mind taking a break," I said, rising to my feet.

"Stay," Cam snapped. He then took a deep breath and looked up at me, suitably abashed. "Sorry, I don't mean to bark orders. But I think you should meet David Benton and hear what he has to say. Two impressions will be better than one, don't you think?"

"Very well." I rolled my chair back to my desk and sat down. "But I'm going to stay over here, out of sniping range."

Cam's eyes narrowed. "It wasn't that bad, was it?"

"It wasn't polite, but you know that," I replied. "I hope."

"Yes, I'm learning." Cam leaned back in his chair, staring up at the coffered ceiling. "Thanks for calling me out on such things, Jane. I really do want to do better."

I cast him a smile. "I know."

"You and Lauren have to keep pointing out when I slip up," Cam said. "I realize I don't always react well to your efforts in the moment . . ."

I couldn't prevent a gurgle of laughter.

Cam continued speaking with only a sharp glance my way. "However, I do appreciate them. And you," he said.

"And Lauren, I hope." I considered my next words carefully. "She does a lot for you. Far beyond her job description, I'm sure."

"I realize that," Cam said stiffly.

"Do you? Perhaps you could show a little more . . ." I cut my sentence short as the tapping of Lauren's heels as well as heavier footfalls resonated from the hallway.

A tall, distinguished-looking older man walked into the room while Lauren waited in the hallway. "Thanks so much," he told her.

"No problem at all," she replied. "Cam, please introduce yourself and Jane. I want to run to the kitchen. I believe Mateo has whipped up some drinks and snacks for your meeting."

Cam stood and crossed to the older man. "Cameron Clewe," he said, extending his hand.

The man, whose tailored gray suit and expertly trimmed silver hair wouldn't have looked out of place on Wall Street, gave Cam's hand a vigorous shake. "David Benton. Very glad to meet you, even if I did have to practically mow down a few reporters at the gate to get here."

"And this is Jane Hunter, a librarian I've hired to catalog my book collection," Cam said, ignoring the comments about the gate while indicating me with a sweep of his hand.

"Ah, my favorite sort of person." David Benton strode around the desk to offer his hand to me. "I love librarians. Can't imagine what the world would be like without them."

"Eternally disorganized," I said dryly as I held out my own hand.

The lines fanning out from David Benton's brown eyes crinkled. "Indeed." He clasped my hand rather than shaking it. "Very pleased to make your acquaintance, Ms. Hunter."

"You can call me Jane," I said, as I extricated my fingers.

"Then you must call me David." He turned to Cam. "You too. I don't need to stand on ceremony with fellow book lovers."

"Won't you have a seat?" Cam motioned to the armchairs.

"I understand you have quite a collection here at Aircroft." As David sat down, his gaze roamed around the library, and I couldn't help but notice that his eyes sparkled with a glint of avarice as well as appreciation.

"This isn't everything," I said. "Cam stores some of his collections elsewhere."

"Is that so? I'm impressed." David turned to Cam, who'd settled in the other armchair. "Well, Cam—I hope I can call you that? Since we're all friends here . . ."

Cam's auburn eyebrows shot up.

". . . I hope, anyway," David continued, without seeming to notice Cam's reaction. "So, what can I do for you, Cam? My auction house is quite adept at finding rare items, books as well as art and antiques. If you have something special in mind, I'd love to help you acquire it."

"Actually, I'm afraid I've brought you here under false pretenses." Cam's fingers drummed against the chair arm in sets of three, like a waltz rhythm. "I'm not looking to purchase items; I'm seeking information."

"Oh?" David settled back in his chair. He appeared perfectly calm, except for a twitch in his impressively sculpted jawline. "What could that be?"

"It has to do with the Anderson family," I said.

"The Last Chapter Bookshop Andersons?" David arranged his face into a mournful visage. "What a terribly sad story that is. First Abby Anderson kills her husband and then her daughter . . ."

"Before you go any further, you should know that I've offered Eloise Anderson refuge here at Aircroft," Cam said, his tone as thunderous as his eyes.

David smiled. "Of course I know that. Why else would your front gates be swarming with reporters? And, I confess, I've heard all about the recent murder and how much you're helping poor, dear, Eloise. Very gallant of you, I must say."

"We're both trying to help prove her innocence," I said, drawing David's amused gaze.

"That's your little hobby, right?" David looked me over. "Aiding your boss, of course. Oh yes, I did my research on you, Cam," he added, turning his head to meet Cam's cool stare. "I always check out potential clients. It's amazing how many crooks and frauds there are in the world, don't you agree?"

"Which is precisely what I wanted to ask you about," Cam said, stilling his fingers when he caught me sending him a message by surreptitiously wiggling my own. "I know there can be some black-market dealings in the world of art and antiques and other collectibles, and rare books are no exception."

"Sadly, that's true," David said. "Although of course Benton House eschews such behavior."

Cam crossed his arms over his chest. "The thing is, during Abby's trial, your mother alluded to the Andersons being involved in illegal acquisitions and sales. I can't speak to the truth of that, but given the possibility, I wondered if you knew whether they'd made any enemies."

"You mean, of the organized crime variety?" David shrugged his broad shoulders. "It's possible, although how anyone other than Abby could've committed that murder is beyond me. But if you want to pursue that white whale, you don't need to look any farther than their business partner."

I sat up straighter. "Neil Knight?"

"That's the guy. Now retired, of course, but he was still involved in the bookstore after Ken's death. Supposedly helping out Eloise, although I suspect he was also helping himself, if you catch my drift."

"You think he was crooked? As in brokering black market deals?" I asked.

David's genial expression never faltered. "I've heard rumors to that effect."

"He is still alive," Cam said softly, as if talking to himself.

"Yes indeed. He retired to a very exclusive, very pricey, golf community." David met Cam's intense gaze with a lift of his eyebrows. "Not something you'd expect for a partner in a somewhat successful, but certainly not extremely lucrative, book business."

I leaned forward, gripping my knees. "You're saying he's the person we should talk to if we want to find out if the Andersons had possibly run afoul of criminal connections?"

"It would be a good start, I think." David's gaze swept over me, examining my face and figure in a way I found distinctly uncomfortable. "If you would like to meet him, I believe I can arrange that. My family is hosting a gala on Friday evening. It's a charity thing, meant to raise money for a local arts school. I could make sure Neil gets a last-minute invite and, knowing him, I'm sure he'll accept."

"Then you'd invite Cam as well?" I asked, sharing a look with my boss. I knew it would be difficult for Cam to attend a large gathering outside of Aircroft, but thought he might brave it, if only for Eloise's sake.

"Well, I wasn't actually thinking of Cam. I know he doesn't enjoy such things." David turned his brilliant smile on me. "It might work better if you come as my date, Jane. No one would question it, and you could mingle freely with my guests. You could even speak with my mother if you felt so inclined. She knew the Andersons fairly well, at least as business rivals. And you could also talk to Neil Knight."

I opened my mouth and snapped it shut again without saying anything.

"That sounds like an excellent idea," Cam said.

I shot him a warning look.

Cam stared me down. "Of course she'll accept, right, Jane?"

Swallowing back a swear word, I shifted my gaze to David and forced a smile.

"Delighted," I said.

Chapter Thirteen

I made my excuses and swiftly exited after that, leaving Cam and David talking about some of the more unique items shelved in the library. As I headed for the kitchen, I ran into Lauren and Mateo, who were carrying trays of snacks and drinks.

"Don't worry, Mr. Benton is still in the library with Cam. I just needed to take a break," I told them when they both sent me inquiring looks.

I wandered through the kitchen and stepped outside into the kitchen garden. Pacing the flagstone paved walkways between the raised beds, I allowed the buzz of bees and the warm breeze to calm me. Finally tired of walking, I sat on a wooden bench at the far end of the garden and watched two monarch butterflies flitting from blossom to blossom on the trellised snow pea vines.

Tilting my head, I stared up into the pale blue sky and amused myself by imagining the clouds as a herd of fluffy sheep grazing on air. But I still couldn't banish the memory of my rudeness to David Benton.

Not a very smart move for a sleuth, no matter how amateur, I chided myself. *We do need to talk to Neil Knight and Benton provided the perfect opportunity.* I sighed deeply as I lowered my gaze. I knew my reaction was because I'd felt ambushed. That had been a tactic my ex-husband, Gary, had frequently used on me—publicly forcing me to agree to some action or event because there was no graceful way to say no. *But Benton isn't Gary and this isn't a real date or anything like that. It's simply a way to speak with some people with knowledge of the Anderson family.*

My cell phone vibrated in the pocket of my navy-blue slacks. Sliding it out, I opened a text from Vince.

Last minute, but could you leave work a little early today and meet me here? They might have some info on Lily, he texted, before providing directions to a local history museum.

Even though I hadn't cleared leaving work early with Cam yet, I immediately texted my agreement with this plan. I felt a few extra hours away from Aircroft might be beneficial to my mental health. Cam would just have to understand.

"Well, speak of the devil," I said, as footsteps on the flagstones alerted me to Cam's arrival. "Has David Benton left already?"

"Just now." Cam's hands were hanging by his sides, but they were squeezed into fists. "I'm sorry for pushing you into a situation you might not find comfortable, Jane, but it really is a fantastic opportunity to speak to people who might shed light on our current investigation."

"I know. After walking off my anger and then sitting here surrounded by nature, I realized that." I patted the seat of the bench. "Come sit down and tell me if you learned anything more from Benton."

"Not much," Cam said as he sat beside me. "He's a pretty clever guy. Doesn't give much away. I felt he was manipulating me as much as I was trying to play him. Which honestly makes me wonder if he's telling the truth about Neil Knight."

"You suspect he wants us to think Knight is crooked to take the focus off of Benton House?"

"That thought did cross my mind." Cam shot me a sidelong glance. "By the way, I told him that I'd hire a car to take you to the gala and bring you home, so you don't have to worry about traveling around late at night with a stranger."

"Thank you. That does relieve my mind," I said. "How did Benton react to that proposal?"

"He pretended not to care, but I think he was disappointed. Whether that was because he wanted the opportunity to feed you more dubious information or because he fancies you, I don't know."

I snorted. "Fancies me? What is this, some Regency romance novel?"

"It seemed to me he was showing a decided interest in you," Cam said, hunching his shoulders.

"That's ridiculous. As you've said, the man can't necessarily be trusted. Besides"—I lightly poked Cam's arm with my elbow—"you aren't the best judge of such things."

"True enough," Cam said morosely.

I decided not to pursue that line of conversation. "Okay, so I'm attending this gala Friday night. The only problem is, I imagine it's black tie or something similar and I have nothing appropriate to wear."

Cam's expression brightened. "That's simple enough. I'll just have Lauren provide you with a credit card and point you toward some shops. She knows what's best in the area."

"Probably some places I've never stepped into before, but as long as it's your money . . ."

"It's really no problem," Cam said, with a dismissive wave of his hand.

I studied his finely etched profile for a moment. "See, that's the thing, Cam. You can't even imagine the obstacles people who don't have a boatload of money face every day. I think sometimes that makes it hard for ordinary people to relate to you. People like Eloise, for example."

Cam turned his head and stared at me, his eyes narrowed. "If you're trying to tell me something, spit it out. You know I don't like veiled comments."

"I simply mean that maybe someone like Eloise feels a little intimidated around you. Your lifestyle is so different from hers. And all that money you've paid out for her defense team and bail also creates a sort of, well, *imbalance* between you."

"You think that's why she wants to keep to herself?" Cam asked, his brow furrowing.

I laid a hand on his forearm. "I believe that's part of it. Not to mention she's experienced a trauma. So don't come on too strong right now. Give her time."

Cam looked away, but I could tell he was processing this information. "I'll keep that in mind. Now—since you do need to buy an outfit for the gala, why don't you take the afternoon off? I'll check in with Lauren and have her meet you in the library with the credit card and her store suggestions." He rose to his feet, brushing a speck of dust from his ivory linen pants.

"Thanks, that will be helpful," I said, standing to face him. I didn't bother to mention meeting Vince later in the day. That could remain my business unless I actually discovered any pertinent information on our mystery woman.

Cam looked me in the eyes, his lips curving into a faint smile. "No, thank you. For helping the investigation by attending the gala, and . . . well, always being honest with me."

A Killer Clue

"It's a bad habit of mine," I said, with an answering smile. "Just ask my daughter. Which, by the way, you might get to do soon, as she's coming for a visit."

"Really? How nice," Cam said, in a casual tone that let me know the depth of his interest in Eloise.

Otherwise, I thought, *he'd been more excited about meeting Bailey, whose photos he's seen, and expressed appreciation for, at my apartment.*

"Alright, I'm going to head back inside," I said. "I'll wait for Lauren in the library, and then take off to do some shopping." I made a face. "Not my favorite thing."

"But remember, you can spend whatever you want," Cam said. "Buy something that makes you feel glamorous."

"I don't think even an unlimited expense account will achieve that. I'd need a fairy godmother," I said, earning a rare laugh from Cam.

Chapter Fourteen

Armed with an unlimited credit card and high-end boutique suggestions from Lauren, I did find something appropriate for the gala—a simple sleeveless black dress with a scooped neckline. A sheer black overlay shot through with multicolor metallic threads provided a higher neckline and short sleeves and gave the dress a touch of sparkle. I glanced at the tag only once, overcame the knot forming in my stomach, and bought the dress, along with an appropriate pair of shoes and some sheer black stockings. Fortunately, I already owned a fancy clutch purse, and as it was May, I wouldn't need a heavy coat. The black cashmere shawl that Bailey had given me as a birthday gift would suffice.

I hope you were serious about spending whatever, I texted Cam.

All part of the cost of the investigation, he responded.

After dropping off my new outfit at my apartment, I headed out to meet Vince at the local history museum. Since Vincent's home was close to the small downtown shopping district, I decided to walk. Maintaining a fast pace, I reached the museum in about ten minutes. An older brick building squeezed between a deli and pet grooming salon, the museum's plate glass window was filled with artifacts and a large, framed, antique map.

A string of bells tinkled as I entered.

"There she is." Vince waved me to the back, where a stocky older woman stood beside a wooden display case. "Jane, this is Anna Martz. Anna, Jane Hunter."

"Are you the curator?" I asked Anna.

Her small hazel eyes sparkled with good humor. "No, just a volunteer. To be honest, everyone who works here is a volunteer, although sometimes we bring in students from Salem College to help us set up special displays. They have a museum studies program, you know."

"I didn't know that," I said. "But I'm still learning about this area. I've lived in North Carolina for many years, but not around here."

Vince tapped my arm. "They have a collection of scrapbooks from the late forties through the early eighties. Newspaper clippings, photographs, and that sort of thing. I thought that might be a good place to start our research."

"I bet you've been here many times before," I said.

"Sure, Vince is a regular. I keep telling him he needs to sign up as a volunteer, but we haven't roped him in yet." Anna tucked a strand of white hair that had escaped her low bun behind one ear.

"Maybe someday," Vince said, shooting me a conspiratorial grin. "The scrapbooks are upstairs," he added, pointing toward a wooden staircase.

I expressed my thanks to Anna and followed Vince up the steps. "Wait a minute—if you're a regular, surely you've looked through many of these scrapbooks before. But you said you never saw anyone who looked like Lily. So what good is this going to do?"

"I haven't looked through them all," Vince replied as we reached the top of the stairs. "And two heads, or pairs of eyes, are better than one. I could've missed something before."

We crossed to an expansive wooden table placed in front of a row of metal bookshelves. Tall bound volumes, their spines marked with dates, filled the shelves. "Wow, that's a lot," I said, surveying the scrapbooks. "Someone spent a good deal of time putting these together."

"That someone would be me," said a man's gravelly voice behind me.

I spun around and came face-to-face with a tall, lanky man whose white hair and lined face told me he was at least a decade older than me. "Hello," I said, extending my hand. "Jane Hunter."

"Gordon Glenn," the man said, giving my hand a surprisingly strong shake.

Vince, who'd climbed up on a stepstool to retrieve two of the scrapbooks, hopped down, the volumes pressed to his chest. "Sorry, I didn't see you there, Gordy, or I would've made introductions."

"No worries." Gordon looked me up and down, his deep brown eyes sunken in his bony face. "So this is the librarian hired by Cameron Clewe. Vince has mentioned you a couple of times, Ms. Hunter."

"Saying good things, I hope," I replied with a smile. "And please, call me Jane."

Gordon's lips parted as he smiled, displaying yellowed teeth. "Then I'm Gordy. That's what everyone's called me since I was knee-high to a grasshopper."

"Very well, Gordy it is." I studied him for a moment, noting the slight hunch of his shoulders. "You must've been a volunteer here for many years to have accomplished all of this." I motioned toward the full shelves.

Gordy shook his head. "I began compiling the scrapbooks long before this museum even existed. It was mostly newspaper clippings back then, but as I got older, I convinced my friends and family, and eventually the town council, to provide me with photographs and other memorabilia. When the museum opened in the eighties, I donated my collection. I didn't feel like continuing with it once digital stuff started taking over, but I thought the earlier years could be useful."

Vince laid both scrapbooks on the table. "Gordy started scrapbooking back in . . . what was that year again?"

"Around 1947," Gordy said. "I was fourteen."

A quick calculation put his current age at ninety, which actually surprised me. *He's very well-preserved*, I thought. "So you started this as a hobby?"

Gordy shrugged. "My family owned a small farm outside of town. It was pretty isolated. I went to school, of course, but my parents were too busy to chauffer me around for sports teams or after-school clubs or anything like that. Except for schoolwork and farm work, there wasn't much to do."

"Gordy's always loved history," Vince said as he took a seat at the table. "And I've certainly picked his brains about things that happened in the area back in the day."

"You have indeed," Gordy said.

I sat down across the table from Vince. "Did Vince tell you what we're researching today?"

Gordy strolled over to one of the bookshelves. "No, just that you're mainly interested in the late fifties on."

"We're trying to find out more information on this woman," I said, fishing the copies of the photograph and drawing from my purse and laying them on the table. "Has Vince shown you these before?"

Gordy cast a quick glance at the pictures before looking away. "Yes. And like I told him then, I don't know anything about her."

"We have some new information. Apparently, her first name is Lily, and she dated Calvin Airley in the late fifties, right before his unfortunate death," Vince said, flipping open the scrapbook.

"Sorry, doesn't ring any bells," Gordy said. His back was to us, but I could see his grip tighten on the edge of one of the shelves.

"You never saw her around town?"

Gordy released his hold on the shelf and turned to face us. "No. But I wasn't around much. I'd gotten into farm equipment sales and traveled a lot."

"You kept up with the scrapbooks, though," Vince said, waving his hand over the open pages.

"That was still my hobby, when I was at home." Gordy flashed a tight-lipped smile. "Now, if you'll excuse me, I'm going to head downstairs and see if Anna needs help with anything."

After Gordy's footfalls on the stairs faded away, Vince looked over at me, his bushy eyebrows raised far above the frames of his glasses. "Is it just me, or does he seem very tetchy about our research on our mystery woman?"

"Not just you. He seemed distinctly uncomfortable," I said.

Vince slid the closed scrapbook across the table. "Maybe they dated? If she dumped him for Calvin, he might still be bitter."

"I don't know. From what Ruth Young said about her being around the same age as Calvin, she'd be in her mid-nineties by now. So she'd be older than Gordy by several years."

"That doesn't always matter." Vince lowered his head to peer at something in his scrapbook. "Here's photos from some party at Aircroft in 1956, but unfortunately, I don't see any signs of Lily in these." He turned the book around so I could see the page.

"I'm not surprised. Ruth said Calvin and Lily were keeping their relationship a secret." I studied the newsprint photos. "I guess this was from the society page. There's Calvin, appearing rather glum."

"He does look like he'd rather be anywhere else," Vince said. "Even while surrounded by all those pretty girls."

"This must've been about one year before he died." I sat back in my hard wooden chair. "It's a little spooky, seeing him in these pictures and knowing what happened to him."

Vince shoved his drooping glasses back up the bridge of his nose. "But we don't really know, do we?"

"True. Was it an accident, a suicide, or a murder?" I pushed the scrapbook back across the table. "Do you think we'll ever know?" I asked as I opened the other volume.

"If I have anything to say about it, we will."

"It would help if we locate Lily." I cast Vince a speculative glance. "She might know, or at least have the information you need to put it all together."

Vince's jaw clenched. "Which is just one more reason we need to find her."

Chapter Fifteen

V ince and I scoured the scrapbooks until the museum closed for the day but found no evidence of Lily in any of the pages. There were a few discolored spots on the scrapbook pages that made me think that photos had been removed at some point in time, but when we asked Gordy, he said he "reckoned people took out a few pictures of their parents or grandparents or something."

As Vince and I walked back home, I mentioned my theory that our mystery woman had come to the area to work at a local business.

"Perhaps she felt like an outsider," I said, when we reached Vince's house. "She may have kept to herself, which is why there are no pictures of her at community events."

Vince paused with one foot on the step of the porch stairs. "But Calvin met her somewhere."

"It had to be at her workplace." I wiped a little sweat from my upper lip. "Which could narrow things down. If we consider what establishments Calvin would've frequented . . ."

"Great idea!" Vince gave me a thumbs-up. "I'm going to check my notes. With all the facts I've collected on Calvin's life, there should be something in them about his favorite haunts."

I raised my eyebrows. "Haunts? Are we sure we want to call up spirits?"

"Wouldn't do any good, anyway," Vince said with a rueful smile. "You've said you haven't seen any evidence of ghosts at Aircroft, and if any place was going to be haunted, I think that estate would be it."

"I haven't seen or heard anything *yet*," I replied, with an answering smile. "Maybe Calvin just isn't ready to talk to me."

Vince's expression grew serious. "Have you ever asked Cam if he's experienced anything paranormal at the estate? He's lived there all of his life."

"You want me to ask Cam about ghosts?" A bark of laughter escaped my lips. "Can you imagine his reaction?"

"Yeah, okay. Maybe not my smartest idea. Forget I said that." Vince grinned and wished me a good evening.

Not long after I settled on the sofa in my apartment, sipping a glass of wine and enjoying the next chapter in my latest read, a loud series of knocks rattled my front door. Swearing under my breath as I set down my book and wine, I padded in my bare feet across the tile floor of the kitchen.

I peered through the peephole. Seeing a middle-aged woman in a tailored navy suit, I cracked open the door, leaving on the chain. "Yes, can I help you?"

The woman flashed a badge. "Ms. Hunter, I'm Terry Lindover, a detective with the Chapel Hill police department. I just have a few questions for you. May I come in?"

"Can I see your badge again?"

The woman pressed it into my palm. I examined the badge and identification card, confirming that this was indeed Teresa Lindover, before I slid off the door chain.

"Sorry, I wasn't expecting anyone," I said, scooping up my kicked-off shoes and my purse and carrying them into my bedroom, which was simply an area cordoned off from the main living space by a set of bookcases. "Please, have a seat."

When I walked back into the living room, Terry Lindover was perched on the edge of my comfortable, but well-worn, sofa. "Can I get you something to drink?" I asked. "I have water, tea, coffee, and a couple of cans of diet cola." I also had wine, but doubted an officer on duty would accept that.

"Just water," she replied, tugging her narrow skirt down over her knees.

Bringing her a glass of water from the kitchen, I took a moment to take a measure of the detective. She was an attractive woman, tall and slim, with wheat-gold hair and blue-gray eyes. Her short, feathery haircut framed her face, softening her angular features.

"Here you go," I said, handing her the glass. "Now, how can I help you?"

"I'm doing a little follow-up from the other day." Terry delicately sipped the water before setting it on the side table next to the sofa.

"More questions? I've already talked to one of your fellow detectives over the phone, and of course I gave my statement at the scene," I said, sitting in my wooden rocking chair.

"This is a little different." Terry settled back against the sofa cushions. "Full disclosure—this isn't exactly an official visit."

I gripped the smooth arms of the rocker. "Oh? What is it, then?"

Terry met my dubious gaze with a humorless smile. "I'd just like to know more about your impressions of the scene. It's somewhat personal. You see, the victim, Detective Parker, was my partner for many years."

Blinking rapidly, I searched for the proper response. "I'm very sorry for your loss," I said at last.

Terry inclined her head. "Thank you."

"But what do mean by my impressions of the scene?" I pushed one foot against the floor, sending the rocker into a gentle motion. "I told the detectives at the scene everything I saw, and I reiterated those points when they called me."

"But those are just facts. I'd like to know how you felt when you entered that office." As Terry crossed her hands in her lap, I noticed her meticulous manicure. Her nails were buffed, not painted, but I had no doubt that she'd had them professionally done.

"Confusion, at first. It was dark, so all I saw were shapes. It wasn't until I was able to find the switch and turn on the lights that I realized what I was looking at."

"The lights were off?" A tiny spasm twitched the corner of Terry's lips. "Are you sure?"

"Absolutely. Which is odd, don't you think? Ms. Anderson claims she left the office and went into the storeroom to look for a book that Detective Parker had requested. There was no reason for her to turn off the lights before she left, and I don't understand why your former partner would've done that either."

"If she left." Terry straightened until her back wasn't touching the sofa. "We only have her word for that. It's just as likely that she agreed to meet Bruce in the bookshop office, turned off the lights before he arrived, and ambushed him."

I rocked the chair a little faster. "I suppose."

"You arrived after the fact, correct?"

"I think so. There was no shouting or sounds of a violent struggle while I was in the store," I said. "I did hear a thump, which drew me to the office, but that was all."

"Which means Ms. Anderson's story is just that—her story, which cannot be corroborated." Terry flicked a piece of lint off of her skirt and met my gaze with perfect equanimity. "I know you believe her to be innocent, as does your boss, Mr. Clewe, but you both should seriously consider the possibility that she is not. For one thing, how did someone else kill Bruce and leave without you seeing them?"

"Perhaps they fled before I arrived," I said. "I imagine the official time of death and other evidence will prove whether that was possible or not. And the back door to the loading dock was unbolted."

"The official report said it was locked," Terry said, her nostrils flaring.

"Yes, but the dead bolt wasn't thrown. That was something I noticed even before I discovered the murder scene." I stopped the rocking of my chair by skidding one foot against the floor. "That doorknob is the kind you can lock and pull shut once you're outside. The killer could've fled out the back, and the door would've locked when they let it slam behind them."

Terry pursed her lips and looked me over, her expression unreadable. "Not an impossible theory, but a little far-fetched, wouldn't you say?"

"Not as strange as Eloise Anderson stabbing someone for no reason."

"But she had a reason. Bruce was the detective who helped convict her mother," Terry said.

I stared at Terry's implacable face. She seemed determined to pin the murder on Eloise, but then apparently so did the rest of her department. And Bruce Parker had been her partner, which gave her a personal motive for seeing justice done. "Yes, but Eloise claims that he was the one who wanted to meet with *her*, to provide some sort of update on the case. She thought he'd discovered new information that might exonerate her mom."

"I don't see how that would be possible." Terry sat up straighter, gracefully crossing her legs at her ankles. "Bruce retired four years ago. He wouldn't have, actually couldn't have, still been investigating the case, especially since it was considered solved." She frowned. "He did visit Abby Anderson in prison a few times, but I thought that was simply his way of trying to understand her motive for killing her husband. He always found that incomprehensible, to tell you the truth."

So Bruce Parker visited Abby in prison. Which meant he could've been the one to slip her the mysterious note. Perhaps he grabbed a book from the prison library and made sure it was delivered to her. I leaned forward, resting my palms on my thighs. "Tell me, Detective Lindover, why are you really here? You said this wasn't an official visit, and frankly, I have nothing to share with you beyond what's in my statements to your colleagues."

"Oh, I just wanted to see if you were a reliable witness." Terry flashed a humorless smile. "It's important to me that the case be solved, and I started to have my doubts about your reliability when I heard that your boss had taken the chief suspect under his wing. But you've confirmed everything I read in your statements, so I now believe you can be trusted to present the facts as you know them."

"I'd always do that, especially under oath," I said. "Besides, the truth is important to me. I won't bend the facts just to protect someone. I'll describe the events as I experienced them, whether that's beneficial to Ms. Anderson or not."

"I'm glad to hear that." Terry stood up and smoothed down the front of her jacket. "I won't take up any more of your time." She turned and strode toward the front door.

I followed on her heels. "I truly am sorry that your former partner was killed," I said as I held open the door to allow her to exit.

Pausing on the landing. Terry looked back at me with a searching gaze. "There was one more thing. Not really important, since I think it's all bunk, but since Ms. Anderson claims Bruce sent her to find some mysterious book, I wonder what book that might be. Did she say?"

"No, because she says she didn't know."

"That seems odd, don't you think? In her statement she claimed she only had an inventory number, but if she was telling the truth about Bruce's request, I can't imagine him knowing such a thing. The title of a book, yes. But not some random number." The lines around Terry's lips deepened. "Another thing that makes me think Ms. Anderson is lying."

"Perhaps it was something Abby Anderson told him before she died." I looked the detective directly in the eyes. "You said he'd visited her in prison a couple of times."

"Yes, but I don't think she was passing him messages. Anyway, I just wondered whether Ms. Anderson has embellished her story after the fact, like mentioning the actual book title? I thought she might've provided more details later, to you or Mr. Clewe. But apparently not." Terry rolled her shoulders, as if casting away some burden. "It doesn't matter, of course. I simply find it a curious alibi. Goodbye, Ms. Hunter," she added, as she descended the stairs.

Closing my door, I made sure it was securely locked and the chain was engaged. If anyone else came knocking, I wasn't home.

Chapter Sixteen

L auren told me to go home early on Friday, assuring me that she'd inform Cam. "You need time to get ready for the gala tonight, and since Cam asked you to go, he really can't complain," she told me.

"He might anyway," I said with a smile.

Lauren rolled her eyes. "Let him. I'll just ignore it like I usually do."

Back at the apartment, I took a leisurely shower, using the time to think up questions to ask the Bentons and Neil Knight. Since my hair was short, it was pretty much wash and dry, no styling required, but I did spend more time than usual on my makeup. Fortunately, Bailey had shown me some tricks she'd learned as an actress, so I was able to enhance my features while still looking natural.

When I finally checked myself out in the full-length mirror that I'd hung in my bedroom, I was pleasantly surprised. My new outfit was slimming but still had style and a little sparkle. "It's definitely going to be my go-to for any fancy events in the future," I told my mirror self.

Cam had been as good as his word and arranged for a car to pick me up at the apartment. I wasn't surprised when it turned out to be a luxury sedan, with a driver in uniform, but chuckled nonetheless. Cam was so used to luxury, he had no idea that this was a bit of overkill.

The driver got out and held the back door open for me. "I'm Taylor," he said. Tall and broad-shouldered, with short blond hair covered by a hat, he looked more like a bodyguard than a chauffeur. *Which isn't really the worst idea*, I thought as I slipped into the vehicle.

"Will you be driving me home as well?" I asked, fastening my seat belt.

"Yes. I'll just wait outside in the car until you text me." Taylor handed me a business card. "I may have to park a few blocks from the venue, but I'll pull up to the main entrance as soon as I get your text."

"You have to just sit in the car for a few hours? That doesn't seem quite fair," I said.

"It's fine. The weather's good, and I have a book to read." As Taylor backed the car out onto the road, I could see his eyes in the rearview mirror, bright blue as cornflowers.

"What book?" I smoothed down the long skirt of my dress. "Sorry, I shouldn't be so nosy. It's just that I'm a librarian, so I'm always interested in what people are reading."

"No worries. I like to talk about books too." Taylor turned onto the main road through town. "It's *Piranesi*, by Susanna Clarke."

"Oh, I love that book!" I adjusted my expression to hide my surprise and internally chided myself. *Just because a guy looks like a bodyguard, it doesn't mean he doesn't like literary fiction.*

"Don't tell me how it ends," Taylor said with mock severity. "I'm only two-thirds through."

I crossed my heart. "I would never do that. But I'm interested in your comments about the story. I mean, how it all ties together."

"I have some ideas. But I don't know if they're right," Taylor said, as he turned onto the highway that led to High Point.

"I wouldn't worry about that," I said. "Personally, I think there can be multiple interpretations of this story, which is one of my favorite type of books."

We discussed the novel for the remainder of the drive. I was enjoying our conversation so much that I was disappointed when we reached our destination.

Taylor pulled up and parked in front of a large, cream-colored brick building. It looked more like a warehouse than a store, although there was one large plate glass window displaying antique furniture and paintings on easels, and the windows in the entrance doors were emblazoned with *Benton House* in an elegant script.

"I didn't realize they were holding the gala at their store," I said as Taylor opened my door. I climbed out, careful not to catch the hem of my gown on the heels of my dressy black sandals.

"It's a big space. I imagine they can move things around and make a sort of ballroom," Taylor said.

Pulling the front edges of my cashmere shawl together with one hand and holding my clutch purse in the other, I thanked Taylor and followed a finely dressed couple into the building.

David Benton, looking quite handsome in a well-tailored black tuxedo, was waiting just inside the door. "Jane, how splendid you look," he said, looking me over with a practiced eye. "Do you want to hold on to your wrap, or leave it with the coat check?"

With the crowd of people milling about, the space would be warm. "Coat check is fine," I said, slipping off my shawl and handing it to him. "And, thank you."

David turned to a young woman standing behind a carved mahogany table that I assumed was one of the company's antiques.

Behind her, temporary rolling racks had been set up to handle coats and other outerwear. The young woman traded a ticket for my shawl.

"Is this your main showroom?" I asked David as I tucked the ticket inside my purse.

David took my arm and guided me through the press of people near the entrance. "Yes. Of course we moved out most of the stock and brought in rental tables and chairs for tonight."

"I'm sure you didn't want your valuable items damaged," I said.

It was a large, open room with tall ceilings and plain white walls. *The better to display art and antiques*, I thought as I surveyed the space. Standing-height circular tables, covered in white linen tablecloths, dotted the central area, while groupings of chairs and short cocktail tables lined the walls. There were flowers everywhere—extravagant arrangements in shades of pink, yellow, and white.

"People do tend to spill things at these events," David said, releasing his hold on my arm when we reached a less congested section of the room. "We left the antique light fixtures, though."

I looked up, realizing that chandeliers, lamps, and other light fixtures of all descriptions hung from the black metal rafters above our heads. They cast a golden glow over the room. "Is that a Tiffany?" I asked, pointing toward a light made from vivid, intricate pieces of stained glass.

"It is indeed," David said, his voice brimming with pride. "Quite a find, actually. One of the original Clara Driscoll designs."

This meant nothing to me, but I smiled and nodded as if it did. "You have so many beautiful pieces, and that's just the light fixtures. I'll have to come back to see some of your antiques and art sometime."

"I'd be delighted to give you a tour one day," David said.

He did have a charming smile, but that was not why I was here. "Has Neil Knight arrived yet?" I asked, glancing around the crowd.

"I saw him earlier, near the bar." David hmphed. "No surprise there."

I looked up into his chiseled face. "He drinks? I mean, more than most?"

"Definitely more than is acceptable," David said, his brown eyes narrowing. "Not a very intelligent choice for someone who has things to hide, but then, most criminals aren't too bright."

I looked away as David's gaze lingered on my face a little too long, and caught a glimpse of an older woman standing behind a cluster of chattering society matrons. We made eye contact for only a second before the woman turned and walked away, leaving me with an image of bright blue eyes and a cloud of white hair styled like an early twentieth-century Gibson Girl. There was something about her face that made me want to chase after her, but at that moment David tapped my shoulder.

"There he is." David surreptitiously gestured toward a short, bald man wearing a white tux jacket and a magenta cummerbund and bowtie. "Neil Knight. He always wants to stand out, even though it would be wiser for him to fly under the radar."

"Can you introduce us?" I pulled the narrow strap from inside my purse and slipped it over my shoulder. I wanted the use of both my hands, just in case.

"Of course." David led me over to Knight, who was throwing back a glass of amber liquid while a tall, almost skeletally thin woman wearing a white silk one-shouldered gown talked at him.

"Sorry to interrupt, Chelsea," David said, "but I have someone I'd like Neil to meet."

Chelsea lifted her barely existent eyebrows. "Of course, darling. I'll just go a grab another one of those delicious glasses of champagne." She side-eyed me as she slinked away, obviously not impressed.

David offered Knight a broad smile. "Neil, this is Jane Hunter. She's a librarian who currently works for Cameron Clewe out at Aircroft. She knew you were once in the book business and wanted to say hello."

Knight's gaze swept over me with indifference. "So you're working at Aircroft. Living there too?"

"No, I have my own place," I said.

"Good for you. Best to separate work from home life," Knight said, before finishing off his drink. "I'm going to grab another. You want anything?" he asked, addressing both me and David.

"Nothing for me. I need to make the rounds and try to drum up some support for the beneficiary of this event. Get these folks to open their wallets or purses and write big checks." David flashed another smile. "Hope you don't mind."

"Of course not. Mr. Knight and I can chat about books," I said.

David gave my arm a pat before he strode away.

"Let's talk and walk," Knight said, heading for a long, linen-draped table set up at one end of the showroom.

I followed him, increasing my pace to keep up. "I understand you were a partner in the Last Chapter Bookshop for many years," I said, huffing a little.

Reaching the bar, Knight demanded another whiskey on the rocks and took a swallow before he answered. "That's right. It wasn't my only business venture, of course, and I didn't have much to do with the day-to-day running of the place."

I asked for a white wine. Holding the glass by the stem, I stepped away from the bar to allow other guests access.

Knight trailed me over to a small alcove set up with a bistro table and two chairs. Sitting down, I took a small sip of my wine while Knight plopped down in the chair across the table from me. "I love vintage books. It's what I'm cataloging now, for Mr. Clewe, and it's so fascinating." I set my wineglass on the table. "I bet you've run across some interesting things in the past. Book-wise, I mean."

After taking another slug of his drink, Knight glared at me over the rim of his glass. "What are you getting at, Ms. Hunter? I know you must have some agenda other than talking about books. No one wants to meet me to talk about books. They know I'm really not an expert. When I partnered with the Andersons, I was mainly an advisor. They knew about books and I knew business."

"I guess you're glad you retired before the latest tragedy," I said, keeping my tone light.

"You bet I am." Knight took another long swallow. "It was bad enough the first time," he said, banging the now-empty glass down on the table. "All the suspicion and investigations and inquiries. A total cluster-you-know-what."

"But I thought it was a pretty open-and-shut case," I said, widening my eyes. "Abby Anderson killed her husband, pure and simple."

Knight snorted. "That's the part I don't buy, no matter what the police and courts said. "Abby Anderson couldn't kill a fly. Naw, it wasn't her, although she took the rap."

"If it wasn't Abby, who was it?" I asked, curling my fingers around the stem of my glass.

"Who do you think? Same person who stabbed that detective years later." Knight met my astonished gaze with a sardonic smile. "Dear little Eloise."

Chapter Seventeen

"Surely you don't mean that," I said, sliding back in my chair.

"Surely I do." Knight rattled the ice cubes in his empty glass. "I was in the shop the evening before the murder and heard Eloise arguing with Ken. She was angry because he'd forbidden her to go to some concert. It was a pretty heated confrontation."

"Did you tell the authorities about this?" I picked up my wineglass and took a sip.

"No. I didn't see the connection at the time. It was only later, when I was mulling things over, that it occurred to me. By then Abby had been arrested and I decided to stay out of it."

I tapped two fingers against my glass. "Even if the wrong person went to prison?"

"I figured Abby would tell the police about the argument, but I guess she didn't. She wanted to protect Eloise, I suppose." Neil shrugged. "My assumption has always been that Abby discovered Eloise standing over Ken's body or something equally damning, and decided to cover for her daughter." Neil lowered his eyelids, as if seeing that image in his mind. "Abby was that sort of woman."

"But you continued to work with Eloise for several years after the murder," I said. "How could you do that if you thought she was a murderer?"

Neil's lips curled back, revealing his small white teeth. "I don't worry about the morals of my business partners. That's far too limiting. Besides, I don't think Eloise remembered killing Ken. That was my impression, anyway. She had some kind of amnesia about it."

I met his gaze with a neutral expression. "I thought Eloise stayed overnight with a friend and wasn't even in the bookshop when Ken Anderson was stabbed."

"Oh, I think that was a bit of subterfuge," Neil said, wagging a finger at me. "We only have Abby and Eloise's word for that."

I set my glass back on the table. "And the friend and her mother. Why would they lie?"

Neil leaned back in his chair, crossing his arms over his chest. "I don't think they did. Yes, Eloise did stay overnight at her friend's house, but she left early the next morning. That's what was in the full statements from her friend and the friend's mom. Eloise explained this by saying she wanted to take a walk to clear her head before she went home, but what if that was the lie? She had a key to the shop and could've entered quietly and killed Ken before Abby was awake."

"This is only your theory, of course," I said.

"True. But it kind of ties together, don't you think? I mean, considering someone else got stabbed in the shop recently, and Abby is no longer around to take the blame."

I studied his face for a moment, wondering why he was so adamant that Eloise was the killer. Was it because he'd loved Abby and wanted to clear her name, or was there a more sinister reason? *If he's the murderer, he may be trying to cast the blame on Eloise to protect his own interests*, I warned myself. *You can't take what he's saying at face value.*

But I couldn't ignore it, either. I'd have to tell Cam about this new information and see if he could find a way to verify it. "Now that the police think Eloise stabbed Detective Parker, do you plan to finally talk to them about your suspicion that she also killed her father, and that Abby covered for her? Or are you still going to remain silent for some reason?"

Neil's expression grew stony. "I haven't decided yet. I doubt the authorities need any more evidence to convict Eloise this time, and honestly, I prefer to mind my own business."

You mean you don't like to get too involved with law enforcement, I thought. "Well, if we're being honest, I must admit I've heard a few rumors about you, Mr. Knight."

"Such as?" he asked in a belligerent tone.

"Oh, just that you might've done deals with people who are, shall we say, on the wrong side of the law. And perhaps incurred some debts that needed to be paid off sooner rather than later."

"Even if that were true"—Neil leaned forward, resting his lower arms on the table—"it wouldn't have anything to do with these murders. It's not like killing Ken would've yielded a windfall. He didn't even have life insurance."

"I wasn't suggesting that *you* killed anyone," I said, which was a lie, but necessary as a tactical maneuver. "I was thinking more like one of your more disreputable business associates. You know, to send a message about paying debts, or something along those lines."

"That's ridiculous." Neil snatched his glass off the table. "I need another." His chair squealed as he shoved it back and stood up. He stared me down, his expression full of repressed rage. "I won't say it was nice to meet you, Ms. Hunter, because it wasn't. But I will give you a little advice, free of charge—if you value your health, you'd best keep your baseless accusations to yourself." He stormed off toward to bar.

I grabbed my own glass and finished off the wine in two gulps.

"Was Neil behaving badly? I can have him tossed out on his ear. Just say the word."

I looked up at David, who was standing next to an older woman in an elegant, crystal-pleated sage-green gown. "Thanks, but that won't be necessary." Rising to my feet, I extended my hand to the woman at his side. "Hello, I'm Jane Hunter. You must be Gloria Benton."

The woman inclined her head. She was tall, like David, and had the same eyes, silver hair, and strong features. But despite the resemblance, it was clear from the lines etching her face that she was a good twenty years older. "I am," she said, clasping my hand for only a moment. "It's nice to meet you, Ms. Hunter."

"Please, call me Jane, and I'm glad to meet you too," I said. "As I told your son, I'd love to return one day to explore your collection of art and antiques. Not that I can probably afford anything, but perhaps I could encourage my boss to consider a purchase."

Gloria tilted her head slightly to one side. "Ah, you mean Cameron Clewe. His father did buy a few things from us, but I'm afraid the younger Mr. Clewe has never visited our showroom. I'd certainly be pleased if you could persuade him to do so."

"I can't promise that, but I'll see what I can do," I said, with a little smile.

"Speaking of Aircroft, I understand that Mr. Clewe is hosting Eloise Anderson at the estate," Gloria said, pursing her lips. "Do you think that is wise? I do feel pity for the girl, but sheltering a murderer . . ."

"Alleged murderer," David interjected, giving his mother a sidelong glance. "Innocent until proven guilty, remember?"

"Yes, yes," Gloria said, with a lift of her chin. "Still, it would make me uneasy to work with Eloise in the house."

I clutched the strap of my purse. "I'm not bothered by that."

"Jane is made of stronger stuff." David laid a hand on his mother's shoulder. "She's a librarian, after all."

"Really? How interesting," Gloria said, in a tone that told me she didn't find it interesting in the least.

"Anyway, you must admit that Eloise has suffered a lot of tragedy in her young life. I suppose you knew both Ken and Abby Anderson when they were running Last Chapter?" I asked, widening my eyes in what I hoped was an innocent expression.

"Not well. But we ran into each other from time to time. Often bidding on the same rare books at auction," Gloria said.

"We won, most of the time." David's genial tone didn't mask his pride. He motioned toward the empty wineglass on the table. "Would you like another, Jane?"

"Yes, thanks. White, please."

"Got it. No, just leave that glass, I'll get you another." David lifted his hand from Gloria's shoulder. "What about you, Mom?"

"Champagne, of course," she replied, offering him a smile.

I could tell that they had a close relationship. *Which means either one would probably do anything to protect the other*, I thought, as David strolled away to fetch our drinks.

Gloria looked me over. "That's a lovely gown, Jane. Did you buy it locally?"

"Yes," I said, before mentioning the shop Lauren had directed me to. "Thanks, I'm glad the dress is appropriate. I wasn't sure what to wear to an event like this. I don't attend too many black-tie functions."

Gloria waved one hand through the air. "Oh, we aren't that fussy. Or stuffy. I mean, my son even allows people like that reprobate Neil

Knight to attend our functions." She made a face. "Magenta, my heavens."

"You know him as well?" I asked.

"Unfortunately. He's purchased a few items from us. I don't approve of some of his rumored business associates, but what can you do? A customer is a customer." Gloria brushed back a thick lock of hair that had fallen over her forehead. "But I'd say he's a bad influence. I don't know what Ken and Abby were thinking when they brought him in as a partner, but I suppose they needed the infusion of money, poor dears. Their bookstore was really struggling at one point."

"Did they have to start from scratch?" I knew the answer to this, but hoped to get Gloria to say more about the Andersons' money troubles.

"No, the store had been there for many years. The Andersons actually purchased a good deal of stock along with the building. Ken apparently found a few very nice items that fetched a good price in among the old stock, which did help them out in the beginning," Gloria said.

This was information that would probably interest Cam. If the store held hidden treasures, perhaps one had been discovered around the time of Ken's death. *If Neil wanted the money from the sale of a valuable book for himself* . . . I realized that Gloria had said something else and refocused my attention on her. "Excuse me, I drifted there for a moment. What were you saying?"

Gloria's smile was strained. "Nothing important. Just that I hope Eloise has a good lawyer. Even if she did stab that detective, I'm sure there was some reason. Self-defense, perhaps? One never knows what men get up to these days."

"She does have an excellent legal team. Cam, I mean Mr. Clewe, has made sure of that."

"How nice of him," Gloria said, looking off to her right. "Ah, here's David with our drinks. Shall we change the subject?"

I preferred not to, but knew I had to acquiesce if I didn't want to blow my cover. David handed us our drinks, and we made small talk for a few minutes before Gloria said she supposed she'd better circulate among the guests.

"Wait," David said, as his mom took a step away. "I meant to tell you earlier, Mom, but with everything going on it slipped my mind. I talked to Terry this morning about that property in Chapel Hill. She says she thinks the owners are finally willing to play ball."

"Great. We'll talk more later," Gloria said, giving David an approving smile. Turning to me, she added, "Very nice to meet you, Jane. Please do come and visit us when we can show you our lovely art and antiques."

"Terry?" I asked, as Gloria walked away. It seemed like a strange coincidence, considering the encounter at my apartment. "How funny. I just met someone with that name."

David gave me a quizzical look. "It's not uncommon, but this is a real estate agent in Chapel Hill. We're looking at some investment property there. I doubt you know her, but her full name's Teresa Lindover."

Chapter Eighteen

I loosened my tight grip on the stem of my wineglass, afraid it would snap. "That can't be right. It was my impression that she was a detective with the Chapel Hill police department."

"She was, but she left about five years ago to go into real estate. Much more lucrative, I'm sure," David said.

I considered the badge Terry had shown me. *I thought they had to turn those in if they left the force. She must've somehow stashed a copy of her old one, or had a fake one made.* "I'm sure you're right." I took a swig of my wine. "Also a lot less dangerous."

David eyed me with curiosity. "That's certainly true. Look at Detective Parker. He was retired and still died due to his entanglement in an old case."

I had no intention of telling David about Terry's visit to my apartment. Despite his friendly overtures, he was still on my list of suspects. "Well, what do you say we avoid talking about murder for the rest of the evening? I noticed that you had quite a spread of hors d'oeuvres on a table near the bar and I do like to eat a little something when I drink."

"That sounds like an excellent plan," David said, slipping his hand through the bend of my elbow. "Let's grab a little snack and then I can introduce you to a few more of the guests."

I acquiesced with this plan, primarily because I wanted to remain alert and already felt the two glasses of wine going to my head.

After we enjoyed some tea sandwiches and other finger food, I requested a glass of sparkling water from the bar. It didn't escape my notice that David did the same. *One point in his favor*, I thought as I followed him back into the milling crowd.

The truth was, despite my initial impression when he visited Aircroft, I found David to be a very pleasant companion. He was eager to discuss books as well as art and antiques.

"It must be exciting to work with such materials," he said, after I shared information on some of the items in Cam's book collections. "I always feel a rush when I'm holding a particularly rare book."

"I know that feeling," I said.

"Wonderful, isn't it? As a matter of fact, I have a pending acquisition that would certainly make your eyes light up."

"Really? What is that?"

David pressed a finger to his lips. "Sorry, can't talk about it yet. I'm still in negotiations with the owner. But once I have it in my hands, I definitely let you know. I'm sure you'd be thrilled to see it."

I agreed with this plan, my mind racing with the possibility that David's new acquisition could be the same book that Eloise was sent to look for by Bruce Parker. *Which means he may be in on the murder*, I reminded myself, as I laughed at one of David's quips. I couldn't let my guard down, even if David, and his mother, seemed like decent people on the surface. The investigations that Cam and I had undertaken over the past several months had taught me that devils were quite adept at hiding behind masks.

By the end of the evening, I'd been introduced to numerous people I was sure I wouldn't remember the next day. Longing to go home and kick off my heeled sandals, I thanked David and Gloria for their hospitality and once again promised to return to the showroom to view their collection of art and antiques. Elbowing my way to the main doors, I retrieved my shawl and texted Taylor.

He drove up to the building entrance two minutes after I stepped outside.

"Did you finish *Piranesi?*" I asked him as I settled into the back seat.

He flashed me a smile in the rearview mirror. "I did, and was truly blown away. It wasn't what I expected, but it was absolutely perfect."

"I thought so too," I said, buckling my seat belt.

We continued to discuss the book on the drive back to my apartment. At a certain point, impressed with his insights, I asked him if he was interested in writing as well as reading.

"You just display a certain approach to the text that makes me wonder," I told him.

"Guilty," he said. "I actually have a degree in creative writing. Which is why I'm working as a chauffeur," he added, flashing me a grin over his shoulder.

"I guess it does give you time to read and think, or maybe even jot down some scenes?"

"That's one benefit. I also need the money, of course. I've sold a few short stories, but I'm still trying to break into the business as a novelist. And even then, I might need to keep driving. Most authors don't make enough from their work to live on."

"I've heard that. It's a pity," I said, collecting my purse and shawl as Taylor pulled into the parking spot in front of Vince's house. "Do you have a website or anything? I'd like to keep an eye out for your stories, and that novel I'm sure you'll eventually sell."

Taylor jumped out to open my door and help me out of the car. "Not yet, but I'm planning to make one soon," he said. "All my contact information is on the card I gave you. It's for my car-for-hire business, but I write under the same name."

"Ah, Taylor Iverson. Good name for an author," I said.

"Let's hope so." Taylor lifted his hand in a brief acknowledgement before he wished me a good night. He didn't get back in the car, though. "I'll wait until you're safely inside your apartment," he said.

I made a mental note to tell Cam to send Taylor a tip, then lifted the hem of my gown and ascended the staircase. Opening my door, I was surprised by the flood of light that spilled out onto the landing.

"Didn't think I left the lights on," I muttered, before waving to Taylor to let him know it was okay for him to leave.

When I stepped inside the apartment, I heard sounds that made me stop in my tracks. I considered running back outside in hope that Taylor hadn't driven away yet, but grabbed a walking stick from my umbrella holder instead. Stalking into the living room area, the stick raised over my head, I glanced at the flickering images on the TV screen.

It was a scene from the 1995 version of *Sense and Sensibility*. I lowered my arms and turned my attention on the sofa. "Bailey, what on earth are you doing here?" I asked.

My thirty-one-year-old daughter looked up at me, a bright smile lighting up her face, which wouldn't have looked out of place in a Pre-Raphaelite painting. "Hi, Mom. Your landlord let me in, once I was able to prove who I was. Hope you don't mind."

A Killer Clue

Bemused, I studied her for a moment, marveling as I always did over how two rather average people could have produced such a beauty. Her wavy chestnut hair glinted with crimson highlights, her wide brown eyes were framed by impossibly thick black lashes, and her lips formed the perfect sensuous bow. "Of course I don't mind, but I wish you'd let me know you were arriving this evening. How'd you get here anyway?"

"The usual way—plane and Uber. Now, don't make that face. As I keep telling you, Ubers are perfectly safe." Bailey paused the film on the TV before uncurling her long, lithe, body and gracefully rising to face me. "I'm glad I didn't tell you I was coming today. Otherwise I know you'd have missed whatever event you attended this evening." She whistled. "Very nice outfit. I hope you were on a date?"

"Not exactly," I said, sweeping my shawl from my shoulders and tossing it onto the sofa. "I did attend a gala, but it was in support of an investigation, not because I was out with some guy."

"Too bad, because you look lovely." Bailey stepped forward and pulled me into a hug.

Hugging her back, my fingers brushed her shoulder blades. "Goodness, you're so thin. Haven't you been eating?"

"Oh, Mom, you know how it is in my business. Have to stay slim if I want to land the primo roles." Bailey stepped back, sliding her hands down my arms so she could clasp my fingers. "You look great. This new job must agree with you."

"I do enjoy it," I said.

"The amateur sleuthing parts as much or more than cataloging?" Bailey's eyes twinkled. "I know you enjoy playing Nancy Drew."

"I'm a little old to be Nancy Drew," I said, with a smile.

Bailey grinned and released my hands. "Miss Marple, then."

"And I'm too young for that," I said, playfully swatting at her.

"So this evening's event is part of some investigation you're running along with your rather eccentric boss?" Bailey asked, gracefully sitting back down on the sofa.

I plopped down beside her. "Yes. We're trying to find evidence that a young woman is innocent of murder, while simultaneously proving her mother didn't stab her father to death many years ago."

"Wow, this sounds more intriguing than the soap opera scripts my agent keeps sending to me," Bailey said.

Kicking off my sandals, I sank back into the sofa cushions. "It's more like a Greek tragedy. Or one of those whodunit plays where there are too many suspects and not enough clues."

"Hmmm. If it's like a play, maybe I could help." Bailey swung her legs up and stretched them out across the seat cushions as she leaned into the decorative pillow pressed against the arm of the sofa. "I've studied enough scenarios to understand motives and all that."

I patted her ankle. "This is real life, not the stage. Things don't always mesh together so easily. Not like when you see something in an earlier scene that portends what will happen later."

"So no Chekhov's gun? Too bad." Bailey yawned. "Sorry, it's been a long day."

"For me too," I said. "Why don't we both get some sleep and talk more in the morning?"

"Sure thing. Only, I need you to promise me two things," Bailey said.

"What's that?" I asked, standing again and gathering up my shawl and shoes.

"One, that you'll tell me all about the various investigations you're pursuing right now, and two, that you'll introduce me to your quite intriguing-sounding boss as soon as possible."

Glad my back was to Bailey, I grimaced. "Alright. But don't expect too much."

"From the details about your sleuthing or meeting your boss?" Bailey asked.

"Both," I called over my shoulder as I strode into the bedroom.

Chapter Nineteen

O ver breakfast, I filled Bailey in on the two Anderson murder cases, as well as the efforts Vince and I had made to track down our mystery woman.

"I'm not sure I want to get involved in investigating murders, but I'd love to help you find out more about Lily," Bailey said, as we washed up the dishes.

I dried my hands with a dish towel. "You could go back to the local history museum and look through some more scrapbooks or other historical documents. I'll give you my copies of the photo and drawing so you'll have a reference point."

"Alright." Bailey placed a coffee mug in the dish rack. "But I don't have a car, so you'll have to drop me off when you head into work."

"The museum doesn't open that early. You'll have to wait until ten. It's okay, though, because it's only a short walk from here." I pulled my keys from my pocket and slipped the apartment key from the ring. "Here—there's a small hardware store a block from the museum. Have them make a copy of my front door key so you can come and go without bothering Vince."

Bailey swept her long hair behind her shoulders. "Thanks, that will help, but I'll have to make sure I'm here when you get home since you won't have a key yet."

"Just be here around six. I usually finish work around five, but I thought I'd stop and pick up something for dinner." I studied Bailey's bright face for a second. "Any new food restrictions I should know about?"

"Nope. Still a vegetarian, of course."

"Of course. Okay, I'd better run." I stopped by the tall, narrow table placed behind the sofa and slid the two photocopies from the drawer. "Here are the pictures." I turned and blew her a kiss. "Love you."

"Love you too," Bailey called after me as I left the apartment.

When I got to Aircroft I ran into Jenna Brown, the new housekeeper for the estate. She was in the main entry hall, providing instructions to the small crew she brought in once a week to give the mansion a thorough cleaning.

A tall woman with dark hair, skin, and eyes, she had the slender but athletic build of a runner. Which she'd been, she'd told me once. She'd even won statewide awards for running cross country in high school. Now in her mid-forties, she still ran, but only for exercise and, occasionally, for charity.

"Hi, Jenna," I said, after the cleaning crew dispersed. "Would you happen to know where Mr. Clewe is this morning?"

"Last I saw he was in the breakfast room," Jenna said.

"Is Ms. Anderson with him?"

Jenna quirked her eyebrows. "No, I haven't seen her yet today. She does tend to sleep much later than anyone else."

Knowing she probably wondered why I cared if Eloise was eating breakfast with Cam, I mentioned something about needing to discuss cataloging issues. "Pretty sure that would bore most people," I added, with a smile.

"It's a mystery to me, that's for sure," Jenna said, before wishing me a good day.

I headed down the corridor that led to the breakfast room, which was larger than most dining rooms in less grand homes. It had floor-to-ceiling windows on two adjacent walls that flooded the space with sunlight. On the longer solid wall, a small table held a silver-plated coffee urn and white ceramic mugs as well as cream, sugar, and all other possible accouterments.

Cam, seated at the far end of the table, looked up as I entered. "Good morning, Jane."

"Hello," I said. "You must have something going on today. You're wearing your power suit."

"I have back-to-back video meetings," Cam replied. "I'm about finished here, but please sit down. Have you had breakfast yet?"

"Yes, I actually ate something at home, because my daughter arrived last night," I said, realizing only after the fact that I'd immediately betrayed Bailey's presence. I bit my lower lip and made a beeline for the small table. "I'll have some coffee, though."

"Bailey is in town?" Cam casually dabbed the corner of his mouth with a linen napkin, but I could tell from the color rising in his pale cheeks that this news had caught him off guard.

"Yes, and she does want to meet you and tour the estate and all that, but I wanted . . ." I paused, considering whether I should mention anything about Bailey's mission. Cam was well aware that Vince, Donna, and I were still searching for the identity of the mystery woman, but considering his frustrating search for his biological father, I really wanted to have more concrete information to give him before I shared the news about Lily. "I mean, Bailey had things to do today."

"How long will she be staying with you?" Cam asked.

"I'm not really sure. Her last acting gig just ended, so she's waiting on news from her agent about auditions." I stirred cream into the mug I'd filled with coffee.

"We'll have to arrange a little dinner party," Cam said, as I sat down at the table near him. "Maybe next week, if Bailey plans to stay that long?"

"I'm sure she will. She told me she wanted some time off before tackling auditions or anything like that." I blew across the surface of my hot coffee. "She's been touring for over a year, you know. She needs a break."

"No doubt." Cam placed his napkin on his empty plate and pushed his chair away from the table. "You did attend the gala?"

"I did, and that's why I sought you out this morning. Figured you'd want a report," I said, before taking a sip from my mug.

Cam scooted his chair sideways so he could stretch out his legs. "Definitely. Did you learn anything new about the Bentons, or the questionable Mr. Knight?"

Setting down my mug, I launched into a recounting of the previous evening. "The Bentons didn't raise any particular red flags, although I don't think we can rule them out as suspects, if only because they do have quite an interest in rare books. David really lit up when he mentioned some special volume he's hoping to acquire."

"David, huh?" Cam raked his inquiring gaze over my face. "Are you two getting chummy?"

"Chummy?" I rolled my eyes. "You need to modernize your vocabulary, Cam. But, for your information, I did find his company pleasant enough. However, that won't cloud my vision, I assure you."

"Good to know," Cam said. "Because my research and some reports from business contacts has revealed that Benton House is not immune to engaging in some questionable deals."

"Such as?"

"Buying pieces from sellers who don't provide provenances, for one thing. Not to mention, in terms of motive, one of my contacts told me that when Ken Anderson acquired a rare first edition copy of Ernest Hemingway's *In Our Time*, Gloria Benton accused him of basically stealing the purchase from her. Apparently, she'd introduced Ken to the seller as a courtesy. She didn't mind Ken working with the seller on future acquisitions, but then he went behind her back and bought the book she dearly wanted."

"That could create some bad blood between them, for sure," I said. "But is it a motive for murder?"

"That particular book is worth at least three hundred and twenty-five thousand dollars," Cam said dryly. "Or at least it was around sixteen years ago. It's probably worth a lot more now."

"Oh." I drank a few more gulps of coffee. "That would've been around the time Ken was murdered, too."

"Which is why the Bentons stay on the suspect list."

"I agree. They seem nice enough, but you never know. And David would've been working for the company back then. He would've been in his forties, so he undoubtedly knew about that deal." I ran my finger around the rim of the mug. "But I've heard rumors that Last Chapter was struggling financially around that time. How could Ken have purchased such an expensive book, and wouldn't he then have been able to fill the bookshop's coffers if he sold it for a profit?"

Cam lifted his hands. "You'd think. The thing is, Neil Knight had apparently borrowed a great deal of money from people who were not too forgiving if someone didn't pay them back. Maybe that Hemingway deal simply paid off a few debts."

"Speaking of Neil Knight, he certainly did not impress me." I filled Cam in about Neil's drinking and aggressive behavior. "He was adamant that Eloise killed her father, as well as Detective Parker."

"That sounds like someone who wants to divert suspicion from themselves," Cam said.

"I thought the same thing. If he killed Ken, perhaps he also murdered Parker. He probably still had a key to the bookshop. The locked doors of the first murder and the quick exit from the scene in the second wouldn't be impossible if he's the culprit."

Cam sat forward in his chair. "Perhaps he somehow learned that Parker *had* found evidence to exonerate Abby and point the finger at someone else, so he decided to silence him."

"It makes as much sense as any of our other theories." I mulled over the other information Neil had shared. "Knight did say he over-heard a harsh argument between Eloise and her father the day before Ken died, and that she could've come home earlier from her over-night visit than she claimed."

Cam's eyelashes fluttered. "Probably more lies," he said, drumming his fingers against his thigh. "But I will certainly question Eloise about that."

"I do think I've made a solid connection with both David and Gloria Benton, so I can always talk to them again," I said. "Especially now that I know that story about the first edition Hemingway."

"I also want you to question Knight again." Obviously observing my grimace, Cam held up one hand. "In a safe situation, of course. I've discovered that Knight likes to frequent one of the area country clubs. According to my confidant, he's there almost every day, mostly hanging out at the bar. That might be the best place to approach him."

As I finished off my coffee, I considered this request. "Alright, text me the directions to the place and I'll check it out."

"Just don't go off anywhere with him alone," Cam said. "Stay in public areas where there are lots of people around."

"Will do. I definitely don't trust him," I agreed.

Remembering my confusion over Terry Lindover's career status, I opened my mouth to share this other bit of information with Cam, but was cut off when Lauren dashed into the room.

"Sorry to interrupt," she said, breathlessly. "But we can't find Eloise anywhere."

Chapter Twenty

C am met Lauren's frantic gaze calmly. "Why is that a problem? Eloise isn't a prisoner here."

"Cam, think for a minute." Lauren shoved her tight black curls back from her forehead with one hand. She left her hand pressed against her forehead like she was battling a headache. "You vouched for her with the authorities. You'll be responsible if she flees the area or, heaven forbid, the country. You could lose all the bail money, and be placed under suspicion yourself if Eloise does a runner."

I stood as Cam leapt to his feet. Leaving my briefcase and purse on the floor where I'd set them, I followed Cam and Lauren out of the library and down the hall that led to the kitchen.

"You've looked over the entire house?" Cam asked, the corner of his lips twitching.

"Yes. I got Jenna and the cleaning team involved. They've checked every room. Or at least, every space that wasn't locked. I mean, Eloise doesn't have keys to anything but her own room. But then there's the attic and wine cellar and a couple of storerooms . . ."

"Have Jenna and her team check those too," Cam said. "Jane and I will search outside."

"I'll tackle the attic." Lauren said. "I don't want to send the part-time staff up there."

Mateo, obviously hearing the commotion, appeared at the door to the kitchen. "What's going on? Can I help?"

Lauren flashed him a grateful smile. "Ms. Anderson has gone missing. You know the layout of the wine cellar and storerooms. Would you please search those areas?"

"Sure thing." Mateo pulled off his white chef's jacket, revealing a plain black T-shirt. "I'll just hang this up and grab a flashlight and head downstairs."

I cast a concerned glance at Cam, who appeared frozen in place. "Cam," I said, placing a gentle hand on his shoulder, "why don't we go out into the kitchen garden and then work our way through the formal garden and beyond?"

"Okay, let me check in with Jenna and search the attic." Lauren held up her cell phone. "Call or text if you find her." She sprinted off down the corridor toward the main entry hall.

Mateo waved his own phone. "I'll text everyone if I see Ms. Anderson anywhere," he said, as he dashed into the kitchen.

Cam took off his suit coat and hung it on the row of hooks just inside the kitchen before we exited the room. Outside, we both checked the kitchen garden's raised beds and shed, then jogged over to the entrance to the formal garden.

"I'll take the left path, you take the right, and we'll meet at the pavilion," Cam said as he strode away.

Traversing the path at a fast walk, I searched all the beds on my side without any glimpse of Eloise. Of course, the formal section was so carefully trimmed and weeded, it would be hard to conceal anyone. *The wild portion of the garden was a more likely hiding place*, I thought as I approached the water feature. Cam was already there, standing by the koi pond and staring down into the water. His hands were hanging at his sides but he was rhythmically clenching and unclenching his fingers.

"I didn't see anything," I said, with a quick glance at my phone. No messages. "Shall we check the back garden? That's where I'd head if I were trying to escape notice."

Cam didn't answer. He simply turned on his heel and climbed the stairs of the pavilion, taking two steps at a time. Since I didn't have his long legs, I had to follow more slowly.

"Hold up," I said, leaning into one of the Grecian-style pillars that supported the wooden roof. "We should probably search the wilder area together. It would be easy to miss someone in all that lush vegetation."

Cam stared out over the back section of the garden. "Do you believe I was an idiot to trust Eloise? It seems Lauren thinks so."

"I think we don't know what's happened yet," I said, glancing at my phone again. "I tell you what—let's approach this with the idea that Eloise may have simply fallen or gotten lost or something. Whatever the case, if she's still on the estate, she needs our help."

Cam expelled a gusty sigh and looked at me, abashed. "You're right."

"That happens sometimes," I said, strolling closer and patting his tense arm. "Come on. There's no messages from anyone in the house yet, so we really do need to tackle this area."

We walked down the steps that led to the back section of the garden, an area that had been designed almost like a maze, its narrow beaten-dirt path winding through bushy shrubs and thick stands of trees. Every so often, a small wooden bench, its boards faded to silver from age and moisture, popped up like a mushroom.

I searched the areas close to the path, while Cam plunged into the lush vegetation, beating aside climbing vines and arching branches to create his own walkway. But neither of us saw any sign of Eloise, or any evidence that she'd come this way. When we reached the far end of the wild garden, we stepped out into a closely mowed field.

Blinking in the sudden burst of sunlight, I shaded my eyes and gazed at the field. "Where does this lead?" I asked.

"To the quarry," Cam said, and took off at a sprint across the field.

I followed, but more slowly. There was no one standing at the far edge of the field, at what I assumed was the lip of the quarry. If Eloise had done something foolish, we were probably already too late.

Although she could simply be injured, I thought, picking up my pace.

Reaching the edge of the field, I realized that the earth below my feet disappeared precipitously. I stopped dead, then took two steps back. The dark-gray walls of the quarry were jagged and steep. Peering down, I noticed pools of black water and chunks of stone that sparkled like fool's gold.

"Jane, over here!" Cam shouted from somewhere to my right.

I turned and caught sight of him, waving his arms over his head. Behind him was a small grove of trees. I moved away from the dizzying edge of the quarry and strode through a patch of tall orchard grass to reach Cam.

"There'd better not be snakes," I muttered, as spiny burdock seeds snagged my slacks. When I reached the small clearing at the base of the closest tree, I found Cam kneeling beside a hunched Eloise.

Her glasses were askew and one earpiece was bent, and her hair was a tangle of burnished gold. She had her back pressed into the rough trunk of the tree, with her knees pulled up and enclosed by her arms. As she rocked slowly, a dark piece of fabric slid off her shoulder and fell to the ground.

Cam looked up at me, his sea-green eyes clouded. "She was blindfolded and forced to walk here from the front garden."

"What? By whom?" I asked, squatting down to look Eloise in the face. "Who did this to you?"

"I don't know," she replied, her voice crackling like glaze on pottery. "I never saw them."

Cam stood up and offered his hand to Eloise. Pulling her to her feet, he threw one arm around her shoulders as she wobbled.

I grabbed the black cloth and straightened. "Evidence," I said when Eloise cast me a wide-eyed look. "I assume this was the blindfold?"

She bobbed her head. "Whoever it was, they grabbed me from behind and tied on the blindfold before I could get even a glimpse of their face. Then they forced me to walk here." A tear, dangling from Eloise's eyelashes, fell and splashed onto her pale cheek. "They shoved something in my back. I think it was a gun. Couldn't be sure, but I was too scared to try to escape, just in case."

"Did they speak to you?" Cam removed his arm from Eloise's shoulders but kept his palm pressed against the small of her back. "Could you identify their voice?"

Eloise shook her head. "They didn't say anything. Just stuffed something in my pocket and left me here. I didn't leave or take off the blindfold because I had no idea where they were. I thought they might shoot me or something if I moved." Her eyes widened as she stared over the swath of tall grass. "What's that? Where the ground seems to fall away."

"It's an old quarry," I said, sharing an anxious glance with Cam. Had Eloise's kidnapper planned to toss her off the edge, only to change their mind for some unknown reason?

"I'm calling the police," Cam said, sliding his cell phone from his pocket.

"No, no." Eloise grabbed his arm. "Please don't. I don't want to have anything to do with the police right now."

"But someone kidnapped you. They might've harmed you if they hadn't heard us rustling through the grass." I motioned toward the trees. "I bet they ran off that way when they heard us coming. Where does that lead, Cam?"

"Through the woods, which separate this area from an old farm road. It isn't used now, but it does end up close to an actual county road."

"So someone could've gotten away easily enough," I said.

"Yes," Cam said, his expression grim.

Eloise cast a wild gaze from Cam to me and back again. "Please leave the police out of this. I don't want to give them any new reasons to distrust me, and since we can't identify my abductor . . ."

"Alright, we'll leave it for now. But I don't think you should leave the house from now on. Sorry," Cam said, dropping his arm to his side.

Eloise offered a wan smile. "It's okay. It is a big house."

"Oh, shoot," I said. "We should let Lauren and the others know we've found you." I texted a couple of messages while Eloise pulled a folded piece of paper from her pocket and handed it to Cam.

He opened the paper and stared at what I assumed was a message.

"What does it say?" I asked, pocketing my phone.

"It's rather cryptic," Cam replied. "Does this mean anything to you, Eloise?" He cleared his throat and read the note out loud. "'Talk and I won't help you. Tell anyone and you'll be sorry you did. You know what I'm capable of.'" He stared at the paper, his jaw tightening. "Written with a computer, so no handwriting to analyze."

Before Eloise lowered her head, I saw panic wash over her face. "No. I mean"—she covered her face with both hands—"maybe it has to do with some things connected to the shop."

"And connected to Neil Knight?" I asked, raising my eyebrows as I met Cam's tight-lipped expression.

Eloise simply burst into tears. I moved forward and pulled her into a hug.

Looking at me over Eloise's shoulder, Cam tapped his temple with one finger.

I knew what he meant. With an abductor who apparently knew what they were doing and the use of a kidnapping to send a warning, this action seemed like the work of someone who had ties to the criminal world.

Which meant Neil Knight had just rocketed to the top of our suspect list.

Chapter Twenty-One

When we guided Eloise safely back to the house, I escorted her up to her room to rest while Lauren argued with Cam about notifying the authorities. Apparently Cam won, since I heard no sirens or other sounds indicating the arrival of the police when I headed back downstairs and made my way to Cam's office.

I knocked on the closed door, hoping I wasn't interrupting a meeting, but when Cam called out a loud "come in" and I entered the room, I found him alone. He was standing with his back to me, staring out at the gardens through the expansive window at the far end of the office.

This room was in complete opposition to the rest of the mansion. Of moderate size, it was furnished with an L-shaped glass desk set on sleek chrome legs, a brushed metal storage cabinet, and several legal-sized, silver-toned metal file cabinets. The light that spilled in from large windows on two adjacent walls sparkled off the pale wood floors and an arrangement of floating shelves that filled a windowless white wall.

I stared at my boss, noting the rigid set of his shoulders. He'd left off his suit coat and rolled up the sleeves of his sky-blue dress shirt. "I thought you had meetings today."

"Lauren rescheduled them," Cam said, turning to face me. "Please, sit down. I'd like to talk through a few things."

I settled in the plain gray armchair that faced his desk. It was the only seating other than Cam's high-backed, pewter-toned task chair. "Concerning Eloise and the supposed kidnapping?"

The freckles that speckled Cam's high cheekbones blazed against his milky skin. "So you aren't entirely convinced either?"

"I am not." I crossed my legs and leaned back in the chair. "It strikes me as odd that someone would abduct Eloise just to send her a message. Why not simply make a phone call?"

Cam strolled over to the desk and sat down in his chair. "Perhaps they didn't want her to recognize their voice."

"Then send a text." I flexed my dangling foot. Hiking through gardens and fields in my thin-soled loafers hadn't done my feet any favors.

"On the other hand, a direct attack would show Eloise, and us, that her assailant was capable of getting to her, even at Aircroft."

"True." I examined Cam, whose expression had grown pensive. "Do you trust Eloise? I can't help but consider the possibility that she faked this kidnapping in order to make us, and the police, think she's innocent."

Cam sighed. "I don't trust her completely. There's something she's hiding. Every time we talk, there's a thread of nervous agitation in her manner, no matter how mundane the conversation."

"It could be related to the murder, but I also think it has something to do with financial matters related to the bookshop," I said. "She even admitted as much this morning."

"And we know that Neil Knight was still a partner in the business when Eloise was in charge." Cam drummed his fingers against the arm of his chair. "I suspect she knew he was involved in some illegal activities and looked the other way."

"That's my guess as well." I frowned. "She probably thought it was the only way to save the business. As long as Knight brought in enough capital to keep the shop afloat, she may not have wanted to dive too deeply into where the money came from."

"Into such murky waters, you mean." Cam pressed his other palm over his tapping fingers. "I've attempted to get her to understand that, whatever her involvement in any financial irregularities, it's nothing compared to being convicted of murder, but she still refuses to confess her secrets."

I eyed him, wondering how he'd come across during these chats with Eloise. *Probably like a particularly fierce prosecutor*, I thought, shaking my head. "On the other hand, if Eloise did fake her own kidnapping, why?"

Cam leaned back, rocking his chair slightly. "Maybe she wants us, as well as her legal team, to think someone is tracking and targeting her."

"To come across as a victim rather than a perpetrator?" I winced as I dropped both feet to the floor. "I'm sorry, Cam."

"Why?" he asked, with a lift of his eyebrows.

"I thought . . ." I cleared my throat. "Well, not to get too personal, but you seemed taken with Eloise at first. I thought you might, you know, want to date her or something."

Cam stared at me, his face still and cool as marble. "I don't know where you got that idea. I was driven to help her, but only because it seemed the police and others had already condemned her, before any sort of solid investigation or trial. It was a desire for justice, not romance."

"Okay, okay," I said, lifting my hands. "I must've read things wrong." Of course, I knew I hadn't, but I didn't want to embarrass him any more than I probably already had. "So what now?"

"We still need to talk to Neil Knight again. If anyone is trying to keep Eloise from talking, I bet it's him."

"Right, at that country club. The only thing is"—I clasped my hands in my lap—"can I even get in? I checked into the place and it's a private club. Members and guests only."

"That does make it more difficult." Cam looked up at the ceiling as if he could find a solution there.

"Well, you know lots of the wealthier people in the areas. I thought maybe you could introduce me to someone who could bring me in as a guest."

"I doubt my contracts would do that without far too many questions," Cam said, lowering his gaze to look me in the eyes. "Al had a lifelong family membership and I've continued to pay dues just for the sake of a little community involvement, so I suppose I'm still a member."

"Have you ever been there?"

"No, but I could get you in as a guest." The pained expression on Cam's face told me he was not enthused about this idea.

"You'd have to accompany me. Are you willing to do that?"

He grimaced. "I could try. Anyway, after I get you in, I can simply hide out somewhere quiet, I suppose."

"Why don't we plan on going sometime this week, then?" I asked in a calm tone. I didn't want to make a big deal over Cam deciding to venture out to a new, very public, place, even though I was proud that he was willing to give it a try.

I could tell by the spastic movement of his jaw that Cam was grinding his teeth, but he simply opened his laptop and peered at the screen. "Wednesday would work for me," he said, after a minute or two. "According to my calendar, I don't have any other meetings or appointments that day."

"Great. We can leave from here. It would probably be best to go in the afternoon, if we hope to catch Knight at the bar."

"Alright. That's the plan, then." Cam had resumed his finger tapping, this time on the glass surface of the desk. "Well, I'm going to check with the PI I have digging into Neil Knight's background, so I'll let you get back to work."

I rose to my feet and turned to leave before realizing I hadn't shared all the information I'd planned to give him today. "One more thing," I said, turning back around. "There's something I was going to tell you this morning, but then everything went haywire . . ."

"What's that?" Cam asked without looking up from his computer screen.

"It's about Bruce Parker's former partner, Teresa Lindover."

Cam raised his head and locked eyes with me. "What about her?"

"She came to see me at my apartment. She showed me her badge and I assumed she was still a detective with the Chapel Hill police department, but then at the gala David Benton said she was his real estate agent."

"She's moonlighting?" Cam asked.

"No, not according to David. He told me she was retired from the police force."

"So she lied to you." Cam straightened in his chair. "What did she want?"

"It seemed to me that she was trying to find out if I was going to be a reliable witness." I met Cam's inquiring gaze with a lift of my chin. "I think she was afraid I might change my story to protect Eloise."

"Why pretend to be a police detective, though?" Cam mused, talking to himself as much as to me.

"To give herself a more official status, so I'd let her in and talk to her, I bet."

Cam leaned forward, resting his arms on the desk. "She could be running her own investigation, outside of police jurisdiction. If Parker was her partner for many years . . ."

"Which I think he was," I said.

"Then perhaps she wants to exact justice on her own terms." Concern shadowed Cam's eyes. "If she's convinced that Eloise killed her former partner, she could be set on seeking revenge."

I nodded. "Which means we need to keep an eye on her. Especially if Eloise is exonerated by the court."

"Another person's name to add to the list of suspects, if only to protect Eloise," Cam said, in a bleak tone. "It seems this investigation is growing exponentially."

I offered him a wry smile. "Good thing you don't have to handle it on your own."

"A very good thing," he said, returning my smile.

Chapter
Twenty-Two

I spent the rest of the day engaged in my actual job, finally finishing cataloging all the books and other materials related to Helen McCloy.

Around four, my phone buzzed with a text from Bailey.

Don't get takeout, it said. *Dinner at Vince's house.*

Hoping this meant that Vince or Bailey had some more information to share, I drove home with my mind a jumble of thoughts and theories about Lily as well as the two Anderson-related murders. As I parked next to Donna's emerald-green compact hybrid, Bailey waved to me from Vince's porch.

"I locked up the apartment, so just come on in. Vince and Donna have dinner almost ready," she said.

I grabbed my briefcase and purse and locked the car. "As long as no one cares about my disheveled directly-after-work appearance."

Bailey laughed. "Like I dressed up." She flourished her hand to draw attention to her old *Phantom of the Opera* T-shirt and cutoff denim shorts.

"Sure, but you'd look good in a potato sack," I said as I joined her on the porch. "My pants have more pills than a pharmacy."

"Yeah, what happened?" Bailey asked as she looked me over.

"Long story. I'll save it when we're inside." I hoisted my slipping purse strap higher on my shoulder and followed Bailey into the house.

"There you are." Donna bustled forward to give me a hug. "Hope you don't mind that we made plans without consulting you. Bailey let Vince know that she'd gathered some interesting information at the museum, so we thought we might as well share that along with dinner."

"As if I'd ever complain about someone else cooking for me," I said, setting my purse and briefcase on a console table near the front door.

Vince, standing behind the kitchen island, raised a wooden spoon in greeting. "Hey there. Hope you like Thai food. I've been experimenting."

"It's vegetarian," Donna said, as she ushered Baily and me to seats at the sleek birchwood dining table. "Bailey let us know she doesn't eat meat, so Vince found a recipe that would work for everyone."

"Sounds good." I sat down across from Bailey. "I didn't know you'd taken up cooking as a hobby, Vince."

"Have to keep busy somehow, and everyone needs to eat," he said.

"He tries things out on me. Most are good, a few questionable." Donna made a comical face as she sat down at one end of the table. "Only one was truly ghastly."

"We don't talk about that." Vince carried a large bowl of rice and set it on the table, then headed back to the island to grab another bowl.

Donna shaded her lips with her hand. "It was supposed to be goulash, but it tasted more like galoshes."

"Very funny." Vince set down the second bowl, which was filled with an appetizing mixture of lightly cooked fresh vegetables and fried tofu in a dark-brown sauce. He crossed to Donna and planted a kiss on her temple before circling around to sit at the other end of the table. "Alright everyone, dig in."

We passed the bowls around, each taking large spoonfuls of rice and the vegetable mixture. "Mmmm, very good," Bailey said after taking a bite.

It was delicious. I ate a good portion of what was on my plate before I dove into describing the day's confusing events.

"So someone kidnapped Eloise but she didn't want to report it?" Vince quirked his bushy eyebrows. "That sounds a little odd, as do the contents of that note."

"She said her abductor didn't speak, but who knows if that's true?" I said. "Maybe she did recognize the person and just doesn't want to expose them for some reason."

"What reason could that be?" Bailey asked.

I shrugged. "Cam and I have uncovered information that could cause her additional legal problems. It seems that Neil Knight, a former partner in her bookshop, has conducted some questionable financial transactions with a few shady people in the past. Maybe Knight was her abductor and she doesn't want to expose him because he could reveal her involvement, or at least acquiescence, with some less-than-legal deals."

"That would fit the wording of the note, too," Vince said.

Donna laid her fork across one edge of her empty plate. "Neil Knight, you say? I've heard that name before, but I can't recall where or when."

"From me, probably," Vince said. "I looked into the guy as part of some reporting on suspicious art deals. Remember the woman who said she'd found a Grandma Moses painting at a flea market but it turned out she'd stolen it from a gallery? She was caught and convicted, but although she mentioned Knight along with a few other dealers, nothing could ever be pinned on him."

"Sounds like a pretty untrustworthy character," Bailey said, laying down her fork. "That was delicious, by the way."

"Yes, it was. But getting back to Neil Knight—I met him the other evening and he did come across as rather unpleasant," I said.

Vince's expression turned solemn. "You talked to Knight? At a public event, I hope."

"It was at that gala I attended." I studied Vince for a moment. "He's a pretty aggressive type of guy."

Vince tapped his fork against the edge of his plate. "I'd say dangerous."

"Oh dear. And Cam wants me to track him down at his country club to try to speak with him again." I dabbed at my mouth with my paper napkin. "I guess you don't think that's wise?"

Bailey shot me a concerned look. "It doesn't sound like it, Mom."

"Well, certainly not if you go alone. I tell you what"—Vince stood and began collecting the dishes and silverware from the table—"why don't I accompany you? I'd feel a lot better about that, to be honest."

"So would I," Bailey said.

Donna, who'd also stood up, grabbed the rice bowl. "I agree. Vince should go with you, Jane, just to make sure nothing bad happens."

"No need," I said. "Cam agreed to go with me." I shrugged when Vince and Donna reacted with surprise. "He has a membership at this particular country club, so he can get me in as a guest. I'm not sure they'd let me in otherwise."

"I thought Cam didn't like to leave the estate," Bailey said. "Isn't that what you've told me, Mom?"

"Yes, but he has done so, a few times, more recently."

"He's been here, and visited your mother at her apartment," Vince said, as he returned to the table to pick up the other bowl. "But that's not exactly out in public. Certainly not as public as a country club. Is he really up to that sort of expedition?"

"I think we should let Jane worry about that," Donna called over her shoulder as she carried the bowl to the counter near the sink. "Besides, it's about time Cam overcame his reluctance to mingle with strangers. He's still such a young man. He needs to expand his horizons."

"Well, I hope it all works out," Vince said. "Now, sit tight. Donna made one of her famous apple pies for dessert." He carried the stack of dishes to the sink.

Bailey groaned. "This is torture. I know I should refuse dessert, but who can say no to apple pie?"

"Oh now, dear, you have nothing to worry about. You're thin as a whippet," Donna said, as she lifted the pie off a cooling rack and set it on the island. "It's folks like me who should be refusing dessert. But you know what? I don't. Because you only live once so you might as well enjoy it."

Vince waited until Donna had cut two slices of pie and topped them with vanilla ice cream, then he strolled back to the table, setting pieces of pie in front of Bailey and me. "So Bailey, you said you had some information you wanted to share from your visit to the museum?"

"Yes, do tell," Donna said, bringing two more pieces of pie to the table for herself and Vince. "I know Vince is dying to hear what you've learned."

Bailey tossed her shining fall of chestnut hair. "I don't know how important it is, but Mom said you guys wanted news on anything I found."

"Was it something in the scrapbooks?" I asked, after swallowing a delicious bite of pie.

"Nope. Didn't find any match to your phantom lady there," Bailey said. "There were some missing photos, though. I could tell because the color of the background paper was brighter and you could see the outlines where something had been."

"We noticed that in the scrapbooks we checked too," Vince said.

"But that isn't the most interesting info." Bailey licked the last remains of pie from her fork. "Sorry, I inhaled that. But it was so good."

Donna beamed. "I'm glad you enjoyed it."

"Anyway"—Bailey placed her fork on her plate—"I got to talking to one of the volunteers. Someone named Gordon Glenn, although he said everyone calls him Gordy."

"We've met him," I said. "He was the one who created the scrapbooks."

"Yeah, he told me that. But then he left to go help someone downstairs and this older lady came over and chatted with me. She said she was a friend of Gordy's and remarked on how she admired him for his energy and resilience, especially with all the tragedy he'd had to overcome in his life."

"What sort of tragedy?" Vince leaned forward, resting his forearms on the table.

"Well, his parents dying within a year of each other when he was in his late twenties, but before that, he had a sister who disappeared."

The image of Gordy's bright blue eyes flashed through my mind. "When was that?"

"In 1957," Bailey said, casting me an inquiring gaze. "She just vanished and was never seen again."

Vince and I locked eyes. "That's the same timeframe," he said.

I nodded. "Yes, it has to be her."

"Who?" Bailey asked, her deep brown eyes widening.

"Our mystery woman, Lily," I said.

Chapter Twenty-Three

B ailey was excited to learn that the woman we'd been trying to identify was probably Gordy's sister. She offered to return to the museum to speak with the elderly man again.

"I think he'll talk more candidly to me. He seemed to like me," she said, using both hands to sweep her hair behind her slender shoulders.

"Of course he did." I rolled my eyes dramatically but followed that with a grin. "Which is good. Maybe you can get him to share more information on Lily."

"So it's Lily Glenn," Vince said, his expression thoughtful. "That gives me a much better handle on researching her."

"It could be different now. She could've married and changed her last name," Donna said.

"Sure, but when she was dating Calvin she would've been single. I can dig back into some of the archives at the newspaper." Vince made an OK symbol with his thumb and forefinger. "I still have research privileges."

After we talked a little more, Bailey and I offered to help clean the dishes. Donna and Vince vehemently refused our assistance, telling us to go home and enjoy the rest of the evening.

"I know with Bailey's career, you two don't get a lot of time together," Donna said, with a warm smile. "You should take advantage of this chance."

Bailey and I graciously agreed and headed back to the apartment, where we settled on the sofa and chatted about the auditions Bailey's agent had already lined up for her.

"I'll have to fly to New York next week, on Thursday to be exact," Bailey said. "But only for a couple of days. I'd like to come back here while I wait to hear from my agent about the results of the auditions, if that's okay with you."

"Of course it's okay," I told her. "And if you need transportation, don't bother with Uber and give this guy a call." I opened the drawer in the side table next to the sofa and fished out Taylor Iverson's card. "He's very nice." I tapped the card against my palm. "Come to think of it, maybe I should have him take Cam and me to the country club this Wednesday. If I don't have to worry about driving, I can spend more time trying to keep Cam's anxiety under control."

"You know"—Bailey twisted a lock of her long hair around one finger—"I think it's pretty amazing that Cam's willing to go with you. You've often talked about him not leaving the estate."

"I'm not really sure how well it will go, but I certainly don't want to dissuade him." I stared at Taylor's card. "I'm going to call this guy tomorrow morning. Then I'll put the card back in the drawer here." I motioned toward the side table. "You can call whenever you need a ride."

"Won't that be expensive?" Bailey asked "I mean, a private car might be okay for your boss, but for me . . ."

I waved this off. "Don't worry about it. Tell Taylor to send the bill to me. I just want you to be safe."

"Says the woman who runs around playing detective." Bailey made a face at me.

"Now, now, I try to be smart and stay safe," I said mildly.

"Well, it will be good if your boss gets over his fear of leaving the house and accompanies you more often, especially when you're talking to skeezy types," Bailey said.

"It's not as easy as snapping your fingers and getting over it," I said sharply. "It's not like Cam wants to feel the way he does."

Bailey reared back against the sofa arm. "Whoa, don't go all mama bear on me. I'm not trying to diss the guy. It's just . . . peculiar, you know? Not something you expect from someone who's intelligent as well as rich."

"Anxiety and other things like that don't discriminate," I said.

"True." Bailey scooted over and slid her arm around my shoulders. "Actually, I think it's sweet how you defend him." She hugged me to her side. "Shows what an old softie you are."

I hmphed but didn't pull away.

*　*　*

After clearing it with Cam, I called Taylor and asked if he was free to drive us to the country club on Wednesday.

"During the day? No problem," he replied. "Most of my work is at night, so this will be a bonus job."

Still not sure that Cam would actually be willing to accompany me, I decided I'd go on my own if necessary. But on Wednesday, right after lunch, Cam appeared at the door to the library, wearing khaki pants and a kelly-green polo shirt.

"You look ready for the golf course. Or tennis, although I guess you'd wear shorts for that," I said, as I gathered up my purse.

"I never wear shorts," Cam said. "The pale arms are bad enough. I don't need to show off my ghostly white legs as well."

I chuckled as I followed him out the door and down the hall. "But you were a swimmer. You had to wear a bathing suit then, right?"

"That's different. When I went to the pool, I was mostly in the water. I went to swim, not lounge about."

"You know, I'm surprised there isn't a pool here at Aircroft," I said, as we walked out the front doors.

"I've thought about it. But it's just another thing to maintain, and I'd probably be the only one to use it. Lauren already has access to a pool at her apartment complex, and I don't think Mateo or Jenna would be interested."

Taylor, spotting us, jumped out of the sedan and circled around to open the car door.

"I enjoy swimming," I said, giving Taylor a nod in greeting before climbing in the back seat.

"Then perhaps I should reconsider," Cam said, as he slid in next to me.

After Taylor settled in the driver's seat, he wished us both a good day. "It's a nice day to be out playing a round, that's for sure," he said.

"We're not going to play golf," I said, with a little laugh. "I don't know how, to be honest."

"Neither do I. Rich man's game," Taylor replied.

I caught a glimpse of the abashed look in Taylor's eyes in the rearview mirror. "Not all wealthy men play golf, though, do they, Cam?"

"No. Never played the game. Not my thing," Cam said, casting me a sidelong glance. He was clutching the locked door handle for dear life.

"I'm glad you agreed to accompany me today," I said. "I doubt I could sweet talk my way into the country club."

"No, that isn't really your forte," Cam said.

In the mirror, I could see Taylor's eyebrows shoot up.

"My daughter, on the other hand, could convince the devil to do a good deed." I gently placed my right palm over Cam's left hand, which was furiously tapping the leather upholstery of the seat. "My daughter, Bailey, is an actress," I added, directing my words toward Taylor. "She has the gift of charm."

"Would I have seen her in anything? Movies or TV or anything like that?" Taylor asked.

"She mainly works on the stage," I replied. "But she's had a few guest roles on TV. I'll have to show you her picture later."

"Thanks." Taylor took a swift glance over his shoulder. "Everybody okay back there?"

I looked over at Cam. Beads of sweat dotted his upper lip and his freckles stood out like a tattoo. "Absolutely," I said.

"How about some music?" Taylor fiddled with some dials on the dashboard. "There we go, some classical. Is that okay?"

"Fine," Cam said, between gritted teeth.

The calming strains of Ravel's "Pavane for a Dead Princess" filled the car. I sat back against the plush seat cushions but kept my hand over Cam's restless fingers. We didn't talk for the rest of the drive.

As Taylor pulled into the wide driveway of the country club, I lifted my hand and cast Cam a reassuring glance. "You could return to the car, you know," I said under my breath. "Once you get me in, you could leave."

Cam shook his head. He slid a linen handkerchief from his pocket and dabbed the sweat from his upper lip and brow.

Taylor parked under the shade of a large maple tree. "I'll just wait here," he said. "There's a breeze, so with the window down it'll be cool enough."

"You have a book to read?" I asked.

Taylor grinned. "I do. I'll be fine. Just text me when you're ready to leave."

"Please unlock the doors," Cam said, his voice cracking on the last word. "No need to get out. We can exit on our own."

Complying with this request, Taylor turned to look at me after Cam bolted out of the car. "Is he okay?"

"No, but he'll survive," I said, as I climbed out of the vehicle. I hurried around to where Cam was standing, his back pressed against the tree trunk. "Deep breaths," I said.

"I'll be fine." A muscle in Cam's taut jaw twitched. "Everything will be fine."

"Of course it will," I said, with all the bravado I could muster. "Remember—it's *dear friends* jumping into the breach."

Cam looked me in the eyes. "Always a good thing to have, friends."

"Nothing better," I said. "Now—how about you pretend I'm a bit feeble and you need to hold on to my arm to escort me inside?"

"Feeble? I'm not sure anyone would believe that," Cam said, with a wan smile. But he took my arm anyway.

Chapter
Twenty-Four

C am had to riffle through his wallet to produce his membership card at the welcome desk.

"Mr. Clewe, how nice," the attractive young lady at the desk said. "I've seen your name on the membership rolls but I don't recall you ever visiting before."

"No time like the present," Cam said, as he shoved the card back into wallet. "Can you direct us to the bar?"

If the desk attendant was surprised by this clipped demand, she didn't show it. "Just through the main doors and to the left," she said, checking Cam out with obvious interest.

I wanted to tell her not to bother, but thanked her instead. "You really can wait in the car if you want. I can handle Neil Knight on my own."

"Nonsense. I've come this far. Might as well continue." Cam shoved his hands in his pockets.

Probably to keep from betraying any shaking, I thought. "At least the place isn't too crowded. I guess Wednesday afternoon isn't as busy as the weekend would be."

"I assume many of the members are at work," Cam said.

We walked past clusters of round dining tables draped in white linen with simple flower arrangements as decoration. A few tables, obviously the most prized, looked out over the golf course. "As I expected, it's a bit old-fashioned," I said, gesturing toward the dining area, where columns painted to resemble marble rose up from the tiled floor, and framed prints of various famous golf courses hung on the forest-green walls.

"My dad . . . Al, that is"—Cam cast me a tight-lipped glance— "came here almost every weekend. He said a lot of business could be conducted over a round of golf."

"He never brought you along?" I asked, bobbing my head in greeting to the few people who passed by us. I didn't know them, but thought it best to look like we belonged.

"Like I said, I don't play golf, and Al wasn't one to just want to hang out somewhere." Cam stopped in his tracks. "There's the bar. Do you see Knight anywhere?"

I swept my gaze over the area, focusing on the long mahogany bar with its burnished brass accents. Catching a glimpse of Cam and myself in the mirrors that backed the glass shelves filled with colorful liquor bottles, I frowned. Cam looked like he was in physical pain. "No. He's balding and stocky. No one like that at the bar."

"What a surprise," said a deep male voice behind us. I turned and looked up into David Benton's handsome face. "I've never seen you here before, Cam. Or Jane, but I suppose she's your guest?"

David's assumption that I couldn't be a member of this country club rendered my "hello" rather testy. "Cam's the member, of course. His dad came here often."

"I remember. Albert Clewe was a fixture on Saturdays. He was always hosting people for golf and dinner. Different ones most of the time, so I assumed he was courting new financial partners. All business, wasn't he?" David's smile was genial, but I still felt a frisson of unease.

"He was an extraordinarily focused individual," Cam said, tapping the toe of his right shoe against the hard floor.

I bumped his foot with the side of my loafer. "So you're a member here?"

"My family have been members since before I was born," David said. "Speaking of family, here's my mother. I know you've met her, Jane, but I doubt Cam has." David waved Gloria over. "Mom, you met Jane Hunter at our gala, but not her boss, Cameron Clewe. Cam owns Aircroft now. I believe you once acquired a few paintings and antiques for that estate."

"Gloria Benton," she said, extending her hand. "I don't think we've met, although as David said, I did some business with your father in the past." Gloria's eyes narrowed as she looked Cam up and down. "I must say, you don't look anything like him."

Cam slid one hand from his pocket to clasp, and swiftly drop, Gloria's fingers. "I'm told I look more like my mother."

"That's right, Patricia, wasn't it? I only met her a couple of times, but she was a lovely woman. You have her coloring, although her eyes were blue, not green." Gloria smiled. "You're lucky to have gotten her height. Al was rather short."

I cleared my throat. "It's nice to see you both again, but we're actually looking for Neil Knight. We understood that he could be found here almost every afternoon."

"At the bar, you mean?" Gloria arched her feathery eyebrows.

"Now, Mom, don't be unkind." David eyed Cam and me with interest. "I can't really confirm that rumor. The truth is, I'm not here that often. Mom and I came today to meet with someone."

"We don't want to keep you, then," Cam said, curling his hand into a fist at his side.

"Not to worry. Our contact isn't here yet," Gloria said. "As for Neil Knight, I know he lives nearby. Close enough to walk, which I suppose comes in handy . . ."

"Mom." David took Gloria's arm. "I'm sure Cam and Jane aren't really interested in gossip."

I wanted to disagree—gossip could be quite handy when running an investigation. But I simply smiled. "No harm done. I observed Mr. Knight's predilection at the gala. He was knocking them back pretty fast."

"A bad habit," David said, with a shake of his head. "I'm surprised he's done as well in business as he has."

A bright tinkle of notes filled the air between us. "Oh, that's my cell. Excuse me." Gloria pulled her phone from her purse and glanced at the screen. "Terry just texted," she told David. "She says to meet her in the lobby."

Cam and I exchanged a glance. "Isn't that your real estate agent? I thought she worked out of Chapel Hill," I said, keeping my tone as innocent as possible.

"You remembered. I'm flattered." David cast me a look that told me he'd mistaken the reason for my interest. "Yes, it's Teresa Lindover. She agreed to drive over and meet us today with some investment proposals."

Gloria patted her elegantly styled silver hair. "Have to put the money somewhere, right, Cam?"

Staring over her shoulder, Cam shuffled his feet. "Real estate is always a good investment."

"The best, outside of art and antiques, of course," Gloria said, with an arch smile. "Well, we must run," she added, tapping my arm with her manicured nails. "But don't forget, Jane—you're supposed to visit the showroom sometime soon. Of course, you're welcome too, Cam."

"Thanks. Nice to meet you," he said, without looking at her directly.

I said goodbye to David and Gloria as well, waiting until they were out of earshot to turn to Cam. "Perhaps our trip isn't in vain. If Neil Knight doesn't show up, we can still try to talk to Terry Lindover. I certainly have a few questions I'd like to ask her."

"Alright, but I just thought of something." Cam shook out his hands. "Al talked about a private room downstairs. I believe he took some potential business partners there from time to time. I think there's another, smaller bar in that room. Why don't you stay here and keep a lookout for Knight while I head downstairs and see if he could be using that space instead?"

Knowing Cam had reached the end of his tolerance for mingling in a strange new place, I assumed he was looking for a way to escape the busier upper floor for a few minutes. "Fine. I'll just order a drink so I don't look odd hanging out at the bar," I said, flashing a smile. "I promise I'll still be sober when you get back."

"I should hope so," he said, turning on his heel to walk away. "Although," he called over his shoulder, "Taylor looks like a stout fellow. I'm sure he could carry you, if you need help getting to the car."

I bit back a scathing reply and stalked over to the bar, where I ordered a gin and tonic. "Can I charge to a member's account?" I asked the bartender.

"If you're their guest, yes," she replied.

"Then give me the top-shelf gin and put this on Cameron Clewe's tab."

Chapter
Twenty-Five

I nursed my drink and kept watch for Neil, my cell phone lying on the bar top in front of me. When it buzzed and skittered an inch or two, I picked it up, assuming Cam had sent a message. But the text was from Bailey.

Exciting!!! the text said. *Vince and I talked to Gordy. We can visit him Sat. at home. Have address.*

I texted back my thanks and told Bailey we'd talk later.

While I was focused on my phone, someone slid onto the barstool beside me.

"I can't stay long," Terry Lindover said. "I left the Bentons at the table. Said I was heading to the powder room."

I swiveled to face her. "I assume they mentioned they'd run into me."

"You and your boss." Terry waved aside the bartender. "They also said you know I'm their real estate agent."

I examined her meticulously made-up face. "Not a detective, then."

"I was, and I was also Bruce Parker's partner for many years." Terry zipped open her clutch purse and extracted a lipstick tube and a red compact. She flipped the compact open and used the mirror to reapply her pale-pink lipstick. "I left the force before Bruce retired."

I plucked the lime wedge from the rim of my glass and dropped it into my drink. "But you kept your badge?"

"That was a lucky break. I thought I'd lost the one I showed you, so I was given a new one. Then the first one turned up." She snapped shut the compact and slid it and the lipstick back into her purse.

"But you didn't tell your department about that, I assume? Just turned in the second one when you left."

Terry's perfectly tinted lips curved into a smile. "Correct. I thought it might come in handy someday."

"Isn't impersonating a police officer a crime?" I took a sip from my glass.

Terry adjusted the cherry blossom-patterned silk scarf she was wearing at the neck of her ivory suit. "Well, that's the thing. When I learned you were here today, I thought we should have a little talk. Just to clear up any confusion."

"I haven't said anything to the authorities, if that's what you're worried about," I said.

"Good. Do you mind continuing to stay silent? As you may have guessed, I'm following Bruce's case and doing everything I can to help. Not officially, of course, but I still have many contacts in law enforcement."

I set down my drink. "What incentive do I have to keep quiet?"

Terry surveyed me for a moment. "I was right, you are a tough cookie. Alright, how about this—you don't spill my secret, and I'll share any tidbits that might help your little friend Eloise with you and Mr. Clewe."

"Why would you do that? You want to see her convicted."

Terry slipped off her barstool and tugged down the hem of her jacket. "You're wrong. I simply want to see justice done." She thrust out one slender hand. "Deal?"

I crossed my arms over my chest. "Just how will you share these so-called *tidbits* with me?"

Terry dropped her hand. "I know where you live, remember?" She offered me what I assumed was her professional agent's smile before turning and walking away.

The bartender, who'd been busy at the other end of the bar during our convo, crossed back to me. "Another?"

I shook my head. "No thanks. I need a clear head." I picked up my cell phone and checked for any more messages. There was a text from Cam that simply said: *No one downstairs. Coming back up in a minute.*

Glancing down the bar, I noticed a short, stocky man hurrying off in the same direction as Terry. I couldn't see his face to confirm that he was Neil Knight, but he was bald and wearing a vivid fuchsia polo shirt. I jumped off my stool and followed.

I reached an alcove with two hallways leading off of it. The corridors were separated by an elevator wall. Not spying Neil, or Terry, for that matter, I paused to text Cam—*Just saw Knight but he got away from me. Need you to help check 2 halls upstairs.*

It appeared that Cam was texting back, but the message didn't come through. I hit the down button on the elevator. Cam had said he was taking the stairs, but I assumed this elevator would take me to the same general area. We could meet up and discuss tactics before trying to find Neil again.

I stepped out into a large open room that appeared to be a space utilized for parties or other gatherings. Stacks of folding banquet tables and chairs filled one wall. As I looked around, wondering where the main stairway was located, I heard a commotion that sounded like it was coming from the end of a short corridor.

Pocketing my phone, I strode down the hall, but two people wearing the country club's staff uniforms shoved me aside as they ran into the room at the end of the hall.

"Sorry, emergency!" one of the staff shouted.

I leaned against the wall and stared after them. They dashed to the bottom of a wide staircase, where a few other staff were already clustered.

"Did someone already call 911?" one of them called out.

"On their way." The young woman who'd manned the welcome desk stepped back, revealing a figure lying crumpled on the floor.

I squinted, but all I could see was a pale arm and hand and a flash of kelly green.

Running across the room so fast that I almost tripped over my own feet, I reached the circle of staff members and used my elbow to push one of them aside.

"Hey, stand back please. Someone is injured," said a tall man dressed in a black shirt and pants. *A waiter*, I thought.

"He's my boss," I snapped. "Let me through. I need to stay with him."

Cam was lying on the floor, his left leg bent at an unnatural angle. I knelt down beside him, gently grasping his hand. "What happened?"

He just looked up at me, his rose-gold lashes lowered to veil his eyes and his skin gleaming with perspiration.

"Nobody saw it," the welcome desk lady said. "One of our servers just heard a terrible noise and ran over to the steps and saw Mr. Clewe lying at the bottom. He must've tripped and fallen."

I could tell by the panic in her voice and the stress tugging down the mouths of the other staff that they were immediately thinking about lawsuits and million-dollar settlements. "Is an ambulance coming?" I asked.

"Should be here any minute," the tall waiter said.

Cam squeezed my fingers. I leaned in close to his lips. "Check other hand," he whispered. "Get note."

I reached across his body to find and uncurl the fingers of his opposite hand. Crumpled in his palm was a ball of paper. Glancing up, I realized that the staff members were talking loudly among themselves and not watching Cam or me. I plucked the paper from Cam's hand and sat back on my heels. "Got it," I whispered to Cam. I stuffed the note into the pocket of my slacks.

"Good." Cam squeezed my hand again.

I leaned in, brushing a damp strand of hair from his forehead. "You tripped?"

Cam tightened his lips. Pressing the elbow of his other arm against the floor, he attempted to raise himself up.

"No, no." I used my hold on his hand to force him to lay back down. "You've had a bad fall. Your head and neck need to be checked before you move. Stay still until the rescue squad arrives."

With his free hand, Cam motioned for me to come closer. "Paused at the top of the steps to read your text. Was looking down at my phone. Didn't see anyone."

"What do you mean? You didn't stumble or trip?" I glanced back up at the circle of staff, a few of whom were looking at us now. "One blink for yes, two for no," I whispered.

He blinked twice. Touching his lower lip with one finger, he mouthed, *Pushed.*

Chapter
Twenty-Six

The rescue squad arrived and took charge a few minutes later. I told Cam I'd meet up with him at the hospital.

"Phone Lauren," he called out before I was forced to back away by the EMTs.

I gave him a salute, then hurried back to the elevator to reach the main floor. As I made my way to the front doors, I noticed Gloria Benton standing off to one side.

"Oh dear, I hear it was Cam Clewe who took a bad tumble down the stairs," Gloria said, gripping one of my hands.

I extracted my fingers and stepped back. "Yes. Sorry, I need to go."

"Of course, of course." Gloria looked around the foyer. "You haven't seen David lately, have you? He seems to have disappeared. He left our table, saying he wanted to look for Ms. Lindover. Which honestly, I understood at the time. She'd been away from the table for quite some time."

"No, I'm afraid not," I said, tucking away this information. *Terry, David, and Neil were all in the building, out of sight, around the time Cam was pushed down the stairs. It could've been any one of them.* I offered Gloria a harried smile and a goodbye.

I didn't bother to text Taylor. Arriving at the car, I rapped on the driver's side window.

"Ms. Hunter," he said, closing his book. "Is something wrong?"

"I'm afraid so. Mr. Clewe has had an accident."

"I saw the emergency vehicles. I thought maybe someone had a heart attack or something."

"Mr. Clewe took a tumble down a flight of stairs," I said, holding up a hand to forestall any more questions. "I'm going to ask you to drive me to the hospital. After that you can head home."

"I can wait and drive you to your apartment," Taylor said, as I climbed in the back seat.

"No, no. I plan to call my daughter. My car's still at home, so she can pick me up." I flashed a bright smile to calm the concerned look in his eyes. "Don't worry. I'll be fine."

"So sorry to hear Mr. Clewe has been injured. Is he going to be okay?"

"I'm sure he broke his leg. I hope he's okay otherwise. He seemed to be, but I'll feel better once the doctors check him out."

Taylor glanced in the rearview mirror. "I bet. Now, which hospital? There's a couple different ones in town."

I told him what the EMTs had told me, then sat back and stared out the side window as Taylor drove, pulling over once to allow the ambulance transporting Cam to pass by.

Halfway to the hospital I remembered my promise and called Lauren.

"Just the leg, you think?" she asked, in a strained voice.

"From what I could tell. Of course, he'll be checked for a concussion or any other injuries," I said. "Please don't worry too much. He was conscious and didn't seem confused."

"I'll drive to the hospital now," Lauren said. "You said Forsyth?"

"Yes. Emergency room, of course. See you there." I considered mentioning Cam's insistence that he'd been pushed, but decided against it. Revealing that information would be up to him.

But that reminded me of the crumpled note I'd taken from Cam's hand. I pulled the balled-up paper from my pocket and smoothed it out over my thigh.

It was written in block letters on a sheet from one of the complimentary notepads I'd seen scattered around the country club. *So not a pre-planned attack*, I thought, as I peered at the words.

Stop protecting a killer, it said. *Eloise Anderson is a murderer and all your money can't save her from justice.*

I folded the note and slipped it into my purse.

"I really don't mind waiting for you," Taylor said again when we reached the emergency room.

"It's fine. You know how it is—it will be all hours." I thanked him and headed inside.

Lauren was already in the waiting room. I sat beside her. "Any news?"

"They're doing CT scans and X-rays," she said, plucking at a loose thread at the open knee of her jeans.

"You were already at your apartment, I guess," I said, taking in her faded T-shirt, the worn jeans, and battered sneakers. She'd obviously rushed to the hospital without bothering to change.

"Cam sent me home early." Lauren's dark-brown eyes were glassy with tears. "You don't have to stick around, Jane. I can keep you updated."

"It's okay. I don't have plans for tonight." I didn't mention my real reason for staying, which was to discuss the note and a few other things with Cam. "Oh, but that reminds me—I need to call Bailey. She'll have to drive my car here to pick me up."

"I can take you home," Lauren said.

I shot her a questioning look. "Won't you be taking Cam back to Aircroft? I mean, hopefully they won't be keeping him here overnight, so he'll need someone to get him home." I slapped my forehead. "Shoot, I should've told Taylor to stay. He could've helped get Cam in and out of the car. I don't think you can do that by yourself."

Lauren shrugged. "I can manage. He's not that heavy."

"Hmmm, I don't know." I pulled out my phone. "Here, I'll send you Taylor's phone number. He could be a big help, depending on how difficult it will be for Cam to maneuver with a cast or whatever they put him in."

"That's a good point." Lauren bit her lower lip. "It just seems strange, Cam falling like that. He isn't a clumsy person, and is always on alert. I can't imagine him just taking a tumble. I think if he made a misstep, he'd have caught himself."

I stared down at my phone screen and made a noncommittal noise.

Lauren grabbed my arm. "You'd tell me if there was something else going on, wouldn't you, Jane?"

"If I could. You know Cam. Sometimes he likes to share certain information personally."

"So there *is* something else going on. I knew it." Lauren slammed her right fist into her left palm. "Very well. I may not push Cam too hard tonight, given that he'll probably be on painkillers and not himself, but I'll be asking questions over the next few days, believe me."

"I have no doubt." I cast her a sidelong glance. "You really do care about him, don't you?"

Lauren straightened in her hard plastic chair. "Of course. I've been his personal assistant for almost six years. It's normal to grow attached to people you work with so closely."

I patted her knee. "It's okay. Your secret's safe with me."

She opened her mouth but snapped it shut again as a nurse walked up to us.

"Hello, are you here with Mr. Clewe?" the nurse asked.

"Yes, I'm Lauren Walker, his personal assistant. I believe my name's listed as a primary contact on his medical records."

"It is." The nurse turned to me. "And you are?"

"Jane Hunter. I'm also employed by Mr. Clewe. We were actually on a work trip when his accident occurred." Although I kept my eyes focused on the nurse, I could feel Lauren's gaze burning a hole into my temple.

"Okay. Well, Mr. Clewe is quite lucky. He did break his left leg, but the other CT scans and X-rays are clean. No serious injuries to his back, neck, or head. Of course, he'll be badly bruised and may have some aches and pains for a while, but all in all he was fortunate." The nurse shook his head. "With that type of fall, things could be a lot worse."

"Can we see him?" Lauren asked, grabbing her purse and sweater as she stood up.

"We need to check a few more vitals before we can discharge him, but we've moved him to a room. Just follow me."

Lauren and I trailed the nurse through the swinging doors that led to a wide hall. Or it would've been wide if there weren't beds, filled with patients, lining one side of the corridor.

"I guess you keep busy all the time," I said.

The nurse chuckled. "You don't know the half of it." He led us a room with its door slightly ajar. "Mr. Clewe is in here. Feel free to sit with him, but just be aware he's been given something for the pain."

"You mean he might be a loopy? We figured." I tapped Lauren's shoulder. "You go in first. He may want to talk to you privately. There's a chair outside the door. I'll just wait."

Lauren cast me a grateful smile before she entered the room.

As I sat down, I heard Cam say something about an "unusual outfit," which made me grin. Honestly, I thought it was good for him to see Lauren in more casual clothes. It might make him realize that she had a life outside of Aircroft.

After about fifteen minutes, Lauren walked out. "Your turn. He wants to talk to you alone, although I'm not sure why, because he isn't making much sense. I'll go and see if I can arrange things with the driver. What did you say his name is?"

"Taylor Iverson." I gave her a wink. "He's actually rather good-looking, and he's a writer as well as a driver."

Lauren just waved me off and strode down the hall.

Cam raised the head of the bed when I entered the room. "Jane, the note."

Leaning back against the pillows, strands of his hair fanned out behind his head, he looked young and vulnerable. His left leg, encased in a cast from knee to ankle, lay on top of the rumpled sheet. I crossed to the chair pulled up beside the bed and sat down.

"Did you get a chance to read it before you fell?"

He shook his head. "Whoever it was . . . whoever." He blinked rapidly. "Sorry, not thinking straight."

"Did they shove it into your hand before they pushed you?"

Pressing one hand to his forehead, Cam took a deep breath. "No. Slipped it in my back pocket. I thought someone was trying to lift my wallet. When I checked I felt the paper and grabbed it."

I could tell how much of an effort he was making and decided to help out. "You started to turn around and they shoved you before you could?"

"Right, right. Paper in one hand, phone in the other. Couldn't grab the rail fast enough."

"Which is why this was crumpled in your fist." I fished the note out of my purse and unfolded it. As I read it out to him, he frowned. "And, just so you know, it's written in block letters on the club's free stationery."

"Last minute," Cam said, closing his eyes. "Not planned."

"That's what I thought as well." I carefully folded the note. "As you know, both the Bentons were in the building, but so were Neil Knight and Terry Lindover. I just caught a glimpse of Knight, but Terry actually talked to me. Briefly." Slipping the note back into my purse, I considered my next words. "She wanted to make sure I didn't reveal her officer impersonation."

"Think we should talk another time. Head's too fuzzy now," Cam said.

I laid my hand over his. "Good idea. You should rest. I'll see you at Aircroft tomorrow."

Cam's lashes fluttered. When he opened his eyes, they glowed with a hectic glimmer. "No. Take time off. Visit with your daughter. I won't be any use for a few days. Come back Monday."

"Alright." I lifted my hand and stood up. "Should I send Lauren back in? I'm sure she'll sit with you until you're discharged. Besides, she's arranging your transportation back to Aircroft."

"That would be nice," Cam said, closing his eyes again.

I tiptoed out and found Lauren, who told me she'd gotten in touch with Taylor.

"He'll come as soon as I text," she said.

"I'll go, then. Cam gave me tomorrow and Friday off, but I'll call you to see how he's doing." I patted her shoulder. "I think he'd like for you to sit with him. That's what he said, anyway."

Lauren's expression brightened. "Okay. See you Monday, then." She quickly headed back into the exam room.

As I prepared to leave, I heard Cam say something about ruining her evening before Lauren told him to stop being so foolish.

Chapter
Twenty-Seven

It was nice to have a couple of full days to spend with Bailey. We did a little sightseeing and a lot more shopping. Bailey was fascinated with Old Salem, as well the many unique stores on Trade Street in downtown Winston-Salem.

Of course, I called Lauren on Thursday to see how Cam was doing.

"Recovering, but still in pain," she told me. "All the muscle strains and bruises have kicked in and naturally, he's insisting on taking the least amount of pain medication that he can get away with."

"That means he's probably grumpy. Poor you," I said.

"Oh, I know how to handle that. I just leave the room until he stops being such a bear."

"You must be out of his sight a lot then," I said.

Lauren laughed and wished me a good day.

On Friday Vince called and begged off accompanying Bailey and me to visit Gordy Glenn the following day.

"I'd love to hear what he has to say, but Donna's sister took a tumble at home and we're driving to Asheville later to help out for a few days."

"This seems to be the season for falls," I said glumly. "Cam's doing okay, by the way."

"Glad to hear it. Let me know what you learn from Gordy."

"Will do," I said.

Bailey called Gordy to set a time for our visit. "He says eleven," she told me.

"That will work. We can go somewhere for lunch after," I said.

Saturday dawned sunny and warm—the kind of late May day perfect for driving out into the countryside. Bailey entered Gordy's address into my GPS right before we left.

"Apparently it's an old farm," she said, settling back in the passenger's seat. She'd pulled her long, chestnut-brown hair into a low ponytail and only used a touch of blush and lip gloss.

I shot her a sidelong glance. "You went light on the makeup today."

"Just like I did the other day. I figured an older man, like Gordy, would be more receptive to a sweet young thing." She flashed a grin. "I didn't think going all femme fatale would be my best move."

"Look at you, always playing a role," I said as I followed the GPS's instructions and turned onto a narrow gravel road.

Bailey stared out the side window. "Not always. I'm just myself with you, Mom."

"Which I appreciate," I said, tightening my grip on the steering wheel as my car bounced out of a pothole.

"It's so pretty out here, but awfully remote," Bailey observed.

Staring ahead, I took in the vista of slightly rolling fields bordered by stands of trees. A few small brick houses and wood-framed barns and other farm buildings dotted the green and gold fields with splashes of red, white, and gray.

"Not really. We're only about five miles outside of town. It's just that once you leave the cities and towns around here, it quickly becomes quite rural."

"Certainly different than New York or LA." Bailey glanced at the GPS screen. "Looks like we're almost there."

I pulled into a long, packed-dirt driveway. Post and wire fences bent under the weight of honeysuckle vines lined either side of the road. The fields behind the fences were thick with thistles and wild grasses. I didn't see any cattle or sheep or other livestock.

"It looks like Gordy hasn't farmed in quite some time," I said, as I parked in front of a weathered shed. The vintage tractor inside had chipped red paint and bald tires. There was also a battered truck that, while newer than the tractor, still had some years on it.

"He is ninety. I bet he just decided not to bother." Bailey picked her way through the clumps of weeds that filled the small yard in front of a two-story white farmhouse.

When we reached the sagging wooden porch, a flutter of wings made me look up at a bird nest balanced on one of the crossbeams. "You see the traces of a pale blue color?" I asked, pointing upward. "It's more common farther south, but some people around here also painted porch ceilings blue to keep ghosts at bay. The tradition was that the ghosts couldn't cross water, so the ceilings were painted a soft blue to mimic a stream or river."

"You're a fountain of fascinating facts, Mom." Bailey cast me a sarcastic smile as she knocked on the cobalt-blue front door.

"It doesn't hurt to learn something new once in a while," I said.

Before Bailey could throw out a retort, the front door opened.

"Welcome." Gordy Glenn motioned toward the dim interior of the house. "Please come in."

A significant portion of the entrance hall was given over to a staircase that led up to the second floor. The hall ran straight to the back of the house, with doors opening onto rooms on either side.

"Sorry for the condition of the place," Gordy said, as he led us into one of the front rooms. "I try to keep up with it, but my eyesight isn't as good as it used to be, so I'm sure I miss some dirt and dust."

"No worries. We aren't neat freaks." Bailey offered Gordy a warm smile and sat in a wooden rocking chair. An afghan, crocheted in squares of primary colors, hung over the tall back of the rocker.

The room, which I assumed to be a parlor, was sparsely furnished. I sat on a small sofa covered in a faded floral-patterned upholstery, facing Gordy, who'd chosen a well-worn leather recliner. *I bet that's always been his chair*, I thought, noticing it could swivel to face the old television perched on a weathered pine table.

"Where's my manners?" Gordy said, sitting forward as if preparing to jump back to his feet. "I should offer you ladies something to drink. Only have lemonade and tea from the store, I'm afraid. Or well water."

"Nothing for me, thanks," Bailey said.

I murmured my agreement. "We don't want to put you out. We're just grateful you agreed to talk to us about your sister."

Gordy settled back in his chair and fixed me with his bright blue gaze. "You say Lily is this mystery woman you've been looking for. I suppose you're right. The young lady"—he motioned toward Bailey—"showed me some photocopies of a drawing and a photo and they surely do look like my sister."

"Vince and I showed you the same pictures before," I said.

Embarrassment flushed Gordy's face. "I know. I brushed you off then, but I got to thinking about it and decided it was time to be honest."

"Who was older, you or Lily?" I asked.

"Lily, by five years. There was just the two of us, which made things difficult. My pa was always saying he wished he had more kids, because he needed more hands on the farm. But I sort of figured out that Mama couldn't have any more. Her health was never that good, and she lost a couple babies between Lily and me." Gordy's expression grew solemn. "It was a hard life on the farm."

"I'm sure it was," Bailey said, her tone containing just the right mixture of pity and admiration.

She's good, I thought, fighting back a smile. *Very good.* "Lily didn't stay on the farm, though, did she?"

"Nope, she got out as soon as she could. She was a smart one, with lots of plans." Gordy met my interested gaze with a quirk of his thin lips. "My parents hoped she'd marry a fellow who could work on the farm, but that was never in the cards. Lily had other ideas."

"Like marrying Calvin Airley?" I asked.

Gordy snorted. "I can't say. She loved him, that's the honest truth. I never doubted that. But marriage . . ." He stared out the window behind me. "Samuel and Bridget Airley came from nothing, you know. But once they got rich, they acted like they were born with silver spoons in their mouths. They'd never have accepted Lily as Calvin's wife. She knew that, better than anyone."

"If Calvin loved her back, I don't see how his parents could've stopped them from marrying," Bailey said.

Gordy turned to her, a wry smile on his lips. "You're too young to understand how it was back then. Wealthy young gentlemen didn't marry the farmer's daughter. It wasn't done."

"I believe Calvin wanted to defy his parents." I leaned forward, gripping my knees. "I think he planned to run off with your sister, but then he died."

Gordy took a deep breath that rattled his chest. He coughed before speaking again. "He did, he did. Calvin was a decent man. He wasn't concerned about money and position like his parents. When Lily told him she was with child . . ."

Bailey's sudden jerk set her chair rocking. "She had a baby?"

"She was going to. I mean, she did, but she left town and disappeared before she was too far along." Gordy's fingernails dug into the balding leather of his chair arm. "She was frightened, you see."

"Scared that whoever killed Calvin might try to murder her as well?" I asked.

Bailey whipped her head to the side to look at me. "I thought it was an accident."

"That's what everyone thought," Gordy said. "Accident or suicide, although not too many spread that rumor unless they knew it wouldn't get back to the Airleys. But Lily always believed Calvin was murdered."

"Did she have any idea who killed him?" I asked.

"She had ideas." Gordy stared down at his hands, which he'd clenched in his lap. "She thought it could've been Calvin's parents, although they wouldn't have done the deed themselves. Hired it out, most likely."

"That makes no sense. Why would they kill their only child?" Bailey slumped back in the rocker.

"People do odd things sometimes, when they don't get their way. But the Airleys weren't Lily's primary suspects." Gordy pressed one hand against his chest, over his heart. "She thought it was probably our pa."

"Because Calvin had gotten his daughter pregnant before marriage," I said, my thoughts racing. If that was what Lily had believed, not wonder she'd left and never come back.

Gordy's lips twisted. "He was furious. Slapped Lily so hard it left a mark. I don't know what would've happened if I hadn't been there."

"You protected her," Bailey said. "Good for you."

Gordy's sad smile was heartbreaking. "Wish I could've done more. I did keep her secret, though. She told me she was leaving and never coming back. Said she'd find a way to contact me later, and she did. Just a postcard here and there, but at least I knew she was alive."

"Did the Airleys know about the baby?" Bailey asked, her dark eyes wide.

"No, and that was another secret I kept. Well, my parents did too, but that was mostly out of shame." Gordy grimaced. "I wasn't ashamed of Lily or my niece or nephew, but I understood why she never wanted Samuel and Bridget to know."

"They would've taken the child from her," I said.

Gordy met my gaze and held it. "Sure as the sunrise. It was Calvin's child. They would've fought for custody and Lily figured they would've won."

"But the baby, did it live? And was it a boy or a girl?" Bailey asked, toying with the edge of the afghan.

"I know it lived. Lily told me that much. She let me know that her child had survived and was doing well. Grown now, of course. But she never said if it was a boy or a girl, or told me its name." Gordy shook his head. "Saddest thing in my life. I have a sister and a nephew and niece somewhere out in the world and here I am, all alone."

I shifted my position on the sofa to escape the spring poking up against the fabric seat cushion. "When was the last time you heard from Lily?"

"It's been a while. But I'm sure she's still alive. She let me know, in one of her messages, that she'd have her child send a note when she died. I haven't received any word, so I assume she's still alive and kicking."

We chatted for a few more minutes, then I stood up and suggested that it was time Bailey and I left. "We do appreciate your candor, Gordy. May I share this information with Vince Fisher, the gentleman you've met at the museum?"

"That's okay, I guess." Gordy used his arms to push himself up onto his feet. "Lily and I are so old now, what does it matter? The Airleys are all gone, my pa and mama too. I've kept my sister's secret all these years, but I doubt telling it will affect anyone now."

Bailey strolled out onto the porch, but I hung back for a moment. "You know, Gordy, I think it's a good thing for the truth to come out. My boss, Cameron Clewe, has a secret too, and I think if he could uncover the truth, he'd be much happier."

Gordy looked me in the eye. "He's looking for his father, isn't he? Always figured Albert Clewe wasn't his biological dad. I saw them together around town, when the younger Clewe was a kid. He and Al were nothing alike. Not just looks, either."

"You're right," I said. "But it's another secret you must keep."

Gordy patted the hand I'd rested on the door latch. "Don't worry. As you've seen, I'm good at that."

Chapter
Twenty-Eight

Lauren met me in the entry hall when I arrived at work on Monday.

"Cam wants to see you," she said. "He's in the music room this morning."

"How's he doing?"

Lauren rolled her eyes. "Fine, except he's not happy that he has to sleep in one of the downstairs guest rooms."

"I guess the steps are a little much for someone on crutches," I said, glancing over at the sweeping main staircase.

"A great recipe for another fall, or at least that's what all of us have told him." Lauren fiddled with the gold pendant necklace she was wearing to accent her simple but elegant aqua dress.

"Alright, I'll go talk to Cam and then grab a coffee," I said.

The music room, located not far from the main sitting room, featured a glossy black grand piano and shelves filled with LPs and CDs. There were a few music stands clustered in one corner. I was never sure of their purpose until Lauren told me that Cam occasionally brought in professional musicians to entertain his friends or business associates.

Cam was seated in one of the two upholstered chairs facing an elaborate audio playback system, his left leg propped up, with a pair of crutches leaned against the other side of the ottoman. He removed a pair of high-end headphones when I crossed the room to greet him.

"Relaxing before your workday begins?" I asked as I sat down in the chair next to him.

Laying the headphones on an antique walnut side table, Cam picked up a remote control and clicked off the audio system. "Music helps to take my mind off the pain."

I set my purse and briefcase on the floor. "Is it bad?"

"Off and on. The strains and bruises are actually worse than the leg. I suppose it would be easier if I'd take as many of the painkillers that the doctor prescribed, but I don't like the way they make me feel."

"Out of control, you mean," I said. "Likely to say things you think but don't want to express?"

Cam side-eyed me. "Must you always be so on point?"

"What can I say? It's a rare talent." I lifted my hands in a what-can-you-do gesture.

"More like a curse, from my perspective," Cam said, but immediately smiled.

"I have some news that might take your mind off things." I turned slightly in my chair so I could face him more directly. "It's about our mystery woman. I hadn't said anything before this because I wanted to track down additional information, but after a couple of conversations with some elderly area residents, I now know who she was. Or, more accurately, is."

Cam's eyes lit up. "Really? You've tracked her down?"

"With help from Vince and Donna, and Bailey, actually. But we don't know where she is right now. We only know who she is, and that's she's still alive." I launched into a detailed recitation of the facts I'd learned from Ruth and Gordy.

"Lily Glenn," Cam said thoughtfully. "We should be able to locate her eventually, now that we have her name and age. One of the PIs I have on retainer can probably track her down."

"Do we need to, though?" I traced the paisley pattern on the upholstered chair arm with one finger. "We already know who she is, and why she disappeared, as well as her theories about what happened to Calvin Airley. I don't know if we need anything else."

Cam's fingers drummed his own chair arm. "But Calvin's son or daughter is the rightful heir to the Airley fortune. Shouldn't they be told?"

"Is there anything left? Samuel Airley didn't appear to have any living relatives, or at least, not close ones, so the estate and other holdings went to Bridget Airley's family. Her sister eventually sold Aircroft to your stepfather, and I got the impression from Vince, who'd spoken to that family, that there wasn't a lot of money left at that point."

Cam pressed his other hand over his restless fingers. "There are some investments. The bank manages them now. The remaining Airley relatives receive dividends from time to time."

"Oh, that's different. I guess Lily does need to be found, then, since she and her child would be entitled to some of those funds."

"Exactly." Cam winced as he adjusted his injured leg and wiggled his toes, which were peeking out from the end of the walking cast. "I'll need to get someone on that right away. Now—tell me about this detective turned real estate agent, Teresa Lindover."

I shared the details from my last encounter with Terry, adding, "She seems determined to make sure her former partner's killer is brought to justice."

"And she has ties to the Bentons. A rather curious connection, don't you think?"

"It does feel rather . . . convenient," I said. "But she was working for the Bentons before Bruce Parker was murdered, so if she's keeping tabs on them because she suspects them of any involvement, that would be quite a coincidence as well."

"Stranger things have happened." Cam propped his elbow on the chair arm and leaned his chin against his fist. "Neil Knight was at the country club as well."

"True. He was scuttling around, like he was trying to stay out of sight."

"The note definitely cast the blame on Eloise," Cam said. "And she was here, so . . ."

I swiveled in my seat. "Wait—do you suspect Eloise now?"

"She's hiding something," Cam said, before a rap on the door silenced him.

Lauren poked her head around the door. "You have a visitor, Cam. It's Gloria Benton. May I bring her in?"

Cam grimaced. "I suppose. But you'll need to pull up another chair."

"I can leave," I said, sliding forward.

"No, stay. You should hear whatever Gloria has to say."

Lauren grabbed a folding chair while Gloria strolled over. "You sit here," I told her, grabbing my purse and briefcase and rising to my feet. "I'll use the other chair."

"I'm fine with this," Gloria said, as Lauren set up the folding chair so it faced the two armchairs.

"No, no, you're a guest." I sat in the folding chair. "Please, have a seat."

"You might as well," Cam said dryly. "Once Jane makes up her mind, there's no changing it."

Gloria settled into the armchair, holding her red leather purse in her lap. "Thank you," she told me, before turning to Cam. "I hope I didn't drop by too early, but I was out and thought I'd see how you were doing." She glanced at Lauren, who nodded and left the room.

"It's fine, and I'm doing well," Cam said.

Lauren returned almost immediately with a large bouquet of flowers that she set on a console table under the windows. "These are lovely, Ms. Benton."

Cam glanced briefly at the flowers. "Lauren, why don't you pull up a chair as well. You should stay."

"In case you need anything?" Lauren's eyes were narrowed even though she kept her tone sweet.

"There is that," Cam said, with a lift of his eyebrows. As Lauren went to fetch another folding chair, he turned his head to look at Gloria. "Thank you for the flowers. It was very thoughtful of you, especially since we just met."

"Yes, but we were present when your accident happened, and I did have a connection to your late father. Besides"—Gloria twisted the strap around her hand—"I have an ulterior motive."

"Oh, what might that be?" I asked.

"I know you've offered Eloise Anderson refuge here, and are helping with her legal expenses," Gloria said, her gaze fixed on Cam. "Which is lovely of you, of course. But, given that, I just thought you should know something I should've told the authorities in the case involving Ken and Abby Anderson."

Cam sat up straighter, his eyes glittering with excitement. "Really? What might that be?"

"It involves that police detective that Ms. Anderson is accused of killing, Bruce Parker." Gloria pursed her lips. "He should never have been allowed to investigate the Abby Anderson case."

"Why not?" Lauren asked, her dark lashes fluttering.

Gloria slid a tissue out of the pocket of her linen jacket and dabbed a few beads of sweat from her forehead. "The truth is, he couldn't really be impartial. You see, he and Ken Anderson were close childhood friends."

Chapter
Twenty-Nine

"Why was he allowed to be in charge of the case, then?" I asked.

"No one knew about their connection." Gloria crumpled the tissue in her hand. "They both moved to Chapel Hill after college, but they were raised in High Point. I was acquainted with both of them because they played on the same soccer team as David. He was a little younger, and never really got along with Bruce or Ken, but we knew them."

"David also said nothing to the police about this connection?" Cam asked.

Gloria took a deep breath. "I asked him not to. You see, I was questioned by the Chapel Hill police because of some of the conflicts Benton House had had with Last Chapter. It was common knowledge that we'd had a falling-out over a rare Hemingway. When they questioned me, I realized from a comment one of the officers made about his boss that Bruce Parker was the lead detective on the case. I thought that was odd, but didn't say anything. Then when David was about to be questioned, I asked him to stay silent about that fact too."

Cam studied her for a moment. "Because you thought contradictory statements would make you look suspicious?"

"It was more that I was afraid it might cast suspicion on David." Gloria stuffed the tissue back in her purse. "He was younger then, and a lot more brash. He was the one who'd engaged in some truly contentious email exchanges with Ken Anderson. I thought if the authorities learned that David knew Ken from childhood, especially with them often being at odds even back then, that would make him a prime suspect."

A little groan escaped Cam's lips as he shifted his leg position again. "Sorry, can't seem to get comfortable. Anyway, what about Parker? He didn't disclose his connection to Ken or David?"

"Not that I'm aware of," Gloria said. "It seems no one in Chapel Hill knew about Bruce and Ken's past friendship. I closely followed the case and there was never any reporting that mentioned that fact. Also, Bruce continued as the lead detective until Abby was convicted, which I was certain would not have happened if the police department had known the truth."

"Why tell us this now?" I asked.

Gloria fluttered her hands. "I know it doesn't seem to have any connection to the current case, but I thought if anything ever came out about David knowing both Ken and Bruce . . ."

"I see. You're concerned about your son; afraid he might get dragged into the current case because he knew Bruce better than most people would assume," Cam said.

"That's exactly it." Gloria stood up, clutching her purse to her chest. "I thought, with Eloise here, she might share things with you that she hasn't told the police, and if she mentioned David being one of Ken's childhood acquaintances you might draw the wrong conclusions." Gloria cast me a quick glance before focusing on Cam. "I've heard of your avocation—about how you help people with your private investigations. I didn't want you to hear something related to the past and drag David into this new murder case."

We already have, I thought, keeping a pleasant smile plastered on my face. The truth was, Gloria's revelations just made David a bigger target. But of course I wasn't about to tell her that.

"Thank you, Gloria, that's very helpful," Cam said. "And I assure you neither Jane nor I will ever accuse anyone of a crime without evidence. Now, forgive me if I don't get up to say goodbye."

"Of course. I hope you recover quickly." Gloria took a few steps forward and wished us all good morning.

Lauren leapt out of her chair. "Let me show you out. I don't want you to get lost." She escorted Gloria into the hall.

"One thing before you go, Lauren," Cam called out.

Lauren paused in the open doorway. "Yes, what is it?"

"See if you can find Eloise and send her in here to talk to me, would you?"

After a sharp bob of her head, Lauren followed Gloria out into the hall.

"Do you want me to leave or stay?" I asked.

"Stay. And please, take the more comfortable chair." Cam tilted his head back and closed his eyes. "What did you make of that?"

"Gloria Benton is worried about her son," I said, switching chairs. "The question is whether she wants to protect him from the inconvenience of being questioned, or feels uneasy about his possible involvement."

"Okay, so play along with me here—why do you think David Benton would kill Bruce Parker?"

Sinking into the comfortable chair cushions, I cast him a side-long glance. "Because David murdered Ken Anderson and somehow, after all these years, Parker found out?"

Cam turned his head and met my gaze, his eyes shadowed by his lowered lashes. "My theory exactly. Not that I think he's the only suspect at this point, but he could have an understandable motive."

"Only if he murdered Ken, though. Otherwise, I don't see it."

"Hmmm, good point." Cam stared back up at the ceiling. "By the way, why don't you and Bailey join me for dinner tomorrow night? Say around seven? You can go home early and then bring her back here around five so Lauren can give her a tour of the house and gardens before dinner."

"I know she wants to see Aircroft and meet you, but are you sure you're up to company that late in the day? I imagine you get tired easier, with your cast and the crutches and all."

"It's fine. Lauren and Jenna will arrange everything and Mateo will make the meal. All I have to do is show up." Cam's smile faded. "Sometimes I think that's all I ever have to do."

The sound of footsteps stopped me from making any response.

"Come in, Eloise. Sit with us," Cam said, sweeping one fine-boned hand through the air to indicate the folding chair.

Eloise gave me a questioning look before she sat down. "Hello, Jane. I didn't know you'd be here."

"I wasn't expecting it either," I said, earning another confused glance.

Eloise turned her gaze on Cam. "Lauren said you wanted to talk to me?"

Cam flashed a cool smile. "That's right. I wanted to check with you about something."

"What's that?" asked Eloise, clutching a fold of her full-skirted pink sundress between her fingers.

"Gloria Benton was just here—one of the owners of Benton House."

"I know who she is." Eloise's grip on her skirt was so tight her knuckles blanched.

"She was at the country club when Cam was injured," I said, hoping to diffuse the sense that Eloise was being interrogated. "So she stopped by to see how he was doing, and brought flowers." I gestured toward the bouquet.

"That was nice," Eloise said, lowering her gaze.

Cam bent forward, resting his palms on his thighs. "However, she also mentioned something that I wanted to double-check with you. She claimed that your father and Bruce Parker were childhood friends. Did you know anything about that?"

Eloise raised her head with a jerk. "No. How could that be?"

I shared a quick glance with Cam. "Your father was from High Point originally?"

"Yes, but he no longer had any family there, so I never visited the area. He moved to Chapel Hill before I was born. Before he met Mom, actually," Eloise said, her blue eyes clouded behind the lenses of her glasses.

"So I assume the first time you met Bruce Parker was when he was lead detective on your mother's case?" Cam asked, sitting back.

"That's right. I'd never seen him before the day of Dad's . . ." Eloise audibly exhaled. "Before my father was killed."

"Interesting." Cam steepled his hands and tapped one forefinger against the other in patterns of three.

"I'm not sure what that would have to do with anything, anyway." Eloise looked over at me.

"Well, Ms. Benton seemed to think that Parker should've revealed his conflict of interest in your mother's case. If he was your father's close friend, even if only when they were younger, it could've biased his investigation," I said.

"Oh." Eloise dropped her gaze again. She released her grip on her skirt and tried to smooth out the resulting wrinkle. "You mean we could've gotten a mistrial if anyone knew the truth."

"At the very least," Cam said.

When Eloise looked up, I was taken aback by the anger distorting her face. "Gloria Benton knew about Parker and Dad and said nothing?"

"I'm afraid so. David Benton knew as well and also stayed silent." Cam lowered his hands. "Do you remember your father having a feud with the Bentons?"

"When I was little," Eloise said, biting her lower lip. "It was something about a book. I didn't really understand all the details back then, but I heard later, from Neil, that the Bentons were angry over Dad acquiring a rare Hemingway they wanted."

"So there was bad blood between your dad and Benton House?" I asked.

Eloise nodded. "Mom didn't like it. She always said that we should work with colleagues, not try to best them."

"Bruce Parker asked you to find a book," I said. "Could that have been the Hemingway?"

"No, Dad sold that book several years before he died. It was what kept us afloat for many years," Eloise said.

"You honestly have no idea what book Parker was requesting?" Cam asked, his voice as sharp as a well-honed blade.

I shot him a warning look, which of course he ignored.

"No idea at all?" he continued, still using a prosecutorial tone.

"Like I've said many times, I haven't the faintest clue what it was." Eloise stood up, a hand pressed to her cheek as if hiding tears. "Now if you'll excuse me, I'd like to go. Thanks for filling me in on the Bentons' duplicity, but I have a call with my lawyers later, and I'd like to prepare for that." She stalked out of the room without any goodbye.

"You were a little harsh," I told Cam.

"I wanted to provoke her," he replied, wincing as he rolled his shoulders.

"And you did."

"But not far enough." Cam glanced at me, his gray-green eyes troubled as a stormy sea. "She's lying, Jane. She knows what book Bruce Parker wanted, but for some reason she won't reveal it."

"You think she's guilty now?" I asked, standing to face him.

Cam shook his head. "I still don't believe that she stabbed Parker, but she's lying about the book. And I want to know why."

"You don't think she stabbed him, but do you harbor any suspicions about her arranging his murder?" I asked.

"Now that is an entirely different story," Cam said, meeting my gaze with a sad smile.

Chapter Thirty

Lauren immediately took charge when Bailey and I arrived at Aircroft late Tuesday afternoon.

"Cam says I'm to give you the full house and garden tour," she told Bailey after introductions. "That will take a little while, but since it's only five and we aren't eating until seven, we'll have plenty of time."

"I think while you're doing that, I'm going to get a little work done," I said, taking Bailey's purse so she could tour without worrying about it. "There have been so many disruptions lately, I feel I'm falling behind on my cataloging."

"Then I'll bring Bailey to the library when we're done. We're eating in the small dining room this evening, by the way," Lauren said.

Bailey looked at me, amused, and mouthed "the small dining room" over Lauren's shoulder before they walked away.

I headed for the library and dove into cataloging a novel, *The Unfinished Crime*, by Golden Age mystery author Elisabeth Sanxay Holding, who was not well-known by current readers, despite having garnered high praise from famous authors such as Raymond Chandler and Dorothy L. Sayers. As I researched her life and works, I was also intrigued to discover that one of her later books, *The Blank Wall*, from 1947, was actually used as a basis for two films—*The Reckless Moment* in 1949 and, even more surprising, a 2001 movie starring Tilda Swinton called *The Deep End*.

"You never know when a book will be picked up for a film," I said, when Bailey, looking a little ragged from her hike through the gardens, arrived at the library. "This one had an adaption fifty-four years after publication."

"Long after the author was dead, I assume?" Bailey plucked a few tiny briars from her form-fitting black jeans and the rust-red short-sleeved cotton sweater that showed off her slender figure and complemented her dark hair and eyes. "I didn't realize we'd be tramping through the wilderness. Is there a restroom close by where I can freshen up?"

"This hall to the right and two doors down," I said, handing over her purse. "And it's not exactly the wilderness, although I know the back garden is a little wild."

"I'll say." Bailey flashed me a smile. "Lauren was adept at navigating the paths, even in her pumps, but I kept crashing into shrubs and vines."

I glanced at my watch. "It's six forty. Hurry and fix yourself up and meet me back here. As you may have seen, the house is a bit of a maze, so I'll have to escort you to the dining room."

"The *small* dining room," Bailey said, with another smile.

As we headed to dinner about fifteen minutes later, Bailey cast me a sidelong glance. "So I finally get to meet the elusive Cameron Clewe, the owner of all this extravagance," she said.

"Yes, and I'll ask you not to seduce him, please."

Bailey pressed her hand to her heart. "Moi? I'd never think of such a thing."

I snorted and took off at a faster pace, which Bailey, with her longer legs, easily matched. "I've explained his challenges to you, so I expect you to be understanding."

"Don't worry. I've dealt with numerous peculiar people in the theater," Bailey said.

"I didn't say he was peculiar . . ." I stopped and pressed a finger to my lips as we reached the smallest of the house's three dining rooms.

The door was ajar. I pushed it fully open and entered, with Bailey on my heels.

"Good evening," I said to Cam and Eloise, who were already seated facing one another across an oval table draped in white linen. The table, which only seated six, was adorned with a flower centerpiece of lilac, baby's breath, and greenery. A chandelier overhead dripped with faceted crystals that cast rainbows across the white china dinner plates.

Cam rose to his feet. "Hello, you must be Bailey," he said, hobbling forward to take her hand. "It's nice to meet you at last. Your mother mentions you quite often."

I could see Bailey assessing him, and tightened my lips as I noticed her smile broaden.

"And you're Cameron Clewe. Mom talks about you a lot too," she said

"Does she?" Cam raised his eyebrows at me. "Only good things, I hope. And please, call me Cam." He guided Bailey to the chair beside his at the table. "Jane, if you could please sit next to Eloise."

"Of course," I said, crossing to the other side of the table. "You should probably introduce Eloise," I added, forcing Cam to tear his gaze away from my daughter.

His expression slightly abashed, Cam gestured toward Eloise. "Bailey, this is Eloise Anderson, who's staying here at Aircroft for a little while. Eloise owns an antiquarian bookshop."

"How fascinating." Bailey offered Eloise a warm smile. "I'm Jane's daughter, Bailey Hunter. I'm sure you and my mom have a lot in common. I don't do anything nearly as intellectual. I'm an actress."

Eloise, who was wearing an off-the-shoulder black dress that was more sophisticated than her usual attire, smiled sweetly. "That sounds exciting. Much more so than my life, I'm sure."

"I love it, but it can be something of a grind," Bailey said. "As a matter of fact, I have to fly to New York Thursday morning for some auditions, and then turn around and come back Saturday afternoon. No rest for the wicked," she added, casting Cam a glance from under her dark lashes.

"Is Lauren not joining us?" I asked, as Mateo rolled in a cart holding several covered platters and bowls.

"No, she had other plans." Cam turned to Bailey. "Lauren is my personal assistant, but unlike my chef, Mateo"—he gestured toward the other man—"Lauren doesn't live in. She prefers her own apartment."

"I save a lot of money living here," Mateo said, as he placed the serving dishes on the table. "But I can understand why a young woman like Lauren would want her own space."

He didn't add, *especially after dealing with Cam all day*, but when I caught his eye, he winked.

"Thanks, Mateo," Cam said, when all the bowls and platters were on the table. He glanced at Bailey. "We're eating family style this evening. I hope you don't mind."

"Of course not." Bailey whipped her linen napkin through the air to unroll it before she draped it across her lap. "When I'm on the road, I'm happy to get takeout or grab something off the snack table in the green room. This is much more elegant, believe me."

She offered Cam a charming smile and then looked across the table at me and Eloise. "And when I was growing up, Mom and I tended to eat dinner off of TV trays." Obviously noticing my frown, Bailey hastily added, "Not because Mom was lazy or anything; mainly because she had to work all day and do household chores at night and didn't have time to make fancy meals."

"I'm sure you helped out," Cam said, as he passed her a silver basket filled with dinner rolls.

"Well, sometimes." Bailey wrinkled her nose at me. "I was in a lot of theater productions from the time I was in middle school, so that kept me busy."

"It paid off, in the end." I turned to Eloise. "How are you feeling today? Everything okay?"

"I'm fine," she replied, staring down at the spoonful of glazed carrots she'd just ladled onto her plate.

Looking across the table, I watched Bailey shift her intense gaze from Eloise to Cam. *Probably trying to calculate the depth of their relationship*, I thought. My daughter was a flirt, but she had strict rules about not interfering with established couples. I knew she'd never make a move on Cam if she thought he was romantically involved with Eloise.

But that ship has sailed. I took the bread basket from Bailey and set it beside Eloise. Grabbing a roll, I slathered it with the dollop of butter I'd placed on my bread plate. *I think Cam's interest in Eloise evaporated as soon as he suspected she was lying about something connected to her case*, I thought as I chewed a bite of the soft roll. *Albert Clewe lied to him all his life, hiding the fact that he was Cam's stepfather. Al also told Cam's biological father that Cam died around the same time as his mother. I can understand not wanting to become involved with a liar after discovering that.*

"Is this fresh flounder?" Bailey asked, as she used the serving spatula to slide a piece off the platter and onto her plate. "It must be difficult to find since you're four or five hours from the beach."

"I think Mateo has an arrangement with someone who supplies the local restaurants," Cam said. "They fly in seafood daily."

"Ah." Bailey sent me a comical, wide-eyed look.

I gave my head an almost imperceptible shake. "It's delicious, however it got here."

"Cam and Eloise, if you'll indulge me, I have to tell a story about my mom," Bailey said. "It involves a batch of cookies she was making for the school bake sale."

I groaned, while both Cam and Eloise turned to me, their eyes bright with interest. "Oh no, not that again."

"Come on, Mom, it's hilarious." Bailey laid down her fork and proceeded to tell the tale, complete with hand gestures and a few sound effects. "Then the entire tray of cookies fell to the floor and guess what happened—they bounced!" she said, sitting back when she finished her impromptu performance.

"You used salt instead of sugar?" Eloise asked. "Didn't you taste the batter?"

"No. I mean, it was for a bake sale. I was trying not to stick my fingers in it, or anything like that. But Bailey's right, those cookies had the texture of sponges. I think I could've scrubbed the dishes with them, to be honest. In my defense"—I lifted my hands in a mea culpa gesture—"I was totally exhausted that day. We'd had a full week of inventory at the library, and someone who shall remain nameless . . ."

"Me!" Bailey chimed in.

"Had rehearsals every night that week." I smiled. "It was funny, after the fact, even if I had to dash to the store the next day to buy something for the bake sale."

"I suppose it's good to have a sense of humor about that sort of thing," Cam said, examining me and Bailey in turn.

"It's an absolute requirement for being a parent," I said. "Especially when you have a high-maintenance type of child."

"Hey, wait a minute," Bailey said, but then let out a musical peal of laughter. "I was a handful. Always so dramatic." She swept the back of her hand across her forehead. "Poor Mom."

We focused on our meal after that, although Bailey continued to talk, telling some equally embarrassing stories about herself. This seemed to draw Eloise out of her shell a little bit. She even laughed as Bailey shared an incident involving a scene where she was supposed to shoot someone on stage. "The gun refused to fire, so I had to grab a prop knife, and then that broke in half," she said.

"So what did you do?" Eloise asked, her eyes very wide.

"Pulled the scarf from around my neck and pretended to strangle them to death," Bailey said, in a triumphant tone.

Cam, who'd been watching Bailey out of the corner of his eye, a smile dancing on his lips, laid down his fork and sat back in his chair. "It's clear you're someone who thinks on your feet. I commend you for that."

"It's just instinct," Bailey said, casting him a sultry look.

I loudly cleared my throat and pushed my chair back from the table. "Cam, please tell Mateo he outdid himself this evening," I said. "It truly was delicious. But now I think Bailey and I should head home." I shot her a warning look. "She has an early flight tomorrow."

After everyone stood and said their goodbyes, Eloise and Bailey headed out into the hall, while Cam and I lagged behind.

Cam grabbed his crutches and pulled himself up onto his feet. "You and Bailey have a great relationship," he said, a wisp of sadness flitting over his face.

"We do now," I said, patting his hand. "We had some rough years. But it's all good these days. Oh, by the way, I plan to visit Benton House on Thursday. I don't know if I'll find out anything useful, but since I have the standing invitation . . ."

"Might as well use it," he said, tightening his grip on the crosspieces of his crutches. "Just be careful, Jane. I have my suspicions about David Benton."

"Don't worry, so do I. And you know me, I'm not that easy to charm."

Cam's laugh followed me out into the hall.

Chapter
Thirty-One

I t rained steadily on Thursday, which almost made me change my plans. I didn't like driving in the rain. But I'd already arranged to meet David at Benton House at three o'clock, so I decided I just had to ignore my nerves and drive to High Point, rain or no rain.

David greeted me at the front doors, grabbing my wet umbrella and dropping it into an antique metal umbrella stand. "I'll take your coat as well," he told me.

Unsure if he was being gallant or simply didn't want me dripping all over the valuable items in the showroom, I handed over my raincoat and wiped my shoes on the absorbent welcome mat several times.

"Terrible weather, but it does have one benefit—we don't have any other customers right now, so I can give you the full tour," David said, after hanging my jacket on a wood and metal coat tree placed over a rubberized mat.

"Do you get a lot of walk-in customers?" I asked, following him into the showroom.

"Not really. Most of our clients make appointments. We get the occasional tourist, but they almost never buy anything. Of course we're very busy during Furniture Market. We have to add on tempo-rary staff over those five days in both spring and fall."

"That's not open to the public, is it?"

"No, it's strictly for the trade. Buyers, designers, and so on." David paused in front of a display that replicated a Victorian parlor. "We like to group our antiques, but all the pieces can be purchased separately. We just find that setting up display rooms really gives buyers the best experience."

"It is different." I clasped my hands behind my back and leaned in to examine a side-table-height mahogany revolving bookcase. "Most antique stores have things scattered about willy-nilly."

"We have to be a little more intentional, since we serve a more specialized clientele." David walked to the next display, which fea-tured Shaker furniture.

"This is the real thing, right?" I asked, as I looked over a set of ladder-back chairs with woven rush seats.

"Of course. We don't handle reproductions," David said, adjust-ing his blue-and-gray-striped tie.

I glanced over at him, calculating that his tailored pearl-gray suit probably cost more than my entire wardrobe. "Where do you find things? Do you go out on scouting missions yourself, or do you have buyers to do that?"

"A little of both," David said, as he led me past two more displays—one of mid-century modern furniture and décor and the other set up like a gallery, showcasing a number of early American folk-art paintings. "We can come back to this later. I wanted to show you our rare book collection first."

David led me down a hall off of the main showroom. At the end of the hall he unlocked a steel door with a metal mesh reinforced window in the top panel.

As soon as I walked into the room I realized that the Bentons were serious about protecting their book collection. The air felt chilly, but dry, and there were no windows. The books were stored vertically in glass and metal cases, each of which had a humidity monitor that I assumed was linked to a remote system. There was also a large dehumidifier in one corner of the room.

"Sorry for the temperature. We have to keep it around sixty-five degrees, as you probably know," David said.

"Yes, I'm aware. I always kept a sweater on hand when I was dealing with the rare books at the university," I said, rubbing my hands up and down my bare forearms. "I assume you have a special fire suppression system as well?"

"We recently added a clean agent system," David said. "Not dangerous for the materials or humans, and environmentally friendly."

"Ah, it uses a fluorocarbon," I said, thinking how much money the Bentons must've invested in this storage room.

David gave me an approving look. "Yes, pentafluoroethane. When released as a gas it absorbs heat energy at its molecular level faster than the heat can be generated."

"Which means the fire cannot sustain itself. Smart, but expensive, no doubt."

"Yes, but it's worth it. For example"—David led me over to a case containing a solitary book—"this volume alone is worth around two and a half million. It's the jewel of our collection."

I peered into the case, reading the title. "*El ingenioso hidalgo don Quixote de la Mancha*. I'm sure I pronounced that incorrectly, but I assume it's an early edition of *Don Quixote*."

"Not just an early edition, the first edition from 1605." David's sonorous voice was filled with pride.

"How in the world did you acquire it?" I asked, straightening and looking up at him.

"Luck, really. We were working with a wealthy family from Dubai. They wanted a few very specific pieces, including an eighteenth-century Hadley chest. Those can be worth a million or more on their own."

"Nice to have that kind of disposable income," I said dryly. "I buy my storage pieces from resale stores."

David smiled. "I don't use extremely valuable antiques at home, either. Anyway, I traveled with the items to ensure their safe delivery, and while I was there the patriarch of the family showed me this book. We were able to do a deal."

"They traded the Cervantes for some of the furniture?"

"Exactly." David gazed down at the book with an expression I reserved for my loved ones. "We don't usually keep such valuable items for ourselves. My mother is always pestering me to find a buyer, and I know I should sell it, but . . ."

"You can't bring yourself to part with it," I said.

David turned his beatific smile on me. "See, you get it."

I didn't, but decided to keep that opinion to myself. I understood Cam's collecting, which involved books and papers that were more valuable for their research potential than anything else. I couldn't comprehend this, which to me was more like hoarding. I thought the *Don Quixote* belonged in a library or museum, where it could be studied as well as preserved. But I simply smiled back at David. "It's amazing. What else do you have?"

Prompted by my interest, David enthusiastically showed me the other books he'd collected, some of which he planned to put up for auction soon.

"I don't hold onto most of them for long," he said, pointing out a first-edition copy of *Pride and Prejudice*. "As Mom says, this is a business after all."

"Indeed it is," said Gloria Benton as she entered the room, closing the door behind her. "Sometimes my son forgets that, which is how we ended up with a set of Hepplewhite chairs in our dining room."

"Now Mom, you love those chairs," David said.

"I'd love what they'd fetch at auction even more." Gloria turned to me with a bright smile. "It's good to see you again, Jane. How is Mr. Clewe doing?"

"Pretty good. He's mastered getting around on crutches, although he's not tackling the main stairs at Aircroft yet."

"I'm glad to hear it." Gloria gaze swept around the room. "We are proud of our little book collection. I just have to remind David that they aren't ours to keep. Buying and selling is the name of the game."

"You make it sound like I'm a dragon hoarding gold, when you know there are only one or two books I've refused to sell over the years." David cast me a smile. "Mom likes to exaggerate sometimes."

"Well, I hope you'll be willing to part with your next acquisition," Gloria said. "I know how excited you are about it, but it can't become another one of your personal treasures. Not with that estimated value."

"What book is that?" I asked, genuinely interested.

David waved his hands. "I really can't say, not until the deal is done. It's just a superstition, but discussing an acquisition before we buy it always seems to portend bad luck." He cast his mother a sharp glance. "Mom knows that as well as anyone."

"Very well. Sorry, Jane, but you'll have to come back and see it once we have the book in hand," Gloria said. "If you'll excuse me, I need to get back to the office. Balancing budgets waits for no man, or woman." She flashed me a smile before leaving the room.

"We should go as well. There's still a lot more to see on the showroom floor." David held the door open for me, carefully locking it once we were both outside. "I really would like to tell you about that book, Jane, because it is extremely exciting, but I'm afraid I'm cautious about such things."

"It's fine," I said as we walked back into the showroom. "It just gives me an excuse to come back for a visit."

David's eyes lit up. "We shouldn't wait that long to get together again. How about dinner sometime soon?"

I bit the inside of my cheek to prevent an immediate *no* from flying from my lips. Regardless of the situation, I didn't want to go on a date with David Benton, or anyone, for that matter. But more importantly, David was still on the suspect list Cam and I had compiled. "How nice of you," I said, staring at a display of Federal-style furniture and décor instead of looking at David. "But my daughter's staying with me right now and we don't get to see each other that often, so I'm not sure when I'll be available."

"No problem. I'll give you a call in a couple of weeks," David said in a cheerful tone that warned me he was not one to give up easily.

After he showed me the rest of the collections on the main floor, I begged off viewing anything upstairs. "I should go. My daughter will be expecting me. Not to mention, after a day at work, I'm afraid I'm a little tired. But I do appreciate you giving me this splendid private tour." Of course, Bailey was actually in New York until Saturday, but David didn't need to know that.

"My pleasure, truly." David helped me on with my coat and then clasped my hand for a little longer than necessary.

I extracted my fingers and grabbed my umbrella. "Thanks again, and good luck with acquiring that book," I said as I hurried out the front doors.

The rain had lightened up, but I still sat in my car for several minutes, mulling over the coincidence of David Benton seeking to buy a valuable rare book not long after Bruce Parker had requested Eloise find a specific item from the bookshop's stockroom.

According to Gloria, David and Parker had known each other as children. I couldn't help but wonder if David and Parker had been working together to acquire the book now missing from Last Chapter's inventory. Had they worked out some sort of ruse to fool Eloise into giving Parker the book, something connected to Parker claiming to use the book to clear Abby's name? Parker could've planned to tell Eloise that there was a letter or something in the book that implicated the real killer.

But if David grew suspicious and decided Parker was planning to cheat him, he could've followed the former detective to the bookshop and hidden in the stacks until Parker entered the office, then crept behind the service desk and heard the conversation between Parker and Eloise.

Maybe Bruce Parker decided to keep the book for himself, I thought, as I turned the key in the ignition. *If David was there, and realized Parker truly was double-crossing him, he may have struck the detective down in a fit of anger and fled, even without obtaining the book. Perhaps he figured he could buy it from Eloise later, not realizing she'd be implicated in the crime . . .* I pulled out onto the main road, gripping the steering wheel so tightly that I had to shake out my fingers when I reached my apartment.

As soon as I got inside, I called Cam and gave him all details on my visit to Benton House, as well as my new theory about David's possible motive in Detective Parker's death.

"Interesting," he said. "Greed does make more sense than some type of business animosity."

"Yes, and David Benton definitely has the potential to be obsessive, based on his attachment to that copy of *Don Quixote*. I don't think most people would kill someone over a book, but he just might."

"I'm always surprised at what drives someone to murder," Cam said. "Your theory about David Benton is perfectly logical, as far as I'm concerned." The tapping of his fingers could clearly be heard in the pause he took to clear his throat. "Which makes the mysterious book that Parker asked Eloise to retrieve all the more important to this case."

"Because that book and David's exciting new acquisition could possibly be related," I said.

Cam's sigh reverberated across the ether. "Because I'm beginning to think they definitely are."

Chapter
Thirty-Two

When I picked up Bailey at the airport on Saturday she was brimming with excitement and eager to tell me about all her auditions. But by the time we got back to the apartment, her effervescence had faded to exhaustion.

"I think I need a nap," she said, as she rolled her small suitcase through the apartment.

"Use the bed," I said, "not the cot you've been sleeping on."

Bailey gave me a grateful hug before kicking off her shoes and collapsing across the bed. Not wanting to make too much noise, I opted for reading. I was in the middle of a re-read of Mary Stewart's romantic suspense books, with one of my favorites, *Airs Above the Ground*, next on my TBR.

Later, Bailey offered to help me make a stir-fry for dinner. "Although you don't have a ton of veggies, or at least you won't once we use stuff for this meal."

"Then I'll go to the farmers market tomorrow afternoon," I said. "Do you want to come along?"

"Sure. Anything to keep busy and not sit around thinking about whether I got a decent role or not," she replied.

* * *

Sunday was a lovely day—warm, but with lower humidity than usual for our area. I threw some reusable grocery bags in the trunk and drove the short distance to one of the region's largest farmer's markets, which was located right outside of Greensboro.

"I'm impressed," Bailey said as she hopped out of the car. "It looks like there are tons of vendors."

The market had two covered outdoor pavilions as well as an enclosed building, a restaurant, and a plant nursery. I parked near the first pavilion and grabbed my bags from the trunk. "Here, take a few of these. It's easier to carry lots of different items if you have a bag or two."

We strolled down the center aisle, pausing to check out the fruits and vegetables for sale. There was also an extensive array of garden plants and flowers, which unfortunately I couldn't use. "Apartment, remember?" I told Bailey when she picked up a potted geranium, its ruby red flowers glowing against the dark green leaves.

"You could grow this inside," she said.

"Where, exactly? The apartment is nice, but it doesn't have deep windowsills, and I don't have room to add more small tables or anything like that."

"You just don't want to take care of it," Bailey said, tossing her single braid over her shoulder.

"True enough. But to be fair, I've spent plenty of years taking care of things"—I bumped her arm with my elbow—"and believe I've earned a break."

"Very funny," Bailey said, rolling her eyes. "Oh look, there's some organic lettuce and other veggies. We can stock up at that booth." She hurried on ahead.

I followed more slowly, allowing my gaze to take in the riot of colorful flowers, shrubs, and small trees. The one thing I missed about not having a single-family home anymore was the loss of a yard. I'd always enjoyed gardening, but preferred to take care of outside plants rather than house plants. Of course, I could enjoy the gardens at Aircroft, but it wasn't quite the same as growing my own flowers and vegetables.

Admiring a lovely cut-leaf Japanese red maple, I looked up and caught sight of someone I'd never expect to meet in this sort of venue. I walked closer, weaving my way through a forest of small trees, until I was face-to-face with Neil Knight.

"Fancy meeting you here," I said.

"Do you really think it's a coincidence?" he asked, pulling the brim of his cap lower on his forehead.

"What else could it be?"

Neil's strong fingers encircled my wrist. "A convenient way to talk to impart some important information."

"Let go of me," I said, futilely pulling against his grip. "I could scream, you know."

"But you won't," Neil said, his eyes narrowed into slits. "Because I brought along some friends today, and they could prove to be quite a nuisance for your lovely daughter. I don't think you want that."

I glared at him. "Alright, say your piece."

"Not here. Follow me," he said, releasing my wrist and turning on his heel. He strode off across the parking lot, toward a stand of trees.

Not sure it was wise to walk into the woods with this man, but also not wanting anyone to harass Bailey, I trotted behind him. When we reached the woods, Neil walked in a few feet. I pushed aside an arching vine of brambles to follow.

"Great, now I have a thorn in my thumb," I said, waving the offending digit.

Neil hadn't gone far. He'd stopped beyond the first row of trees—just far enough so we were hidden from view by anyone in the market pavilion.

"Appropriate, since you're a definite thorn in my side," Neil said.

I placed my clenched hands on my hips. "Just trying to get at the truth."

"As you see it, anyway." Neil planted his feet slightly apart, adopting a fighter's pose. "Listen, Ms. Hunter, I know your boss is convinced that Eloise Anderson is innocent, but there's things you don't know. You two keep digging and you might turn up some information that will only serve to bolster the prosecution's case."

"Such as?"

Neil tipped his head to one side. "You really don't know? Can't say much for your sleuthing skills if you haven't discovered that Ms. Eloise Anderson isn't as squeaky clean as you seem to think."

I considered my next words carefully. Concerned that Neil was fishing for information, I didn't want to tell him anything he didn't already know. On the other hand, there were the reports that Neil may have doctored the books at Last Chapter, as well as brokered some deals with less than reputable clients. "We've learned some things about you, Mr. Knight. Like how some of your acquaintance walk on the wrong side of the law."

Neil's bark of laughter rang through the trees. "And you think Eloise had no hand in that? That she didn't know we were selling some rare books with, shall we say, questionable provenance? Of course she knew. She practically begged me to help her make money by any means necessary. All to keep her precious bookshop afloat."

I took two steps back. Sadly, it made sense that Eloise would cover up Neil's nefarious actions if it meant the doors of Last Chapter would remain open. She probably felt she owed it to her parents, who'd both been dealt a bad hand in life, to continue their legacy. *By any means necessary*, I thought with a frown.

"She knew what was going on," Neil said. "The juggling of numbers to aid in reducing taxes, the sales of questionable merchandise, the loans from businessmen who might be on the FBI's radar—she was aware and a willing participant in all of those activities."

I lifted my chin to meet his sardonic gaze. "Says you."

"Says the facts." Neil shrugged. "At any rate, I don't think it would help her credibility, or her case, if all this came to light, do you?"

"It wouldn't be ideal," I admitted.

"So why don't you and the messed-up master of Aircroft step back and leave the investigating to the professionals." Neil bared his teeth in a humorless grin. "Unless you want all this information to become public knowledge, of course."

I looked him up and down. "But you'll implicate yourself if you go to the authorities with anything you've just talked about. I don't think you'll do that."

"You want to play chicken with me? You'll lose. I've got pals who'll leak just enough information to send Eloise's defense team into a tailspin. Sure, my name might be mentioned too." Neil yanked off his cap and pressed it over his heart. His bald scalp gleamed from a shaft of light falling between two trees. "But I have powerful friends, as well as influential enemies who won't dare speak out about me . . ."

Because you're blackmailing them, no doubt, I thought, my face flushing with anger.

"So I'm protected. Eloise, not so much." Neil slapped the hat back on his head. "Something to think about, Ms. Hunter."

"I'll definitely be mulling over everything you've said today." I plucked a burr from my cotton blouse. "May I go now? My daughter will be concerned if I don't show up soon."

Neil spread wide his hands. "Of course. You've always been free to leave. I'm not a kidnapper, after all."

I wasn't so sure about that, but decided this wasn't the time to voice my suspicions. "Then I'll head back. I won't say *good day*, Mr. Knight," I called over my shoulder. "Because I really don't wish you a good anything."

A burst of foul language followed me out of the woods.

Chapter
Thirty-Three

Nothing out of the ordinary happened on Monday, allowing me to actually get some cataloging done. I did share my encounter at the farmer's market with Cam, who was ready to call the police until I reminded him that Neil hadn't actually done anything illegal.

"I agreed to go with him, and he didn't keep me there by force," I said, when Cam demurred. "Anyway, he gave us some information that should be shared with Eloise. If she really was involved with Knight in some questionable activities, I think she needs to come clean to you and her legal team," I suggested. "We don't want them blindsided by something halfway through the trial. Better to get ahead of it."

"True." Cam studied me for a moment. "I'll talk to Eloise and urge her to be completely honest with her lawyers. But you do realize that Knight might simply have been trying to deflect suspicion off of himself, right?" Cam shifted the position of his injured leg on the stool in front of his office chair. "What if Bruce Parker was conducting a new investigation into the death of Ken Anderson? He might have started to suspect that he helped to convict the wrong person and was trying to make things right. If he was turning up information on shady deals associated with the bookshop, Knight might have killed him to keep him quiet."

"A good theory, especially since Parker was stabbed before he could conclude his business with Eloise." I pressed my palms against the glass top of Cam's desk. "Think about it—Parker may have asked for that book because it contained evidence of some kind. A letter or note or even a confession. Something that would implicate Neil in Ken's death."

Cam nodded. "I've been considering that possibility. But Jane, it's clear Knight runs with a dangerous crowd, so just be careful, okay?"

"I'll try," I said. "I don't seek out danger, you know."

"Yes, but it still seems to find you, and I can't lose my talented cataloger." Cam's lips curved into a barely perceptible smile.

I squared my shoulders and lifted my chin. "We are hard to replace."

"You would be, anyway," Cam said, immediately staring down at the book open in his lap.

I knew better than to say anything more and left the room.

* * *

Tuesday was also a quiet workday with no interruptions until late afternoon, when I received a text from Vince asking me to stop by his house when I got home.

I puzzled over this request, particularly because he'd added *urgent* to the text. Driving home after work, I sent up a few prayers that neither Vince nor Donna was ill or injured.

When I pulled in front of Vince's house, I noticed an old truck already parked in the gravel lot. I examined it more closely when I got out of my car. The truck looked familiar. I couldn't place it, but knew I'd seen it somewhere before.

Vince met me at the door. "Bailey's here," he said. "And a couple of other people, one of whom may surprise you."

"Don't worry, I'm not easily shocked," I said, following him into the house.

As soon as I saw who was sitting on Vince's sofa, I realized I'd spoken too soon. "Hello again, Gordy," I said, my gaze fixed on the woman sitting beside him. Her bright blue eyes and snowy hair, pulled up into a distinctive Gibson Girl style, were a perfect match to the elderly woman I'd briefly seen at the Benton House gala. But she also resembled Gordy closely enough for me to guess who she was. "You're his sister, Lily, I assume?"

"Yes, I'm Lily Glenn. And you must be Jane Hunter. I've been enjoying talking to your delightful daughter," she said, gesturing toward Bailey, who was seated in one of the sculptural wooden chairs in front of the cabinets and bookshelves surrounding the flatscreen television.

Bailey's dark eyes sparkled with excitement. "Sit down, Mom."

When I crossed to one of the chairs Vince had obviously pulled from the dining room, he stood up to greet me.

"Can I get you something to drink?" he asked, motioning for Donna to stay seated in the wooden chair that matched Bailey's. "Don't get up, dear. I can handle this."

"White wine would be great," I said, shifting my chair so I could face the sofa more directly. "I've seen you once before," I told Lily.

"At the gala. I know." Lily demurely crossed her legs at the ankles. Although I could tell from the knotted joints of her hands that she suffered from arthritis, and the lines on her face betrayed her age, she still managed to look elegant in her cobalt-blue pantsuit and silver jewelry.

"You were at that event too?" Donna asked. "What a funny coincidence."

"It wasn't, actually." Lily tucked a loose strand of her white hair behind her ear. "I have a friend whose daughter works for Benton House. When she mentioned that a few people from Aircroft had been invited, I asked if I could attend as her guest."

Vince raised his bushy eyebrows. "So this friend and her daughter knew about your connection to Aircroft? I thought you'd kept that a secret from everyone." He handed me a glass of wine and sat down in the chair beside me.

"She didn't even tell me she was in town until more recently," Gordy said, giving his sister the side-eye.

Lily patted his knee. "Now, Gordy, don't get your knickers in a twist. I always planned to contact you, I just wanted to do a little reconnaissance first."

"What for? Another invitation to visit Aircroft?" Donna asked.

Lily toyed with the silver butterfly pin on her lapel. "That was my hope. But when I realized that only Ms. Hunter was in attendance, I decided on a change of plans."

"Oh, were you hoping to see Cam?" Bailey's silky hair fell over her shoulders as she leaned forward.

"Yes." Lily gripped her gnarled hands together in her lap. "As he is the owner of the estate now, I thought I'd have to get his permission," Lily said.

"He doesn't go out much," Bailey said.

"He just isn't into large crowds," I said, shooting my daughter a sharp look. I didn't feel that discussing Cam's issues was appropriate, especially with someone whose own child should've been the Airleys' heir.

"But I don't think I'm here to talk about Aircroft in the present day." Lily's gaze swept over all of us. "You are interested in the past."

Gordy unfastened the collar button of his white dress shirt. "I've already told them some of that stuff."

"I know, dear, but I want to corroborate your story," Lily said, casting him a warm glance before focusing on the rest of us. "Basically, everything Gordy told you is true. I was pregnant with Calvin Airley's child, which infuriated my parents. We were planning to get married, despite all that, but . . ."

"Calvin died," Donna said, tears welling in her eyes. "Which is terribly sad. I know it's been a long time, but I'd still like to offer my condolences."

"Thank you. But Calvin didn't just die. He was murdered," Lily said firmly.

Vince leaned forward, gripping his knees. "You know that for sure?"

"I do." Lily glanced at Gordy again. "I'm sorry, but it was our father who killed him."

Gordy turned to her, his mouth falling open. "What?" He grabbed his sister's hands. "Why didn't you ever tell me?"

"Because I knew you had to still live at the farm, with our parents. I didn't know if you could do that if I told you the truth," Lily said, lifting her and Gordy's clasped hands and pressing them to her heart.

"Did he confess it to you?" Vince asked, his voice cracking on the last word.

I looked at him with understanding. Vince had been trying to prove that Calvin Airley had been murdered for years. This had to be a thrilling revelation for him.

"Not in words, but there was plenty of evidence." Lily placed Gordy's hands on his thigh and gave them a pat before releasing her hold on his fingers. "I didn't even know Dad had gone to Aircroft to talk to Calvin that day." Lily expelled a heavy sigh. "Mom only told me after I arrived at the farm, when Dad had already left. She said he was going to demand money from Cal, enough for me to start a new life. My parents had it all worked out," she added, bitterness edging her tone.

"They wanted you to leave town?" Bailey asked. "Then why not simply allow you and Calvin to marry?"

Gordy leaned back, staring up at the ceiling. "I expect they still thought it would bring shame on the family. The child would've come too soon, and people would've talked."

"That's right," Lily said. "Mom outlined their plan after Dad left that day. Oh, they were clever." Her tight smile resembled a grimace. "They wanted me to go to some unwed mothers' home they'd found in another county, have the baby, and put it up for adoption. Then I was to stay with my aunt for a few more months, to make it look like I'd gone to get my secretarial certificate." She met Gordy's sad gaze. "Remember how I wanted to do that after high school and they said no? Then when I left home and was living on my own, I had to work long hours and couldn't afford to go"

"Yes, I remember." Gordy said, dabbing at his eyes with a tissue.

"But Calvin would've protested your parents' idea, wouldn't he? Giving up your baby, I mean," Donna said.

"Dad didn't believe he would. He thought Calvin saw me as a dalliance. Dad figured if Cal just paid me off . . ." Lily flashed a brittle smile. "Well, more like paid my family off. Anyway, Mom said if we got the money and I followed the plan and everyone kept quiet, we could all go on with our lives as if nothing had happened."

"But Calvin didn't agree with the plan," I said.

"I assume not. Of course, I wasn't there, but he undoubtedly refused, and probably insisted on marrying me and raising our child at Aircroft."

"So they must've fought," Vince said, his expression thoughtful.

"Yes. They had to have met near the quarry, since that was where . . ." Lily cleared her throat. "That was where Cal's body was found," she added, her shoulders slumping.

"The reports said it had rained that morning. The ground was slick," I said.

"And muddy." Lily looked over at Gordy. "Like I said, I'd stopped by the farm to see Mom. She'd begged me to come over; to tell me about the plan involving my aunt, as I later discovered. But you were away that day, buying seeds for the next planting season. You didn't see our father come home, his boots and jeans covered in red clay mud and his hands shaking so hard he couldn't hold a glass of water."

"That must've been devastating," Bailey said, her eyes gleaming with sympathy.

"Not then. I didn't know then." A single tear, caught in Lily's lashes, fell and streaked her cheek. "It was later that day when I heard about Cal. A terrible accident, everyone said." Lily shook her head. "Only, I realized it was no accident. And certainly not suicide. Cal wouldn't have done that. No, I knew what had to have happened. But I couldn't tell anyone."

"Why not?" Donna asked, straightening in her chair. "Didn't you want to see justice done? I know it was your father, but still."

"I would've sought justice. I wanted to. But there was the baby," Lily said.

"You were afraid the Airleys would take your child away from you," I said.

"I knew they would. They had all the money in the world for lawyers, and I had none. They would've easily won a custody case." Lily sighed again. "I knew I had to leave before they knew I was having a baby. So I packed a bag and took the little money I'd saved and fled that night. At first I stayed with my friend, the one I mentioned before. We'd met at work and she lived in a neighboring town, so my parents didn't know her. She was the only other person I told about the pregnancy, except for you, Gordy."

"That's right, you stayed at the farm until I came home and talked to me in secret. You told me everything," Gordy said. "Well, except that our father was a murderer."

"I've explained why I held that fact back," Lily said, a touch of testiness in her tone. "Anyway, after I talked to you I fled the farm and headed out of town that night. I stayed at my friend's house for a week. She lent me some additional money, which I paid back as soon as I could. Then I took a bus to Raleigh and lived in a rooming house until I found a job."

"Wow, that must've been tough," Bailey said. "How did you manage once the baby was born?"

"Not easily," Lily said. "But my job helped. I became the housekeeper for a widowed Episcopal priest. It was a live-in position, which gave me a place to raise a child. I did have to tell my boss a few white lies, like losing my husband in a car accident right before I found out I was pregnant. I also said I had no family to take care of me. Which was pretty much true, at that point."

Gordy huffed. "I would've taken care of you, Lil."

"I know you would have. But I couldn't stay in the area. Not if I wanted to keep my son."

"You had a boy?" Donna asked.

"Yes. Which made me even more determined to keep his existence from Samuel and Bridget Airley. If they'd known that Cal's child was a boy, they'd have moved heaven and earth to get their claws into him." Lily glanced over at Vince. "I know I turned down a glass of wine earlier, but I think I've changed my mind."

Vince leapt to his feet. "Sure thing. Anyone else?"

Donna and Bailey said yes, but Gordy refused. "Just water," he said. "I'm driving."

"I'll take another," I said, holding up my empty glass.

While Vince got everyone their drinks, I decided to pose the question that hadn't been answered by Lily's confession. "You said you stayed away from this area, but you must've returned once. Otherwise, how could Patricia Clewe have drawn your portrait in 1989?"

Lily turned her intense gaze on me. "You're right, I did. Only once. It was quite foolish of me, but my son was traveling at the time and I allowed nostalgia to get the better of me. I drove to Aircroft and parked on an old road that wasn't used any more. I knew I could slip into the gardens from there, because that's how Cal and I would meet."

"Near the quarry," I said.

"Yes. That was difficult, seeing that deep hole and those jagged rocks." Lily closed her eyes for a moment. "But I persevered and entered the gardens. I didn't expect to see anyone, and knew where to hide if I did. But Pat, Patricia Clewe, that is, caught me."

"You allowed her to draw your portrait," Vince said as he handed her a glass of wine and Gordy a tumbler of water. "Why do that if you were trying to keep a low profile?"

"She had her sketchbook and pencils with her, and when she asked, I thought it would be good . . ." The corners of Lily's lips twitched. "Anyway, she was a sweet woman, and I'd trespassed on her property. I felt acting as her model was the least I could do."

Vince brought over my second glass of wine. "That was the year Cameron Clewe was born. Was she pregnant at the time?"

"No, her son was already a few months old. We sort of bonded over that too." Lily took a sip of her wine. "Both having boys, I mean."

"So now the mystery woman is no longer a mystery," Bailey said, giving me an amused glance. "You can call this a win, Mom."

"And Vince," I said, raising my glass to him. "He's been trying to find you too, Lily, ever since I discovered that photo of you in the attic at Aircroft, and the drawing in Patricia Clewe's old studio."

"I had no idea my history would prove so fascinating to strangers," Lily said.

Vince sat back down, cradling his own glass of wine. "For me, it's because it's connected to the Airleys and their estate. You don't know how valuable this information is to me. Now I can actually write my book about the Airleys and Aircroft."

A pained expression flitted over Lily's face. *She isn't too keen on that*, I thought. *I suppose it's because her father will be revealed as a murderer. Although it would've probably been classified as manslaughter if Calvin fell during a fight. Not premeditated murder, anyway.*

"I hope you don't mind me including you in the book. I'll double-check all facts," Vince said.

"It's fine. The truth should come out." Lily shifted on the sofa, almost sloshing her wine.

"I did wait until I had all the pieces," Vince said.

I took a long swallow of my wine and pondered whether Vince did have all the pieces now. Studying the conflicted expression on Lily's face, I wasn't entirely sure.

Chapter
Thirty-Four

On Wednesday I shared the information about Lily Glenn with Cam, who was glad to finally be able to say one cold case, that of our mystery woman, was solved.

I almost said something about having doubts that Lily had spilled all her secrets, but Cam was eager to talk about his latest conversation with Eloise, so I decided to save my doubts for another day.

"She finally admitted that she knew about Neil Knight's illegal business practices and shady deals and never told anyone," Cam said, shaking his head. "Somehow he convinced her it was the only way to save the bookshop from bankruptcy and then, once she overlooked his first crimes . . .".

"He had her over a barrel. She couldn't expose him without also convicting herself, and that would've meant the loss of Last Chapter."

"Exactly. She should've stood up to him, of course, but she was only eighteen when she took over the business. Knight took advantage of her youth and inexperience." Cam tapped a pen against the top of his desk. "I understand her reluctance to confess. It does cast her character in a bad light, and that's the last thing you need when you're on trial for murder."

"I hope she's going to come clean to her legal team now," I said. "The entire world doesn't need to know about her complicity in Neil Knight's crimes, but her lawyers should. Nothing worse than such information coming out in court and blindsiding them."

"She said she'd tell them after I urged her to do so." Cam lifted his hands. "What else can we do? We can't force her, even though I agree it's the best course of action."

"You could inform her that you'll throw her out unless she tells her legal team everything."

Cam looked up at me, his eyes wide with surprise. "I can't do that. I gave my word I'd allow her to remain here until the trial."

"I was just joking," I said, sweeping my hand through the air as if shooing away a gnat. This wasn't entirely true, but his stricken expression had forced me to backpedal. "You've done all you can for her. Now she has to decide what's best."

"I'm not sure Eloise always considers things logically," Cam said.

I clasped my hands together under my chin. "Maybe not, but as tempting as it is to play knight errant, the damsel has to want to be rescued before you ride in on your white horse."

"Want to be rescued . . ." Cam cast me a wry smile. "Sometimes I'm not the best judge of those sorts of things."

I almost said, "Only sometimes?" but held my tongue. Cam was being open and vulnerable, which didn't happen that often. It was no time for teasing. "Let's just see how it goes. I bet Eloise will follow your advice once she really thinks things through."

The rest of the day passed quickly, especially since I'd delved into cataloging a few books written by Virgil Markham, an American writer who set several of his books in Britain. He had a short but illustrious career from 1928 to 1936. Cam had acquired his first book, *Death in the Dusk*, which was set in Wales, as well as 1933's *Red Warning*. Since I'd never heard of this author before, it was fun to research his life and find out more about his books and their status as precursors of later noir fiction.

Bailey texted me not long before I left Aircroft, asking if I could pick up something for dinner. *Not much in the house*, she said, *and I'm in the mood for Thai, if you can find such a thing.*

I knew she meant, "in this area," but despite my well-traveled daughter's doubts, I'd seen a Thai restaurant when I had driven to Hight Point to visit Benton House. It was a little out of my way, but I didn't mind a slight detour, especially if I could prove to Bailey that the local area had plenty of food options. Not like New York, of course, but enough.

The restaurant was crowded, which told me it was popular, but also made it difficult to move around in the small space in front of the counter. After placing my order, I walked back outside. I had to wait twenty minutes for my food and preferred to avoid being jostled by other customers.

Leaning against the driver's side door of my car, I looked across the hood to another restaurant—this one a café with a few tables arranged outside under a green-and-white-striped awning. At one table I noticed someone who looked familiar.

It's Terry Lindover, I thought, shading my eyes against the sun with one hand. *What's she doing here when her business is in Chapel Hill?*

My curiosity was satiated when a tall, gray-haired man in a navy suit joined her at the table. It was David Benton, looking dapper as usual. He sat down with his back to me while Terry, very chic in an amber dress that showed off her slender figure, leaned over the table and began gesticulating with fervor.

They must be discussing the property the Bentons want to buy in Chapel Hill, I thought, although why they had to meet in person rather than discuss such matters over the phone eluded me. Intrigued, I circled around my car to rest my back against the passenger's side. I still couldn't hear everything David and Terry were saying, but I did catch a few words here and there. Strangely, little of what I overheard seemed connected to real estate. There was mention of an estate sale and something about an auction, which I supposed could be related to property for sale, but then David said "provenance," which made me think Terry was dabbling in selling antiques or other items she may have found while handling a property going on the auction block.

Or perhaps, I thought, eyeing them with interest, *they have more than a professional relationship.* It wouldn't be odd, really. David was around my age and Terry was probably ten years younger, but that didn't matter so much when people were older.

I glanced at my watch. My takeout would be ready in five minutes. Strolling back toward the entrance of the restaurant, I heard footsteps behind me, beating a rhythm that sounded like someone jogging, and turned around.

"Jane, what a coincidence," David said. "I didn't realize you frequented any dining establishments here."

"I don't, usually, but my daughter requested Thai takeout tonight and this was the closest place I could find." Looking at my watch again, I added. "My food should be ready any minute."

"Well, I don't want to hold you up, but I saw you and wanted to say hello." David glanced back at the table where he'd been sitting with Terry. "I just concluded a little business meet-up."

"With your real estate agent, yes, I saw," I said. "How's the property hunt going?"

David's broad smile tightened. "Fine, fine. We hope to close the deal soon."

"That's good," I said. "And may I say it's impressive that Terry Lindover would drive all this way for such a short meeting, but I suppose that's the hustle top agents need to have."

David must've heard something in my tone because he quickly jumped in with a disclaimer to a question I hadn't asked. "It's really all work-related. Terry isn't exactly my type, and she's a little young for me. I prefer women around my age. Especially if they're intelligent and well-read."

"I never assumed there was anything else going on." Another white lie, but who was counting? "It isn't any of my business, anyway."

"Maybe not, although I rather wish it was," David said, with a smile that set off alarm bells in my head.

I held up my wrist, pointing to my watch. "Goodness, look at the time. I'd better grab my food before they give it away to someone else."

Dashing into the restaurant without waiting for his reply, I paid for my takeout and lingered by the side window until I confirmed that David had walked back to the café.

"Everything okay, ma'am?" the counter clerk asked me.

They were probably wondering why I was still in the building after collecting my food. "Fine, fine," I said, giving them a wave as I exited.

Parking at the apartment, I stayed in the car long enough to phone Cam and describe my latest encounter.

"Terry Lindover seems unusually close to the Bentons," Cam said. "I know they're working together on a real estate deal but it feels like something else is going on."

"I think so too." I fiddled with the folded top of the brown food bag. "I was considering them being involved romantically, but I don't believe they are because . . . well, for reasons." There was silence on the line. "You still there?" I asked.

"Just thinking," Cam said. "Consider this—you told me about Terry Lindover visiting you at your apartment, pretending to be a detective. Then she approached you at the country club. Both times it seemed she was warning you to stay out of the investigation into her former partner's murder."

"True, but it wasn't that she didn't want the case solved. It was more like she was determined to seek justice, and in her mind that involved Eloise being guilty." I climbed out of the car, leaving my door open. "So what if she's discovered something that made her change her mind? She's been working closely with the Bentons. Perhaps she found out things that have led her to believe David was involved in Parker's murder. She wants to see justice done, so she's playing David, hoping to get more evidence."

Another few seconds of silence. "Hmmm, I'll have to ponder that for a while. You could be right, but there's something that doesn't add up yet."

"Well, you go and ponder," I said, leaning across the car seat to grab my purse, briefcase, and the bag of food. "I'm going to have dinner. It's Thai, and you're welcome to come and share it with me and Bailey if you like. There's plenty."

"Thanks, but I think I'll stay in this evening. However, I did have a thought—what if I have Lauren and Mateo arrange a little cocktail party for Friday night? I could invite you, Bailey, Vince, and Donna. And maybe the Bentons and their real estate agent too?"

"Combining work and pleasure again?" I asked, climbing the stairs to my apartment.

"Mostly work. I'm not sure it will count as pleasure," Cam said.

This was it—the moment to try a little test to gauge Cam's interest in my daughter. "But Bailey will be there." I juggled the food bag to unlock the door. "She's always a pleasure."

"There is that," Cam agreed, with an alacrity I feared spelled trouble.

Chapter Thirty-Five

"Ta-da!" I said, entering the apartment with the food bag held high. "Thai, as you requested."

"That's great, Mom." Bailey took the bag and carried it over to the kitchen counter. "Vegetarian, I hope."

"Of course. There's a curry with lots of vegetables and a stir-fry style dish with tofu, green peppers, mushrooms, and other things. And rice, of course."

"Here, I'll handle this and get the plates and silverware. You go change out of your work clothes into something comfier," Bailey said, setting the various containers on the small kitchen table.

I wasn't going to argue with that. After changing into sweatpants and a loose T-shirt, I wandered back into the kitchen, where Bailey had arranged everything, including placing a candle in a glass jar in the center of the table.

"Perfect for a celebration," she said, lighting the candle.

I pulled two wineglasses off the shelf and an open bottle of chardonnay from the refrigerator. "Are we celebrating?"

"We are, because I received some great news today." Bailey sat down at the table and flourished her paper napkin before placing it in her lap. "I got a wonderful part in a new musical."

"Congratulations!" I filled Bailey's wineglass and sat down to pour my own glass. "What is it, and is it on Broadway or what?"

"It's off-Broadway, but still in New York at a very nice theater, and it's a new play based on *The Last Unicorn* by Peter S. Beagle." Bailey clinked her glass against mine.

"Really? You used to love that story. Well, I did too."

"Yes, remember how we used to read it together?" Bailey sipped her wine, a dreamy expression on her face. "I hadn't thought about it in ages, but then my agent sent me the audition notice and, well, now I'm going to be part of a musical version."

"What part?" I asked, spearing a square of fried tofu along with some green beans and other vegetables.

"The unicorn, of course. I mean, I play the unicorn when she's transformed into a woman. There's going to be a puppet before that. One of those really amazing ones, like they used in the theater production of *Life of Pi*."

"Sounds amazing. When do rehearsals start?"

Bailey turned her wineglass with her fingers. "Soon. I have to fly back a week from today. That's why I'm glad we could hold this little celebration tonight."

"Cam has invited us to a cocktail party this Friday evening. Are you up for going to that?" I asked.

"Sure, why not. Hey, this is good." Bailey concentrated on eating, but laid down her fork and looked over at me after a few minutes. "Is this cocktail party a real party or is it part of your amateur sleuthing?"

I had to chew for a second before I could respond. "I can't lie— it's mainly to bring some people together who may be important to the case."

"Really, Mom? You know, I've been watching you, and it seems to me that you take a lot of risks to help Cam with his avocation. It's not like he hired you to be a detective."

"He did give me a raise because I help him with the investigations, though," I said, sipping my wine.

"Money doesn't make it less dangerous." Bailey stirred the remaining food around her plate with her fork. "I worry about you going off to meet with people who could be killers. Who knows what could happen?"

I couldn't restrain myself from smiling. "Ah, the tables have turned."

"What do you mean?" Bailey took a gulp of her wine.

"You're worried about me just like I worried about you for so many years," I said. "All those late-night rehearsals in high school and college, and then going off on tours for months on end with a group of people you barely knew. Now you can finally understand how I felt."

A mulish expression settled over Bailey's lovely face. "You always encouraged me to follow my dreams."

"Yes, but that doesn't mean I didn't worry." I saluted her with my empty glass.

Bailey pointed her fork at me. "Is this your way of telling me to mind my own business?"

"Bingo. But in all seriousness, I do appreciate that you worry about your old mom," I said, sitting back in my chair.

"You aren't that old," Bailey mumbled. She cleaned her plate and set her fork down with a clang against the tabletop. "Do you want any more? Because I'm full."

"I'm done. We can put away the leftovers and you can eat them for lunch while I'm at work."

"Sounds good," Bailey said, pushing back her chair and standing up. "But I'll save some for you too. For when you come home from work and don't feel like cooking."

"Oh, you mean every day?" I said, with a grin. "Okay, let's clear the table and stack the dishes in the sink."

Bailey cast me a raised-eyebrow look as she carried a stack of plates and utensils to the counter. "Don't you want to wash them right away?"

"Not tonight. Let's sit on the sofa with our wine and chat. I want to hear more about this musical. The dishes can wait."

When we settled at either end of the sofa, wineglasses in hand, I encouraged Bailey to talk through everything she knew about her new role.

"Oof," she said after a while. "I've been going on and on and you haven't said a word."

"That's okay. I like to hear about your work." I set my glass on the side table next to the sofa and leaned back into the pillows. "My work isn't nearly as exciting, unless you're a book connoisseur or collector, I suppose."

"Like Mr. Benton?" Bailey widened her eyes in a perfect depiction of innocent inquiry. "You mentioned that he asked you to dinner. Are you going to go?"

"Doubtful. He's still on our suspect list. And honestly, Bailey, I'm just not interested."

"You always say that. When I was younger I thought it was just an excuse you gave me so I wouldn't feel like I was tying you down, but now"—Bailey looked me over with a critical eye—"I'm starting to believe you always meant it."

"I did, and I never felt tied down by you." I toyed with the fringe on one of the pillows. "I mean, we were always on the go, traveling to rehearsals and auditions. That along with your school activities, not to mention my job, kept me plenty busy."

"But you didn't date. Not even when I went to college and then out on the road. I know it wasn't because you had no offers," Bailey said, with a smile. "I saw how some of your colleagues or my teachers or directors tried to flirt with you."

"Let's get one thing straight. I had a full life without romance, and I still do," I said firmly. "I know some people find that hard to believe, but it's true. It's not that I dislike men or don't enjoy their company, but I don't feel the need to embark on a romantic relationship." I leaned forward to pat the leg Bailey had stretched out across the sofa. "I swear to you I don't feel like I'm missing out."

"Okay, I believe you." Bailey finished off her wine and cradled the bowl of the empty glass between her hands. "You know, there's a term for that."

"There's a term for everything," I said. "But yes, I've done a little reading and I'd say I'm on the asexual spectrum. Not sure exactly where I fall on it, and also not sure I care. And to be clear—it's not because of your dad or some other trauma. This has always been me. I didn't change because something 'happened to me.' It's just that when I was young, no one talked about such things. You were simply forced to feel weird and different and wonder why."

"I get it, and as long as you're content, I am too." Bailey swung her legs off the sofa and slid closer to me. "I just want you to be happy," she added, throwing her arm around my shoulders.

"I am, most of the time." I leaned into her. "So you really haven't told me what you think about my boss. Just so you know, I have the feeling he's developing an interest in you."

"That's unfortunate," Bailey said.

I sat up and slid out from under her arm. "Why?"

"Because it wouldn't work. Trust me, I'm an actress. I dig into character and motivation for a living. Yes, Cam's intelligent and hot . . ."

I snorted, earning the side-eye from my daughter.

"And he's extremely wealthy. I believe he's basically a good guy, too." Bailey leaned back and stared up at the painted board ceiling. "But he needs someone who's going to be around all the time."

"You really think so? He's pretty self-contained," I said.

"Yeah, but not self-sufficient. Not in a relationship, anyway. I mean, he seems standoffish, but I think if he really fell in love he'd *really* fall, if you know what I mean. He wouldn't want a girlfriend who couldn't be by his side because her career required her to go away for months at a time." Bailey turned her head to meet my astonished gaze. "I think he's attracted to girls like me because we make it easy for him. We do the flirting and all those things he finds difficult. But he'd be better off with a different type of woman."

"One who could sit with him quietly and they'd still feel close?" I asked, acknowledging the wisdom in her words.

"Exactly. Someone like . . . well, his assistant seems to understand him pretty well. She's beautiful too, and smart." Bailey bumped me with her elbow. "Admit it, you've thought the same thing."

"I have, but there's a problem. She's too proud to chase him, and he has no clue how to chase her," I said.

"That's where you come in, Mom. Figure out a way to make them see the light." Bailey squeezed my shoulder. "Because despite how attractive he is, I know I'm not the right person for Cameron Clewe, but I think maybe Lauren could be."

I stared at my daughter, pride causing tears to well up in my eyes. "How'd you get so smart?"

"Oh, I don't know," she said with a smile. "I think maybe it's genetic."

Chapter
Thirty-Six

"Are you going to wear that?" Bailey asked as we dressed for the cocktail party on Friday evening.

I looked down at my simple forest-green top and floral-patterned palazzo pants. "What's wrong with my outfit?"

Bailey made a great show of rolling her eyes. "We're attending a cocktail party at Aircroft, not some potluck at the neighbors' house."

"Everyone at the estate knows what I look like, as well as all the guests. Who am I trying to impress?" I examined her crimson dress with its off-the-shoulders neckline and short skirt. "Who are *you* trying to impress?"

"No one in particular," she replied, with a toss of her long chestnut hair. "I simply enjoy dressing to fit the occasion."

"This occasion is partially intended to allow Cam and me to gather some more intel, so I think wearing less flamboyant clothes is my best option." I fastened a hand-painted folk-art-style pin to my blouse. "Besides, no one will be looking at me while you're in the room."

Bailey squeezed her feet into a pair of black stiletto sandals. "I'll be helping your cause, then. I can distract them while you creep around, eavesdropping on conversations."

"Oh, is that the plan?" It was my turn to roll my eyes. "Are you about ready?"

"I just have to do my makeup," Bailey said, heading for the bathroom.

Sitting down on the couch, I called after her, "In that case, I might as well read another chapter or two in my book."

By the time we reached Aircroft, the number of vehicles parked in the circle driveway in front of the mansion told me that we were probably the last guests to arrive.

"The better to make a grand entrance," Bailey said, flinging her lacy black shawl around her bare shoulders and sashaying up the front steps.

I followed her, shaking my head. "You really are on full blast tonight."

Bailey cast a smile over her shoulder as we both stepped into the grand entrance hall. "It's just acting, Mom."

"I don't know why you feel you need to play a role in front of these people," I said.

"It's what I always do at parties like this," Bailey said. "Otherwise I'd be either nervous or bored."

"Well, come on. Let's make our entrance then." I led the way down the hall that led to the library. Lauren had informed me earlier that the party would be held in what she called the *small reception room*. I'd never been in that space before, but had had it pointed out to me once or twice. It was only a few doors down from the library.

Allowing Bailey to make her grand entrance. I paused in the doorway and surveyed the room. Instead of the dark, polished wood paneling that was prevalent elsewhere, this room's wainscoting was painted a gleaming white. A round table draped in white linen sat under a silver-plated crystal chandelier. Board and batten molding, painted a pale ivory, trimmed the white plaster walls above the wainscoting, and the coffered ceiling was brightened by gilt accents. I realized that this room was decorated to match the larger ballroom next door, which made sense. There was a door that I assumed led into the ballroom, so it was probably used as an antechamber during larger events.

Naturally, all eyes remained fixed on Bailey as I slipped into the room behind her. Well, all but one set. David Benton was staring at me.

"Hello, everyone," I said, focusing on Terry and Gloria. "For those who don't know, this is my daughter, Bailey. She's a professional actress and is visiting me between gigs."

Cam was sitting in a chair at the far end of the room, near the table set up as a bar manned by Mateo. Cam's leg was propped up on an upholstered footstool, with his crutches leaning against the wall behind him. He appeared frozen, his cut-glass tumbler held motionless, halfway to his lips. Eloise, standing beside him, simply looked miserable.

"Very nice to meet you," Gloria said, hurrying forward to clasp Bailey's hand. "This is my son, David, and our friend, Terry Lindover," she added, gesturing toward them.

Friend? I arched my eyebrows and tried to catch Cam's eye, but he was still staring at my daughter.

Bailey expressed her pleasure at meeting everyone, adding, "Of course, I know Vince and Donna, and I've met Cam and Eloise before as well." She glanced around the room. "Where's Lauren? Wasn't she invited?"

"Right here," said a voice behind me. "Watch out, Jane, I need to squeeze past you." Lauren slid by me and strolled into the room, balancing a large silver tray filled with hors d'oeuvres. "I told Mateo I'd bring in the food since he was wrangled into manning the bar."

Lauren's dress was a simple scoop-necked sheath with a sheen like molten gold. Her hair had been plaited into numerous thin braids and pulled into a small chignon at the nape of her neck, highlighting the beautiful bone structure of her face.

As Bailey hugged Vince and Donna and Lauren placed the tray on the table, I strolled over to Cam and Eloise. "Good evening," I said. "I hope you're doing well, Eloise. You look very nice tonight."

Eloise ducked her head and fiddled with the lace trimming the short sleeves of her lilac dress. "Thank you, but I can scarcely compete with those two." She motioned toward Lauren and Bailey.

"Who could?" I said, keeping my tone light. "Hi Cam, how's the leg?"

"Still attached," he replied. He was more formally dressed than I'd ever seen him, in a white dinner jacket and a jade dress shirt that complemented his eyes. Of course, he was still forced to wear a pair of loose black slacks that had been slit up the seam to accommodate his cast. "Unfortunately, I can't circulate much tonight."

I knew this was his way of telling me that I'd have to do most of the questioning and eavesdropping. "Your guests will have to come to you."

"And here we are," Vince said, arm in arm with Donna.

They had chosen to go my more casual route, with Vince wearing a navy suit and a paisley tie, and Donna looking very bohemian in a white peasant top over a voluminous plaid maxi skirt and lots of gold jewelry.

After murmuring hello, Eloise drifted off and wandered over to the round dining table.

"I see David Benton and Terry Lindover are having a little tête-à-tête." Cam looked up at me with a glint in his eyes. "I wonder what they could be talking about. Real estate deals, or something else?"

"Perhaps I should go and say hello," I said, taking the hint. I left Donna and Vince with Cam and crossed over to the corner where David and Terry had huddled in front of a glass-paneled door that led to the outside terrace. Bailey and Lauren, deep in conversation, nodded at me as I passed by, while Eloise stood a little off to one side of them, staring morosely at the hors d'oeuvres without touching anything.

"Hello there," I said when I reached David and Terry. "I hope I'm not interrupting."

"Of course not," David said. His welcoming expression was not matched by Terry, who looked like she'd just bitten into a lemon.

She squared her shoulders, flaunting the flowing lines of her royal-blue silk dress as well as her fine figure. "Good evening, Ms. Hunter, and don't worry. We were simply discussing some boring business matters."

"Ah, about the real estate deal?" I asked.

David looked flustered but Terry didn't miss a beat. "Of course. That's the only business that concerns us, right, David?"

"Right," he said, staring down at his expensive leather shoes for a moment. When he lifted his head again, he was back to his genial self. "So good to see you again, Jane. Your daughter is quite something. Of course, I'm not surprised, since she takes after you."

"Maybe in her coloring, but that's about it," I said. "I suppose it's the miracle of genetics—two rather ordinary ducks can sometimes produce a swan."

"You're far too modest," David said, earning a sidelong glance from Terry.

"I was surprised to see Ms. Anderson in attendance," she said. "I knew she was staying here but thought she'd avoid a party that involved people who knew Bruce Parker."

David shot her an angry glance. "That's really uncalled for, Terry."

She shrugged, keeping her gaze locked on me. "What do you think, Ms. Hunter? Is Mr. Clewe's houseguest truly innocent?"

"The law states, innocent until proven guilty," I said.

"Would either of you ladies like a drink?" David asked, already taking a few steps toward the bar.

"Gin and tonic," I said.

"Nothing for me, thanks." Terry looked me up and down as David strode off. "It seems you kept our bargain. No one has questioned me about my visit to your apartment."

"Yes, but what about your side of the deal?" I asked. "Have you discovered anything that might help Eloise?"

"Sadly, no. Although I must confess, I didn't expect to, since I think she's guilty as sin." Terry said the last bit loud enough to carry across the room.

Eloise, now standing in front of the bar, thrust her hand gripping a wineglass up in the air. Droplets of wine sparkled in the light of the chandelier. "I've had enough of this!" she shouted. "All the stares and innuendoes and gossiping in corners." She glared, furious, at Terry and me. "I know you all think I'm guilty, but I'm not. I'm not, I tell you."

Cam reached for his crutches, but Vince pressed a hand on his shoulder to keep him seated. "No one thinks that, Eloise. And if they do, they should leave now," Cam said.

There was a shuffling of feet and sharing of glances, but no one moved toward the exit except Terry, who sauntered into the center of the room. "Then I must thank you and say good night, Mr. Clewe," she said. "Because I do think your houseguest killed my former partner, and I can't pretend I don't." She locked gazes with Eloise and curled her lips in a sardonic smile. "You know what will happen. The truth will come out," she said, turning and sauntering out into the hall.

All the color had drained from Eloise's face and her chest rose and fell like she was gasping for breath. Lauren hurried over to her and reached out to grasp her fingers, but Eloise batted her hand away. "I can't do this," she said in a strangled tone. "I can't keep this up, I can't . . ." She slammed her wineglass down on the bar so hard that the goblet broke off the stem and white wine splattered everywhere. "It's impossible," she said. "Impossible." She covered the lower half of her face with her hands and dashed out of the room.

Bailey, sidling up to me, linked her arm through my bent elbow. "And you thought I was too dramatic," she whispered, as Mateo and Lauren rushed to clean up the mess.

"Well, I suppose that was the performance portion of the evening," Cam said dryly. "I'm sorry that happened, but please, continue to enjoy yourselves."

I glanced over at him, noticing a gleam in his eyes that made me suspect he'd just realized something that might help our investigation.

"I think I'll go talk to Cam," Bailey said, pulling away from me. "I'll tell him about my new show and maybe also drop a few hints about where he should be looking for love."

Thwarted in my intention to talk to Cam myself, I frowned and tapped my foot against the floor.

"Here, this might cheer you up," David said, handing me a tumbler with a lime slice perched on its rim.

"Thanks," I said, taking a sip. "I suppose it was foolish, Cam inviting Ms. Lindover to an event where Eloise would be present. Terry is hell-bent on bringing the killer of her former partner to justice, and I think she really believes that is Eloise."

"Funny thing is"—David sloshed the amber liquid in his own glass—"so do I."

Chapter
Thirty-Seven

I stared at him. "Let's talk outside," I said, after a moment.

"Alright, but how do we get there?" he asked.

"This way." I crossed to the exterior door and opened it, then remembered it would be locked from the outside. "Come on through," I said, holding the door. I kicked off one of my shoes and stuck it between the door and the jamb. "Otherwise we won't be able to get back in," I told David, who was looking at me quizzically.

With the imbalance created by having one shoe on and the other foot only covered by a sock, I walked awkwardly across the flagstones to reach the white railing that enclosed the terrace. Leaning against the balustrade, one hand wrapped around my half-empty tumbler, I gazed out over the hill that fell away below the terrace. The lawn continued, a rolling expanse of grass, until it met up with a grove of pine trees, their spiky branches spectral in the evening light.

"Why are you so sure Eloise Anderson killed Detective Parker?" I asked as soon as David joined me.

He took a long swallow of his own drink, which I guessed to be either whiskey or bourbon based on its color. "She was there and she had a motive."

"What motive?" I swirled my gin and tonic. "I know people say it was a revenge crime, to pay Parker back for leading the charge to imprison her mother, but I think that's quite a stretch."

"I don't think that was it." David stared at the distant trees. "I believe the detective had dabbled in some investigating after his retirement and discovered Eloise's connection to Neil Knight's fiscal crimes. Maybe he even asked to see her so he could warn her he was about to leak the information to someone still on the force, and suggest she get ahead of that by going to the station and confessing to her collusion with Knight."

"It seems you have it all worked out. But how? Did Bruce Parker tell you what he'd found out about Eloise and Neil?" I watched David out of the corner of my eye, looking for his reaction. "You were childhood friends, I believe."

He spun around to face me. "Who told you that?"

"Your mother," I said, taking another swig of my drink.

David swore under his breath. "Sorry, that was uncalled for. But sometimes Mom is just a little too chatty for my own good."

"If it makes you feel any better, she mentioned it because she thought it would help remove you as a suspect in the case," I said.

David narrowed his eyes. "Why would I be a suspect anyway?"

"There was animosity between Benton House and Last Chapter," I said with a shrug. "Something about a first-edition Hemingway?"

"That was years ago." David finished off his drink.

"Right. Around the time Ken Anderson was murdered." I dropped the slice of lime into my empty glass. "Another childhood friend of yours, I believe."

David's thick eyebrows shot up. "What are you suggesting? That I killed Ken? That's ridiculous."

"There was bad blood between your businesses. Maybe you met and things got heated and . . ."

David set his empty glass on the wide top of the balustrade. "You think I met Ken early in the morning to argue with him? And then I just happened to find a knife and stab him?"

"Well, just like with the Parker case, the knife was one that was lying around in the shop. Used to cut string and open packages, I think Abby Anderson said." I laid my free hand on his arm, which was taut as a guitar string. "Look, I'm not saying I believe all this. But it's just as plausible as Abby killing Ken, or Eloise stabbing Parker."

His arm relaxing under my hand, David laughed humorlessly. "I suppose in this scenario I also murdered Bruce because he'd discovered I was the real killer in the Ken Anderson case and was about to tell Eloise?"

"That would be the logical hypothesis, yes," I said, dropping my hand.

David turned his head and gazed off into the distance. "I didn't do either of those things, but I see what you're getting at. There are more people who possibly had motives to kill Bruce than just Eloise Anderson."

"That's my point," I said. "So when people unequivocally state that Eloise is guilty, it makes me wonder if they're simply rushing to judgement, or if they want to deflect the blame because they have something to hide."

"Something to hide." David spoke quietly, as if talking to himself. He looked back at me. "There is something I've been thinking about, in relation to Bruce's murder. It's just one of those coincidences that feels . . . not quite right, if you know what I mean."

I pressed the bottom of my empty tumbler against my palm. "And what might that be?"

"It's not something I want to discuss now." David reached over and took the glass from my hand. "Too many people around."

"Not out here," I said.

David glanced back at the slight opening in the door to the reception room. "Maybe not, but I'd feel better if you'd meet me at the showroom tomorrow. Mom won't be there . . ."

"Ah-hah, so you don't want your mom to hear about whatever this is."

"That's part of it." David grabbed his own glass. "Look, just come to the showroom tomorrow around noon. I promise I'm not luring you there to kill you."

I looked up into his face with a slight smile. "You know, I think I believe you. But as insurance, I'm going to tell Cam and my daughter where I'll be, so if anything does happen to me, they'll know you were involved."

"You're not a very trusting person, are you?" David asked, a little humor returning to his voice.

"Absolutely not," I said.

David's lips twitched into a brief smile. "Let me carry these empty glasses inside and rejoin the party. Are you coming, or do you want to ponder my possible guilt out here for a few more minutes?"

"No, I'll go in with you," I said, following him across the terrace.

I retrieved my shoe and slipped it on before walking into the reception room behind David. We were immediately met by Gloria.

"What were you two doing out there?" she asked, peering into David's face and then mine. "If you want to have a private rendezvous, go on a date."

"Forgive me, Mom, I didn't know I needed your permission to speak with a woman alone," David said, the glint in his eyes betraying his sarcasm.

Gloria lightly swatted his arm. "Oh, that isn't it and you know it. It's just that . . ." She cast a speculative glance toward Cam, who was now talking to Lauren and Vince, while Bailey chatted with Donna. "Well, you've barely spoken to our host."

It dawned on me that Gloria probably hoped to cultivate Cam as a client. "I think I'll grab another drink," I said, walking away as Gloria reminded David about the real reason they'd accepted the invitation.

It's nice to be rich, I thought, looking over at Cam while Mateo made my drink. *Until everybody wants something from you. Preferably your money.*

The rest of the party continued without incident. As everyone prepared to leave, I approached Vince. "Listen, I'd like to stay and talk to Cam about something," I told him. "But I don't want Bailey to have to hang around."

"Don't worry, we can take her home," Vince said. "She has a key to your apartment, right?"

"Yes, and thanks." I waved Bailey over. "Vince and Donna are going to drive you home. I need to stay and speak with Cam for a little while."

Bailey arched her feathery brows. "More of your unlicensed investigators talk?"

"Perhaps. But I'd rather not go into details," I said.

Bailey offered me a mock salute. "Yes, ma'am."

"Hah, like you ever called me that," I said with a grin. "Alright, I'll see you at home soon."

After Bailey left with Vince and Donna, Gloria and David also said goodbye, both thanking Cam profusely.

"I didn't do any of the work," he said. "You should thank Mateo and Lauren, and my housekeeper, Jenna, although she doesn't live in, so she left hours ago."

"I don't live in either," Lauren said, so quickly that she practically cut Cam off. She offered Gloria and David a forced smile. "I mean, I have my own apartment. Although I may crash here tonight, since it's so late. Sorry, I need to help Mateo with the cleanup. Excuse me." She hurried off to assist Mateo, who was piling glasses and other items on a serving cart.

"Aircroft does have a good number of guest rooms," Cam said, his gaze following Lauren. "It comes in handy if people need to stay over after events."

"I'm sure," Gloria said.

I accompanied David and Gloria to the door, where David leaned in to whisper in my ear, "Don't forget—noon tomorrow."

When they left and I crossed back to Cam's chair, he was eyeing me with interest.

"Is there something going on between you and David Benton?" he asked.

"No, there is not anything *going on*, as you so delicately put it." I grabbed a chair that had been left near the bar and set it down in front of Cam's footstool. "It's all part of the investigation."

"I see," Cam said, his eyes sparkling with mischief.

I sat down. "No, you don't. Anyway, I'm going to Benton House again, tomorrow around noon. David is supposed to share some information with me he didn't want to talk about tonight. I thought I'd better let you know where I would be in case, you know, I don't come back."

Cam grimaced. "Don't say that." He crossed his arms over his chest. "You should take Vince with you. Or someone. Don't forget that David Benton is one of our top suspects."

"I know, but then, Eloise is your houseguest, and she's still a viable suspect too."

"Touché," Cam said. "But you should still be careful."

"I will, I promise. Bailey would never forgive me if I wasn't."

"Speaking of Bailey." Cam sat up straighter. "She told me she's gotten a role in a new off-Broadway musical. That's great."

"Yes, which means she'll be leaving soon," I said, studying his face for any reaction to this news.

"That's a shame, but it was bound to happen. It's how her career works." Cam's resigned expression told me Bailey had found a way to let him know she wouldn't be a good fit in his life.

She's a clever girl, I thought, hiding my smile with my hand. Forcing a fake cough to cover this gesture, I slid forward in my chair. "At any rate, the real reason I wanted to talk with you is because I've come to some conclusions this evening, and I think maybe you have too."

Cam bent his injured leg and stretched it out again. "Sorry, this cast occasionally makes my toes go to sleep. Anyway, what makes you think I had a revelation tonight?"

"A look you got when Terry Lindover left and Eloise got so upset."

"I need to learn to school my expressions more carefully, it seems," Cam said with a wry smile. "At least around you, Jane."

"Be that as it may, what occurred to you in that moment?" I asked, waving to Lauren and Mateo as they left the room.

"Oh, just the way Eloise worded a few things. She was angry, but she wasn't proclaiming her innocence."

"True. She said she couldn't keep doing something. That it was impossible," I said.

"Which tells me that she's hiding part of the story. I still have a hard time picturing Eloise stabbing Parker, but she definitely has

247

a secret." Cam absently drummed his fingers against the arm of the chair. "Maybe she knows who the killer is? She was on the scene immediately after Parker was stabbed. She could've seen them."

"Then why not accuse that person? Why allow yourself to be interrogated and arrested? What would be the point?" I asked, my brow wrinkling in concentration. "It doesn't add up."

"Perhaps the killer is blackmailing her. Forcing her to stay silent, at least until the trial."

I pursed my lips. "But what could be a worse charge than murder? Even if someone was blackmailing me over another crime— let's say, covering up fiscal irregularities or selling stolen goods—I wouldn't remain silent when faced with a murder charge."

"Unless the blackmailer promised to provide evidence at the trial that would exonerate you." Cam pressed his other hand over his restless fingers. "What if the blackmailer doesn't want Eloise convicted, and only hopes to delay the reveal of certain information?"

"I don't see how that would work. The blackmailer would have to have evidence targeting the real killer."

"Yes, but if you have enough money and the right connections..."

"You're thinking of Neil Knight or David Benton," I said. "And there's still the book. That's another thing I wanted to talk to you about. I don't want to accuse David of anything else, but both he and Gloria have mentioned a rare book that he's very eager to buy. If it's the same book Bruce Parker was looking for, they could've been working together and had a falling-out."

"So David stabbed Parker," Cam said, stroking his chin thoughtfully. "Or it could be the same scenario, with Neil Knight as Parker's partner."

"Or"—I rose to my feet—"what if our entire premise is wrong? We've been thinking this particular book might've had something slipped between the pages that would exonerate Abby, but what if that wasn't the case?"

"Because the whole crime is actually about that book?" Cam's eyes glazed over, as if his mind had gone blank, but I knew it was the opposite. He was thinking, visualizing puzzle pieces and locking them together. "The book was the catalyst, not a previous murder."

"But aren't the two murders connected?" I asked, rubbing my temple. "Assuming Abby didn't kill Ken, then his murder was probably the result of an argument with a business partner, like Neil, or a business rival, like David. Then the real killer murdered Bruce Parker because he eventually uncovered their crime. When Parker arranged to meet Eloise and tell her the truth, the killer had to silence him."

Cam leaned back and gazed at me like a tutor with a confused pupil. "Your ideas are sound, but they may be grounded in a fallacy. One I've been basing my theories on too, so don't feel bad."

"What do you mean?" I asked, crossing my arms over my chest. "You don't think there's a link between the murders of Ken Anderson and Bruce Parker?"

"No, I do. In fact, I'm sure there's a connection," Cam said. "But I'm beginning to wonder if they're linked by the same mysterious book, rather than the same killer."

Chapter
Thirty-Eight

I took a moment to absorb Cam's words. "You don't believe the same person killed Ken and Bruce?"

"Let's just say I'm not convinced it was the same individual," Cam said. "I need to do some additional research tomorrow, and call in a few favors. I have a hunch, but I don't have any evidence yet."

"Well, let me see what David has to say tomorrow. That might clarify a few things," I said. "I'll call you if I learn anything useful."

Cam wagged his finger at me. "Call me either way."

Lauren returned at that moment, cutting off my reply. I said goodbye and left the room, but paused right outside the door to look back. As I expected, Lauren was holding Cam's crutches and helping him to his feet.

"No, I will walk with you to your room, and that's final," I heard her say.

"He can figure out complex puzzles, but he can't see the nose in front of his face," I muttered as I headed for the front hall.

When I got home I discovered Bailey lounging on the sofa, her red dress exchanged for the oversized *Les Miz* T-shirt she often wore to bed. She was watching a black-and-white movie on the TV.

"Did you and Cam sort it all out?" she asked.

"Not yet, but we're working on it," I replied, heading into my bedroom to change into my own more traditional pajamas. "What are you watching?" I called out.

"*The Maltese Falcon*," she said. "You know, *the stuff that dreams are made of.*"

I joined her on the sofa as soon as I changed. Flopping down beside her, I said, "Maybe that's what we need—our own Sam Spade. He could solve this case and look good doing it."

"I think you look pretty good doing it too, Mom," Bailey said, which earned her a hug.

* * *

The following day, Bailey decided to finally take advantage of Taylor Iverson's services to take a drive up into the mountains. "It's less than two hours to Boone," she said, "and I'd like to tour that area and Blowing Rock. I hear there are lots of fun shops as well as beautiful scenery."

"Sorry I can't come with you, but I have that meeting with David Benton today," I said while we were finishing up a simple breakfast of toast and scrambled eggs.

"A meeting, huh? Not a date?" Bailey took a tiny bite of her toast.

I blew across the surface of my white ceramic mug. "I told you, it's not a romantic relationship and it never will be."

"I know, I know." Bailey waved her fork at me. "I just like to tease you."

"I've noticed that," I said, taking a sip of coffee.

Bailey speared another bit of egg with her fork. "I was going to work out an itinerary, but Taylor said he knew the area, because he went to college in Boone."

"Is that right? Well, you should also ask Taylor about books. He's very knowledgeable."

"More than I am, I bet. You said he's a writer?"

"Working at it, anyway," I said. "He's had a few things published."

Bailey's eyes were bright with interest. "I wonder if he's ever considered writing plays."

I stared at her, shaking my head. "Well, if he hasn't, I'm sure he will after talking with you for a few hours."

Bailey struck a pose. "I could become his muse."

I made a noncommittal noise and focused on finishing my coffee.

After Bailey left for her day trip, I spent an hour straightening up the apartment before getting ready for my visit with David. I didn't want to overdress, but decided I should wear something flattering and chose my favorite black slacks and a silky maroon blouse. If David was willing to share information with me because he was hoping for a date in the future, I didn't mind using that to my advantage.

David met me at the door of Benton House.

"How lovely you look," he said, ushering me into the showroom. "That shade of red looks good on you."

"It's maroon, but thanks." I looked around the showroom. "No customers today?"

"No, it's our slow season. Anyway, there's a girl in the back office who'll hear the bell if anyone else arrives. This way." David headed for a pair of elevators, one regular size and one that looked like it was intended for freight.

"I suppose you have to have that to move furniture up and down," I said, as we entered the smaller elevator.

"Yes, that and a strong back." David flashed a wide smile. "Not that I move anything but smaller decorative pieces anymore. We hire young people for that."

"The mind is willing, but the back is weak?" I asked.

"You hit it on the nose," David said. "I used to be able to do a lot of things my body now refuses to do."

I glanced over at him, trying to picture him as a murderer, and failing. "I understand that only too well."

We got off on the third floor, which David claimed offered the best place to sit and talk. I wasn't sure what he meant, since the large, open space with exposed beams and pipes we walked through resembled an old warehouse. But when we reached the far side of the room, David opened a door onto a lovely terrace that overlooked downtown High Point.

"Now I see what you mean," I said, admiring the view as well as the potted trees and shrubs and painted iron bistro tables and chairs that lent the terrace the air of a French café.

"This is my own private getaway when things get too hectic downstairs," David said. "Or when I need to escape my mother," he added with a wink.

I sat in one of the sky-blue chairs. "It's very pleasant."

"And I have refreshments." David opened a mini-fridge placed in a covered corner of the terrace and pulled out a bottle of white wine. Grabbing two glasses and a corkscrew from a rattan shelving unit set on top of the fridge, he walked back to the bistro table.

"You are well-prepared," I said, wondering how many other women he'd brought up to his *private getaway* over the years.

David opened the wine and poured us both a glass before he sat down in the chair next to mine. "Cheers," he said.

I clinked his glass with mine but only took a sip before setting my wine on the table. "You said you had something you wanted to tell me in private. This seems to fulfill that requirement."

"Yes, I didn't want Mom to barge in on us, or overhear anything." David took a long swallow of wine. "The thing is, she knows I'm in negotiations over a rare book, but she doesn't know what it is, and frankly, I don't want her to know."

I sent him a sidelong glance. "Because?"

"Because it's an extremely expensive purchase. I doubt she'd approve ahead of time. But once we own it, well"—he lifted his glass—"then we'll have another great treasure to complement the *Don Quixote*."

"Will you tell me what it is?"

"I shouldn't, because it might mean bad luck, but seeing as it's you, Jane . . . it's a miracle." Obviously sensing my disbelief, David scooted his chair around to face me. "No, I'm serious. It's something that shouldn't exist, but does."

I widened my eyes. "A map to El Dorado?"

"No, but very valuable in its own right." David leaned forward. "It's a copy of *Alice's Adventures in Wonderland* by Lewis Carroll."

"There are many editions of that book. What makes this one special?" I asked

"It's the first printing of the first edition from 1865. I emphasize first printing because that's the important part. You see, after two thousand copies were printed, the illustrator, John Tenniel, had them immediately recalled because he was unhappy with the way the print turned out. But by that point, Carroll had already given away a few books from the original print run to family and friends." Resting his elbows on his knees, David clasped his hands together. "All the other books from the first print run were destroyed. Only twenty-two copies from that print run were believed to exist, sixteen of which are now in libraries and six owned by private collectors."

"So this book you want to acquire is what? A previously unknown twenty-third copy?"

"Exactly. It's worth somewhere in the neighborhood of three million dollars," David said, his eyes shining with excitement.

"Oh." I mulled over this hefty price tag. It was a lot of money for a single book; certainly enough money to drive some people to kill. "Where did this book come from? Do you know its provenance?"

"Not entirely. The person offering it for sale said she found it while going through an old house she'd been engaged to sell by the heirs of an elderly gentleman who'd immigrated from England many years ago. I assume it was something he'd inherited from his family." David sat back and reached for his wineglass. "I've seen it and verified its authenticity, but the seller and I haven't come to terms yet."

"Hold on—the seller works in real estate?"

David swirled the wine in his glass. "Yes. That's the main reason I wanted to tell you, Jane. I know you've seen us together and I wanted to reassure you that it is strictly business . . ."

"You're talking about Terry Lindover," I said, my mind racing with the implications of this new revelation.

"That's right. Now I know what Terry did, taking the book like that, falls in a gray area, but honestly the heirs had no idea what anything in the house was worth. That's what Terry says, anyway." David stared at me over the rim of his glass as he sipped his wine.

"Gray area? More like outright theft, if that story is true," I said.

"Why wouldn't it be?" David asked, his bewildered expression confirming my hunch that he was telling the truth. Or at least, the truth as he knew it.

"I don't know. I mean, I'm sure it is," I said, pushing back my chair and standing up. "Sorry, I hate to drink and run, but I just remembered something I promised to do and I need to get on the road right now to make it on time."

"That's too bad," David said, rising to his feet. "But we'll still have to have that dinner sometime soon."

"Yes, yes, and thank you, David," I said, grabbing my purse. "Please sit down and finish your wine. I can find my own way out."

"If you insist, but I hope you do understand now why Terry and I have seemed so close. It's just business, I swear."

"I understand," I called over my shoulder as I exited the terrace. *I understand more than you think.*

Waiting until I was outside, I punched the shortcut on my cell phone to call Cam.

"Listen," I said, before he could even say hello, "you need to have Eloise sit down in front of you and then you need to ask her about the first printing of the first edition of *Alice's Adventures in Wonderland.*"

"Why must I do this?" Cam asked in a dubious tone.

"To see her reaction." I shifted my phone to my other hand while I unlocked my car. "That's the rare book that David Benton is trying to buy."

"Is there any connection to Last Chapter?"

"There might be. I think if you question Eloise, knowing this, you'll be able to find out. By the way, guess who the seller is," I said, sliding into the driver's seat.

"Neil Knight?" Cam asked.

"No. Terry Lindover. The former partner of Bruce Parker, who was the childhood friend of Ken Anderson. Does this add some missing pieces to the puzzle?"

There was a momentary pause. "It does," Cam said at last. "It will also help me with my own inquiries, which I was planning to tackle later today. Oh, by the way, I do have some more intel on your friend Neil Knight."

"He's not my friend, but go on," I said.

"It seems from my source, who knows these people pretty well, that Knight was bragging to some of his shadier pals about pulling off some sort of heist not long before Ken Anderson died. Worth millions, he told them. But the odd thing was, Knight never said another word about it again, and never appeared to have made a big score around that time."

"Interesting," I said, turning the key in the ignition. "Just so you know, I plan to stop by Aircroft so we can chat some more in person, especially since Bailey is out on a day trip . . ."

"I know. She mentioned her plans last night."

"Anyway, I *will* drop by, but I need to check something out first." I started to say goodbye, until another thought popped in my head. "Has the code changed? The gate code, I mean."

"No, we usually do that once week, on Sunday," Cam said. "It's the same as yesterday."

"Okay, no problem then. I'll see you later." I wished him a good day before I hung up and pointed my car in the direction of the country club.

It was a long shot, but if Neil Knight was at the bar, I intended to ask him a couple of questions that might shake loose some of the last few puzzle pieces.

Chapter
Thirty-Nine

I was walking into the country club before it occurred to me that I had no membership card and no member to vouch for me.

Lingering in the lobby, I waited until the desk attendant was busy before I sauntered into the main portion of the building. *Confidence is the key*, I told myself. *Act like you belong.*

My tactic appeared to work. No one stopped me, but then again, who would question a woman in her sixties, tastefully dressed? I'd discovered it was one advantage to being older, especially when it came to a little sleuthing. Christie understood that very well. There was definitely a reason Miss Marple could go everywhere and hear everything without drawing too much attention.

I made my way to the bar, keeping an eye out for anyone who might interfere with my plans. Fortunately, I reached the bar without incident and noticed Neil Knight sitting at one end. I took a deep breath and marched over to the stool right beside him. Not wanting to drink liquor on top of the wine I'd had at Benton House, I ordered a seltzer water.

"Why come to a bar if you aren't going to drink?" Neil said, without looking up from his tumbler of amber liquid and ice.

"I don't know. Maybe just to talk," I replied.

Neil jerked upright. Spinning his stool, he stared at me with bloodshot eyes. "Ms. Hunter, how not-at-all-delightful to run into you again."

"It's great to see you too." I took a sip of my drink and looked him over. "It's a little early for the hard stuff, don't you think?"

"Never too early. Besides, it's Saturday." Neil chugged the remainder of his drink and held up his empty glass, rattling the ice cubes to get the bartender's attention. "Another," he said when she paused in front of us.

"This is the last one," she told Neil, as she slid the drink across the polished wooden surface of the bar.

Neil grumbled and took another swig before turning back to face me. "To what do I owe this little visit? Still digging into things that are none of your business?"

"Perhaps." I waited for the bartender to walk to the other end of the bar. "The thing is, I've been given some information that's quite puzzling, and I thought you could help me sort it out."

Neil snorted. "Me? What would I have to do with it?"

"Well, this involves a book. You were part-owner in a bookshop at one time, weren't you?"

"Yeah, and why are you asking? You know I was. The Last Chapter," he said, with a sneer. "More like the Last Chance. Never did me much good, to be honest. Had to bail that place out more times than I can count."

I took a sip of my seltzer and nodded. "I've heard you had to do some financial finagling to help out the Anderson family, A few questionable deals, some loans from shady lenders . . ."

"What is this?" Neil's expression grew wary. "Have you come here just to insult me?"

"No, I'm simply trying to establish why Ken Anderson, and then his daughter, seemed to owe money to people I can't imagine them dealing with." This was actually an educated guess on my part, but Neil's reaction confirmed it was true.

"That store would've folded in the first five years if not for me," he said, fixing me with a ferocious glare.

I shrugged. "No doubt, although I find it strange that they were short of cash when Ken Anderson was making deals like the first edition of Hemingway's *In Our Time*."

"We did get a substantial amount of money from the sale of that item, but it didn't last forever." Neil swiveled his stool to face the bar. "Besides, Ken had to pay down his mortgage. He and Abby bought the place with quite a bit of stock included, so it wasn't cheap."

"Right, I've heard Eloise mention the old books that were already stored in the shop when her parents took it over," I said. "Most of them weren't terribly valuable, she said." Eloise hadn't said anything of the kind. I was simply working my way around to my primary question.

"Lot of junk. Although . . ." Neil took another big swig of his whiskey and water.

"There was one diamond among all the coal?" I asked, idly swirling the ice around in my glass.

Neil spun around; his eyes narrowed. "What do you know about that?"

"I know Bruce Parker asked Eloise Anderson to retrieve a book by a specific inventory number right before he was killed. She told the police she couldn't find it, or the matching inventory pages, but I wonder if that's true."

The look that passed over Neil's face was a mixture of despair and sardonic hilarity. "It was there, then, all the time. While I was in and out, thinking he'd hidden it somewhere else, it was right under my nose."

"A first printing of the first edition of *Alice's Adventures in Wonderland*," I said, not framing it as a question. "So tell me, Mr. Knight, did you murder Ken Anderson over that book?"

"No!" The word was as explosive as a gunshot. The bartender, busy wiping glasses, looked up, but Neil waved her away. "No, I did not," he added, in a quieter voice. "I've done some questionable things in my life, but I've never stabbed a friend."

"But you knew about the book and how much it was worth?"

Neil finished off his drink. "Sure. I was there when Ken found the thing. I could tell by his reaction that it had to be worth a pretty penny."

"Millions," I said.

"Right. Millions." Neil's expression faded from angry to gloomy. "Ken didn't tell Abby about it at first, or Eloise either, of course. He said he wanted to use the money from the sale to pay off all his debts."

I ran my fingertip around the rim of my glass. "Some of which Abby didn't know about, I guess."

"Yeah, he didn't tell her everything."

"But something happened," I said. "The book disappeared."

The lines bracketing Neil's mouth deepened. "Yeah."

I casually swiveled my stool back and forth. "Because you stole it."

There was a span of silence filled with the buzz of voices from the dining room and the clink of ice in Neil's glass. "It was half mine anyway, and I figured it was the bonus I was never going to get from that store. I took it and started looking for a buyer."

"So what happened? Did you change your mind and give it back?" I asked in a soothing tone. I had him talking now; I could afford to be nice.

"Oh, I gave it back, but only under duress," Neil said, his tone bitter as rancid cooking oil. He shot me a sidelong glance. "Ken had a friend in the police department, someone he'd known since childhood."

"Bruce Parker," I said, my mind whirling.

"Yeah. Ken sent him to visit me. On the down-low, you understand. Not official police business. But Detective Parker said it could become official if he shared all the information he'd dug up on me. I couldn't have that, not even for millions." Neil lowered his head. "There were people I worked with who didn't want their names to appear in any official reports. They'd have killed me if I'd allowed that to happen."

"I see. So you gave the book back, and then what?"

Neil lifted his head and gazed blankly ahead, his expression reflected in the bar mirror, drawn and defeated. "Never saw the blasted thing again. I assumed Ken hid it somewhere, outside the shop. Safe deposit box or something. But it seems he didn't." Neil tipped up his empty glass, seeking the last drops. "Apparently he simply switched out the cases. Many of the older books were stored in acid-free boxes, you see, with nothing but inventory numbers labeling the spine of each box."

"Ken must've told Abby the number at some point," I said. "And she must've eventually shared it with Parker, although I can't figure out why."

"He probably threatened Eloise." Neil turned his head to meet my gaze. "Parker knew about me and my connections. He could've used the same sources to learn how Eloise covered up for me over the years. For the sake of the shop, of course."

"Bruce Parker wanted that book for himself," I said, talking to myself more than to Neil.

He held up his tumbler in a little salute. "Brava. You are clever, I'll give you that."

"You didn't kill him either, I suppose?" I asked.

"Nope. I had no idea that book was still in the storeroom at Last Chapter, much less anything about a switched inventory number or Parker having any knowledge of such a thing."

This tracked with what Cam had told me. Neil Knight had bragged to some criminal pals about stealing a precious item, but he'd never mentioned selling it or anything more about it.

I slipped off the stool and stepped back from the bar. "Thank you for being honest with me today, Mr. Knight. It's clarified things."

He didn't look at me. "You already knew a lot of it, didn't you? Seems like it anyway. Besides, I've got nothing to lose now. The police have cleared me in Parker's death, and as for the murder of Ken Anderson . . ." He stared morosely down at his empty glass. "That one was solved, wasn't it."

I caught the bartender's eye. "Give the man one more on me," I said. "I think he's sobered up a bit now."

"And who should I charge it too, along with your seltzer?" she asked.

"One of your members," I said. "Cameron Clewe."

At the mention of Cam's name, Neil turned on his stool and cast me a sardonic smile. He raised the tumbler the bartender had just handed him. "To the illustrious Mr. Clewe."

I hurried away without responding. Neil's confession had solidified an idea in my mind that I wanted to share with Cam as soon as possible. He needed to know my new theory.

If he hadn't already reached the same conclusion, of course.

Chapter Forty

I drove straight to Aircroft, dashing inside the house as soon as I parked. Running into Lauren in the hall leading to Cam's office, I asked her if he was free to talk for a few minutes.

Lauren checked her watch. "He should be. His last video meeting was scheduled to end five minutes ago." She cast me a concerned glance. "You aren't usually here on Saturday. Is anything wrong?"

"Not really. I just have information to share with Cam," I said, huffing a little.

"About Eloise's case?" Lauren fastened a button of her ivory jacket over her violet blouse. "I know how preoccupied Cam's been with that lately."

"Yes. Hopefully, with this new info, we'll be able to solve it soon." I tugged down the hem of my blouse. "Why are *you* here on a Saturday?"

"Urgent meetings," Lauren said with a sigh. "One of the businesses in Cam's portfolio is going through some growing pains."

"I hope Cam pays you *very* well," I said.

"He does, actually. Anyway, I was headed to the office to see if he needed anything, so you can tag along," Lauren walked on ahead, her pleated ivory skirt swishing around her legs as she navigated the hallway in her spiky beige heels.

She knocked on the office door and waited for Cam's "come in" before entering. "Jane's here to talk with you. Do you have time right now?"

"Absolutely. She called me earlier and told me she was planning to stop by, so I cleared my afternoon schedule. Please sit down, Jane." Cam leaned back in his desk chair, causing it to rock slightly. He was wearing an emerald-toned dress shirt and a tie patterned with palm fronds in various hues of green. As I sat in the chair facing his desk, he loosened the knot and pulled the tie off over his head, mussing his hair. "No need for that now," he said, tossing the tie onto the desk.

"Do you require anything right now, Cam?" Lauren asked. "I was about to head to the kitchen to check on some things with Mateo and Jenna, but I can delay that if necessary."

"I'm fine," Cam said. "I'll text you if I need anything later." After I shot him a sharp look he added, "Thanks, Lauren."

Her dark eyes widened slightly. "You're welcome," she said, turning and exiting the room with her head held high.

"Alright, Jane," Cam said as he unfastened the collar button of his shirt. "Fill me in."

I launched into a detailed description of my discussions with David and Neil. "I believe both Ken Anderson and Bruce Parker were murdered over the *Alice* book," I said at the end of my account.

"I agree, and since, according to David, Terry Lindover now has the book, it would seem that she murdered Parker." Cam tapped his fingertips together.

"I don't follow," I said. "Even if Terry somehow found out about the Carroll and shadowed Bruce in the hopes he'd lead her to it, she couldn't have snatched the book from him. He never had it."

Cam's eyes sparked with excitement. "It wouldn't matter any-way, since Eloise told the police that she couldn't find the book and returned to the office empty-handed. However, I think we can assume that Eloise is lying about this point."

"That's her secret," I said, sliding to the edge of my chair seat. "She did locate the book, but as soon as she realized its true value, she put it back where she found it and planned to tell Parker it was missing."

"Probably tearing out the related inventory page while she was at it," Cam said. "Which would also explain why she claimed she didn't hear raised voices or a struggle in the office."

"Right." I sat back, frowning. "How did Terry get her hands on the book then? I know she has it, because David said he'd seen it."

Cam leaned forward, placing his forearms on the desktop. "Let's go with Knight's theory that Abby gave Bruce Parker the inventory number on one of his last visits to the prison. She was trying to hold out and only confide in Eloise at some point, but Parker forced her hand."

"Because he found out about Eloise's involvement in some of Neil Knight's schemes. Which explains the timing. Parker only recently attempted to retrieve the book because he didn't have the inventory number before. And maybe, like Neil, he didn't even know the book was still shelved in the bookshop." I pressed my elbow into the chair arm and rested my chin on my hand. "I won-der why Abby didn't tell Eloise about the book sooner? It certainly could've helped with keeping the shop afloat, without any help from Neil's unsavory pals."

"Hmmm . . ." Cam sat back and stared up at the ceiling his eyes half-closed, "Hard to say. Perhaps she wanted to wait until Neil retired so he wouldn't be entitled to any of the proceeds?"

"That makes sense. Abby kept the secret because she wanted all the money to go to Eloise. But then Parker pressured her to share the inventory number, threatening to expose fiscal irregularities at Last Chapter."

Cam frowned. "Ironically, Parker only knew of the book's existence because his childhood friend, Ken, sent him to talk to Neil Knight after Knight stole it."

"More like strong-arm the guy, I expect," I said.

"That's probably accurate." Cam lowered his head and met my questioning gaze. "Which means Detective Parker must've had some inkling about the book's value. Maybe he even researched it, who knows?"

"You think Neil gave the book back to Ken and then Parker decided to cash in? He could've thought he deserved a cut. He'd done Ken a big favor, at the risk of his career."

"I can certainly imagine him demanding a share of the profits," Cam said thoughtfully. "If Ken refused, perhaps Parker decided to get even."

I straightened in my chair. "Kill him, you mean."

"It makes sense. If Parker had been in the shop before, he may have known about the inventory system, and thought he could locate the book later, by consulting the ledgers that matched titles to inventory numbers. He obviously knew the title, since he was the one to retrieve the book from Neil. He probably thought it would be easy to find that title in a ledger and match it to the correct inventory number."

"But Ken had switched out the cases, giving the *Alice* book a new number. Parker could've tried to search for it, but then . . ." I snapped my fingers. "He heard someone coming down the stairs."

"Abby," Cam said. "She was undoubtedly distraught when she discovered her husband's body. All Parker had to do was remain hidden in the bookshelves and then make an appearance as one of the police on the scene."

"Wouldn't he have blood spatter on him, though?"

"Sure, but in the confusion, he could say he'd been first on the scene and had tried to revive Ken, just like Abby tried to do." Cam tapped the desktop three times. "That would explain the locked doors as well. All Parker had to do was claim that all the doors and windows were locked. If he was accepted as the first officer on the scene, who would question him?"

"Especially when he became the lead detective on the case." I shook my head. "I shouldn't say this, but right now I feel like Parker got what he deserved. He ran that investigation knowing Abby was innocent, but railroaded her into a life in prison anyway."

"I think we can assume he wasn't a stellar individual if he was willing to murder his childhood friend," Cam said dryly.

"Okay, but where does Terry Lindover come into this?"

"She and Bruce were partners for several years. Perhaps he confessed it to her?" Cam tapped three times again. "But that doesn't explain how she got the book. Eloise is the one who should have it, not Terry."

"That's the missing piece," I said.

Before we could puzzle out the case any further, Lauren rushed into the room.

"Something wrong?" Cam asked.

"I'm not sure." Lauren twisted her hands at her waist. "After I had a long conversation with Jenna about some household matters, I went to see Mateo, and he told me he'd seen Eloise out in the garden."

"That's not a crime," Cam said.

"No, but Mateo said she wasn't alone. There was someone with her and he thought they were arguing."

I jumped out of my chair. "What did this person look like?"

"He couldn't really see them clearly. They were wearing a jacket with a hood. But he said he thought they had blonde hair," Lauren said.

Cam and I locked gazes. "It could be Terry," I said.

"How would she have gotten onto the estate?" Cam asked as he reached for his crutches.

I slapped my forehead. "She was here last night, for the party. She would've been given the gate code, and you said it only changes on Sunday."

Cam uncharacteristically let fly a string of swear words. "Should've kept the security team, even after the furor quieted down," he said, rolling back his chair.

"Did Mateo see anything more?" I asked Lauren.

She nodded. "Eloise and the stranger headed off toward the back garden. He said they disappeared behind the pavilion and he doesn't know what happened after that."

Cam, who'd hoisted himself up on his crutches, moved toward the door. "Lauren, call the police."

"Where do you think you're going?" she asked, as he approached the door.

"Into the garden, of course," he said, his mouth set in a grim line. "Please move aside."

Lauren placed her hands on her hips. "You can't go out there on crutches."

"I can and I will," Cam said. "Besides, I've already tried it."

Lauren faced him with a fierce glare. "In the formal garden, not the wild garden behind the pavilion. How will you manage that, not to mention the steps to climb and descend to get there?"

"With willpower," Cam said, using the padded tip of one crutch to push her aside and slip out the door.

"I'll go with him," I told Lauren. "Please call the police and guide them to us when they arrive."

"You'll be in the wild garden?" Lauren asked as I moved passed her, jogging to catch up with Cam, who was heading for one of the back doors.

I paused for a second as a frightening thought crossed my mind. Following Cam again, I called back to her over my shoulder, "If not there, at the quarry."

Chapter
Forty-One

C am was able to move through the formal garden with no real problems, but hesitated when we reached the stairs of the pavilion.

"I've learned to go up and down stairs on these things," he said, swinging out the tip of one crutch, "but there's no railing here and the steps are a little slick. It's going to be difficult to get the right leverage."

"Why don't I stay right next to you, on the side with your cast. If you feel unsteady, I can help with your balance."

Cam agreed and we slowly climbed the steps. I only had to put a hand on his shoulder once, and that was just for reassurance. He was perfectly capable of navigating the stairs by himself.

I was actually a little more concerned about the stairs leading down from the pavilion to the wild garden, but Cam simply handed me his crutches and used the handrail to keep his balance as he hopped from step to step. At the bottom, after I handed him the crutches, he leaned heavily on them for a moment.

"There are benches nearby if you want to rest," I said.

"No, we have to keep moving," he said, with a grimace. "I don't know what is going on between Terry and Eloise, but I don't think it's anything good."

I walked ahead, holding back any drooping vines or branches so that Cam could move unimpeded on the narrow, winding path. When we reached the edge of the field, I suggested that I go on ahead. "It will be very difficult for you to move across the uneven ground of the meadow," I said.

"Voices," he replied, as if he hadn't heard me. Or was ignoring me. "I hear voices."

Near the quarry, I thought with a shiver. Realizing Cam would never stay back at the edge of the garden, I stomped ahead, checking for any holes or other obstacles that could trip him.

We straggled out onto the flat rocks and clumps of weeds that surrounded the quarry. A high-pitched voice wailing *"Help!"* was almost immediately silenced by a flood of angry invective.

"Over by the trees," Cam said, swinging around on his crutches. "I'm going to stay close to the quarry, where there isn't so much grass."

"For heaven's sake, don't fall." I ran behind him, trying to maneuver my way between him and the edge of the cliff.

"I'm fine. Other side," he said between clenched teeth.

In front of us was a disconcerting tableau. Terry Lindover, dressed in black jeans and a hooded gray jacket, was holding a gun on a terrified Eloise, who'd slid down to the ground with her back pressed up against the trunk of a pine tree.

"Don't come any closer," Terry said. "I'm happy to shoot Eloise if you make any wrong moves. She's been nothing but an irritation for months."

"So you kidnapped her again, just like you did before," Cam said.

Terry smirked. "Except Eloise was in on the abduction the first time. I told her it would help muddy the waters and paint her as a possible victim instead of Bruce's killer. Of course, she wasn't going to implicate me as her kidnapper, since it was all a ploy to cast doubt on her guilt."

Eloise glared up at her. "You owed that to me. Don't forget, you wouldn't have the book without my help."

I shared a glance with Cam. "So that's what happened? You two were working together?"

"We had a plan. No one was supposed to get hurt," Eloise said, cowering as Terry pointed the gun at her forehead.

"You knew Bruce Parker murdered Ken Anderson, didn't you, Terry?" Cam moved forward a few steps, until Terry brandished the pistol at him.

Eloise looked devastated. "What?"

Terry ignored her. "Foolish Bruce. He confessed it one evening not long before he died, when we met up for drinks for old times' sake. I'm afraid he had quite a few more drinks than I did, and ended up drunk and blubbering about his terrible crime."

"Detective Parker killed my dad?" Eloise stared up at Terry, her eyes wide. She wasn't wearing her glasses. I assumed they'd fallen off when Terry grabbed her.

"Yes, dear. Good old Bruce. He and your father were childhood friends too. Did you know that?"

Eloise, stricken mute, shook her head.

"It was all about the book, Eloise, the one Detective Parker sent you to find. *Alice's Adventures in Wonderland* by Lewis Carroll, first printing of the first edition," Cam said, his gaze focused on Terry and the gun.

Finding her voice again, Eloise looked up at Terry accusingly. "You never said anything about Detective Parker murdering my dad."

"Well," Terry said with a shrug. "It was need-to-know, and you didn't."

"You made me think that Detective Parker was a good guy, sharing information my mom had given him after he changed his mind about her guilt," Eloise said.

Terry sneered down at her. "He never had to change his mind because he knew your mother was innocent. No one knew better than him."

"Now you want to do the same to me," Eloise said, her pitch rising. "You know I'm innocent, but you want me to be convicted so you can get away with murder. Even though our original plan didn't include anything about killing anyone. I was supposed to get the inventory number from Parker and tell him I couldn't find the book. He was supposed to walk away with nothing, while we eventually sold the book to David Benton and split the profits."

"That was *your* original plan," Terry said. "Not mine. I knew Bruce too well. He'd already murdered one person over that book. I figured it was best to get him out of the way, or we'd both be his next targets. Once I heard that he'd given you the inventory number and sent you into the storeroom, I crept into the office and killed him."

Eloise cast Terry a bitter look. "Framing me. You said you'd help clear me at the trial, but you didn't actually plan to do that, did you?"

"Of course not. Once you were in jail, I'd have the book and could keep all the money from its sale. It was a tidy plan, until you lost your trust in me." Terry leveled the gun at Eloise's temple. "I know you're ready to squeal, and I can't have that."

"I suppose I have you to thank for my tumble down the stairs?" Cam asked.

Terry nodded. "A lucky opportunity. I thought it would put an end to your little amateur sleuthing, but it seems I was wrong. Which means I'll simply have to put a stop to it another way."

"There's no scenario in which you can get away with this," Cam said. He appeared very much in control, just as he had when we'd faced a killer with a gun before. It was amazing to me how well he could manage when the chips were down. It was like his logical mind took over, shutting down all emotion.

"I think you're wrong. I scouted out this area ahead of time. There's an old road beyond this little wood. I parked my car there. It won't be that hard to make my escape," Terry said.

So at least the gate code faux pas didn't matter. I stared at Terry, trying to determine if she was coolly rational, or off the rails. "Unless we tell the authorities where you've gone."

"Hard to talk when you're dead." Terry pointed the gun at my chest and then Cam's.

"Hard to escape when you're wanted for the murder of three people. No wait, four," Cam said.

"You think I don't have a plan? I have everything worked out. I can disappear with that very valuable book and sell it on the black market and live quite well," Terry flashed an insincere smile. "Not to mention I've made a lot of money in real estate, most of which has been funneled into overseas banks that don't like to share information with U.S. law enforcement. Of course, just in case one of you survives somehow, I've no intention of telling you where I'm going. That would be stupid."

"You think you're clever, don't you?" Cam asked, raising his eyebrows. "Once Parker confessed to killing Ken Anderson over a book worth millions, you figured out a way to take it for yourself. Using Eloise as a patsy, and playing David Benton for a fool."

"What can I say? It's a gift." Terry grabbed Eloise's arm and yanked her to her feet. "I think we've chatted enough. I'm sure someone called the police and they'll be here any minute, so I need to clean up this mess and get out of here."

Cam took a step sideways, closer to me. "I'm sorry," he said.

"Not your fault," I replied, laying my hand on his shoulder.

At that moment Eloise twisted her wrist, breaking Terry's grip, and kicked Terry in the shin. Breaking away, she ran toward the edge of the quarry.

Terry, hobbling slightly, chased after her.

Cam shifted his crutches as if to move forward, but I tightened my grip on his shoulder, keeping him in place. "Don't," I whispered. "Nothing we can do right now."

"I can't stand by . . ."

Terry reached Eloise, and took aim. She pulled the trigger, a malicious grin on her face.

But the gun jammed, and Eloise, belittled and betrayed, reacted as if possessed by one of the Furies. She launched at Terry, fists flying, slamming the barrel of the gun so hard that Terry instinctively opened up her fingers. The gun sailed off to the right, smashing on the lip of the quarry before clattering into its depths.

Before Cam and I could take any action, Terry grabbed Eloise's shoulders and attempted to fling her sideways, trying to force her to follow the gun's trajectory into the quarry. Eloise, with a wisdom born out of necessity, bent her knees and squatted, yanking her shoulders down and away from Terry's grip. Then, as Terry wobbled from this sudden change in balance, Eloise grabbed Terry's shins and shoved.

Terry's feet slid out from under her, and as Eloise rolled away to safety, Terry tumbled in the opposite direction, disappearing over the edge of the quarry.

Resonating off the rocks, a loud series of bumps and bangs ended in a terrible scream.

And then, silence.

Chapter
Forty-Two

The silence lasted for what felt like an interminable stretch of time. Then Eloise, standing and backing away from the edge of the quarry, began babbling. "We should help her, shouldn't we? She might still be alive. We have to help her."

"We can't," Cam said, his voice harsh as sandpaper. "None of us can climb down there without injuring or killing ourselves. We'll have to wait for the police."

"Police?" Eloise let out one shriek and tried to run past us.

Cam thrust out one crutch, tripping her. She fell to the ground, sobbing.

"Grab her, Jane. The authorities will be here soon. We need to hold on to her until they arrive."

I bent down and clamped my fingers around Eloise's slender wrist. Pulling her to her feet as I stood up, I kept a strong grip on her arm. She didn't try to fight me.

"Terry Lindover played you for a fool, Eloise." Cam's voice cut like a razorblade. "I hope you know that."

"I thought . . ." Eloise took a deep breath. "Terry said Detective Parker told her about the book and he suggested they split the profits from its sale. He had some inventory number my mom had given him."

"Because he forced her to," I said grimly. "He knew about the less-than-legal deals Neil Knight had brokered to keep Last Chapter solvent, and how you overlooked Neil's fiscal crimes. I bet Parker told your mother that he'd expose your cover-up if she didn't give him that number, and I'm sure the last thing Abby Anderson wanted was for you to go to jail, even for a short period of time."

Eloise swore under her breath. "I didn't know anything about that. The truth is, I didn't know much. Not about the book, or how my father died, or . . . anything." Her shoulders slumped. "Terry came to me. She said she'd direct Detective Parker to visit me and give me the inventory number. I didn't know what it was connected to, but Terry said it was an item worth a lot of money. I needed money, you see, to save the bookshop, to keep it going."

"She offered to split the profits with you if you told Parker you couldn't find the book. You were supposed to stash it away somewhere instead," Cam said.

"That's right." Eloise ducked her head. "Terry planned to arrive before Detective Parker and hide in the store until I came back to the office without the book. She said she'd keep watch so he wouldn't hurt me. But what she really did was sneak into the office while I was in the storeroom. I heard noises while I was tearing out and disposing of the inventory page, but I thought it was just Parker, snooping around. Then when I entered the office again, expecting to see him standing there, I found him on the floor, stabbed, and Terry dashing out the door." A little sob escaped Eloise's throat. "I tried to save him, I really did. That's why I didn't go after Terry. But it was hopeless."

"Why did you give Terry the *Alice* book?" I asked, keeping a strong grip on her wrist. I wasn't so much worried about her running away as I was her flinging herself into the quarry in despair. "You had it, and you knew she'd killed Parker. Why let her have such a valuable item?"

"She blackmailed me," Eloise replied. "She said everyone would think I was the killer and there would be no way to prove them wrong unless she agreed to help me. But she'd only help if I handed over the book."

"How in the world did she plan to assist you?" Cam's expression hardened. "She was no longer with the police force. She had no leverage."

"She was going to testify as an eyewitness," Eloise said. "She told me she was a respected member of the community and a former detective so she'd easily be believed. She even claimed to have set up a real estate viewing near the bookshop so it would look natural for her to be in the area. All she had to do was go to the police and say she saw a man run from the bookshop with blood on his hands. She'd already worked up a detailed description of the guy. Of course, he didn't exist, but Terry said her testimony would be enough to cast doubt over my guilt, and I wouldn't be convicted. I might not even go to trial."

"But once she had the book, she didn't plan to do anything to help you. She was happy for you to take the rap," Cam said.

Eloise looked as miserable as a cat in the rain. "I know."

"Still, you could've told the authorities what you just shared with us and cast plenty of suspicion on her," I said.

"That's what she was afraid of." Eloise yanked her arm, but I held fast. "I guess she thought I'd already be locked up, 'cause the bail was so high. That no one would believe a jailbird's story over hers." She glanced at Cam. "But you messed up that plan."

"Glad to hear it," he said.

"When did you realize she wasn't going to help clear you?" I asked. "Last night, at the party?"

"Yes. I could tell by the way she was looking at me, and then she made that comment about me being 'guilty as sin.' That's when I knew she'd lied to me." Eloise touched her face with her free hand. "She knocked off my glasses. They must be in the front garden somewhere."

"We'll find them," Cam said. "More importantly, did you contact Terry after the party and threaten to expose her?"

Tears welled in Eloise's blue eyes. "I thought I could still get her to help me. I told her to meet me in the garden so we could talk it out, but she showed up with a gun."

"I'm sorry, Eloise," Cam said in gentler tone. "You're going to have to tell the police everything, and pay the consequences. I won't be able to bail you out this time, or allow you to stay at Aircroft, but I will still pay for your legal team."

"Thank you, Cam. It's more than I deserve." Eloise cast him a teary smile. "You can release me now, Jane. I won't run, and anyway, I see the police coming."

A group of uniformed officers burst out from the shadowy entrance to the garden, guns drawn. They shouted for us to remain still and raise our hands.

Resting his crutch against his ribs, Cam held up one hand, while I thrust both hands over my head.

"It's me you want." Eloise's face grew still as stone. She lifted her arms and walked forward to meet the officers. "Mr. Clewe and Ms. Hunter are entirely innocent."

After Eloise was taken into custody, Cam informed a plain-clothes detective about Terry. "It's doubtful she survived," he said. "But you should check."

"What happened?" one officer asked.

"Teresa Lindover kidnapped Ms. Anderson and held her at gunpoint. When Ms. Lindover attempted to throw Ms. Anderson in the quarry, they grappled and she fell in herself," Cam said in a clear, monotone voice.

"It was self-defense," I added, marveling again at how Cam, for all his anxiety, could turn completely calm in a crisis.

"We'll require detailed statements from you both," a detective said.

Cam and I shared a commiserating glance. "Of course," he said. "Whatever you need."

Chapter Forty-Three

The following week was blessedly quiet and calm. I had to give statements to the police, as did Cam and Lauren, but otherwise everything was back to normal.

I had planned to drive Bailey to the airport on Wednesday, but she hired Taylor instead, a move I found a little inconsiderate. "I know you really enjoyed your day trip with Taylor and think he is *blazing hot*, as you so charmingly put it. But you're heading to New York. Are you going to continue to flirt with this poor guy all the way to the airport and then leave him longing after you?"

"First of all," Bailey said, as she zipped up her suitcase, "there are such things as cell phones, which allow people to text, talk, and even video chat. Secondly," she added, raising her hand, palm out, to cut off my reply, "Taylor is very mature and has goals of his own, so I doubt he'll waste a lot of time sitting around, daydreaming about me."

"Maybe just a little time?" I suggested, with a smile.

"A little would actually be nice." Bailey gave me a warm hug. "See you, Mom. I'll send tickets."

I saw her to the door, reserving any tears until I was alone again in my apartment.

On Friday, I worked on cataloging more books from Cam's collection, including a first edition copy of Dorothy L. Sayers' *Strong Poison*, the novel in which she introduced one of my favorite characters, Harriet Vane.

After lunch, Cam appeared just outside the library door, leaning on his crutches and wearing a pair of the nondescript black pants that I assumed he'd purchased to save his regular clothes from being slit up the leg to accommodate his cast. He'd maintained a more typical style on top, with his short-sleeved cotton sweater in a shade that reminded me of expensive vanilla ice cream.

"Are you busy?" he asked.

"I'm always busy, or at least I'll always tell you I am," I replied with a grin. "But come in and sit down. I know trekking through Aircroft's maze of hallways on those crutches must be exhausting."

"I've gotten rather used to them," Cam said as he hobbled into the library. "But I think I will sit down for a minute." He settled in one of the armchairs, resting the crutches against the back of the cherry side table. "So, how goes it?"

I rolled my task chair back from the edge of the desk. "Fine. I've finally had a week where I could get a good amount of cataloging done."

"That's great. For my part, I've wanted to stop by and give you an update on Eloise, but I got caught up in some sticky business matters. I don't have any more phone or video meetings this afternoon, though, so I thought this was as good a time as any." Cam slid a footstool over from its place in front of the matching armchair and propped up his leg.

"I would like to hear what's happening with her," I said. "I know she wasn't totally honest with us, but I think she was simply reacting to traumatic events as best she could."

"She didn't do herself any favors, that's for sure. Relying on someone like Terry Lindover to rescue her at the last minute was not a smart move."

"Terry would never have saved her," I said. "Eloise would probably have ended up in prison for life, just like her mom."

Cam leaned back against the chair cushions. "Unfortunately, she may still have to do some time, since she did cover up a murder. But her legal team is working on a plea deal."

"That's great. I'm just glad we were there to witness Terry's fall so we could confirm any action Eloise took was in self-defense," I said, twirling a pen between two fingers.

"I think she'll be okay. In the meantime, I informed the authorities that a certain book they'd find among the late Terry Lindover's effects is actually stolen goods. They've agreed to hand it over to David Benton for safekeeping, since he can store it properly. But"—Cam held up one finger—"David, who is, I must admit, a better man than I initially thought, is only holding the book until Eloise is free to negotiate a deal with him."

"So she will get the money after all," I said.

"And David will get his book." Cam met my approving glance with a disarming smile "I've also engaged a few people to keep Last Chapter up and running. You needn't look so surprised. It's really a selfish move on my part. I don't want to lose my best source for vintage and rare books."

"Sure thing, boss," I said. "Heaven forbid you do anything that could be perceived as altruistic."

A rare grin illuminated Cam's handsome face. "You know me too well."

"I'm beginning to, although . . ." The rest of my comment died away at the sound of footsteps in the hall.

The tapping of stilettos informed me that it was Lauren, but there were two other sets of footfalls, slower and more deliberate.

"It sounds like Lauren is escorting a couple of visitors," I said. "Were you expecting anyone?"

"No." Cam turned in the chair to get a better look at the doorway.

Lauren entered first, looking very professional in her ivory silk blouse and black pencil skirt. Behind her were two elderly people, a man and a woman.

"It's Lily," I told Cam as I leapt to my feet. "Lily Glenn and her brother, Gordon."

"Gordy, please," he said, taking off the tweed cap he'd pulled down over his mane of white hair.

Cam made a move as if to stand, but Lily waved him back into his seat. "Please don't get up. I can see that you're recovering from an injury."

I strode forward and clasped Lily's hand and then Gordy's. "It's good to see you again," I said. "Please, have a seat." I rolled my chair out from behind the desk for Gordy as Lauren led Lily over to the other armchair.

"But where will the two of you sit?" Lily asked, concern shadowing her blue eyes.

"I'm fine standing," I said. "I've been sitting all day."

Lauren used her hands to push her body up far enough so that she could sit on the desk. "And I can just perch here. It's no problem."

"If you're sure. I don't like to sit when ladies are standing," Gordy said.

"Really, it's fine." I glanced over at Cam, who was intently studying Lily and her brother.

"Are you here to tour Aircroft?" he asked. "I know about your connection to the estate, Ms. Glenn."

"Do you?" There was something in Lily's expression that made me think she was amused.

Cam adjusted his leg so he could sit a little more forward in the chair. "You and Calvin Airley were in love, but his parents disapproved."

"As did mine," Lily said, after sharing a quick glance with Gordy. "Yes, that much is true. As is the fact that I found out I was pregnant not long before Cal was killed."

"Murdered, you mean," Cam said, gripping his chair arm.

Probably to avoid tapping, I thought.

Lily turned her head to look at Cam more directly. "I think it was more along the lines of manslaughter, but you're right, my father fought with Cal and caused his death. When I realized that, I fled my home and started a new life."

"You came back once." Cam fixed Lily with his intense stare.

"Yes, when you were just a baby." Lily examined Cam carefully. "You look very much like your mother."

"So I've been told. I never knew her, unfortunately," Cam said. "She drew a sketch of you. May I ask why?"

Lily clasped her gnarled fingers tightly in her lap. "We bonded, even in that short time. I suppose it was partially because we were both mothers of sons. She was a lovely woman. I'm sorry you lost her so young."

"Your child was a boy?" Cam asked, the tension in his jaw causing it to twitch.

Lily smiled. "Yes. A healthy, handsome boy."

"The heir to Aircroft." Cam glanced at me before focusing on Lily. "This should all rightfully be his."

"Ah, no." Lily shook her head. "He wouldn't want it. And I think Aircroft is now in the best of all possible hands."

Lauren swung her legs, banging one heel into the front skirt of the desk. "You never told your family about your son?"

"No one but Gordy, and even he didn't know I'd had a boy until recently," Lily said, sending him a sweet smile. "Anyway, I knew he'd keep my secret." She shifted her focus back to Cam. "As you may have heard, or guessed, I was afraid if Samuel and Bridget Airley heard that I'd had Cal's son, they'd demand custody."

Cam nodded. "And probably would've gotten it, knowing the power their wealth would have afforded them, especially at that time." He shifted uneasily in his chair. "Your son is still alive?"

"Oh yes. Or at least, I hope so. That's the real reason I've come here today, you see." Lily's eyes appeared luminous in her lined face. "I've heard that you and Ms. Hunter sometimes help individuals who are experiencing difficulties. That you've cleared the names of a few individuals charged with crimes, and have also found missing valuables, and even people."

"That's true. We are happy to help, depending on the case," Cam said in a slightly hesitant tone. "Is there something you think we could do for you, Ms. Glenn?"

"It's Lily, and yes, I would like to engage your services." Lily straightened until her spine was not touching the back of the chair. "After enduring a couple of tragedies when he was younger, my son began traveling the world. He's a photojournalist, so that lifestyle fits in well with his career. But even though he was always traveling, he kept in touch with me. Once a month at the very least." Lily turned her gentle smile on Cam. "Of course, he's a grown man in his sixties, so perhaps I shouldn't worry so much, but I haven't heard from him for four months now and I've become quite concerned."

"I'm so sorry. I know I'd be frantic if I hadn't heard from my daughter in all that time," I said.

Lauren's expression was filled with sympathy. "Yes, that's certainly understandable."

"You want us to try to locate him?" Cam stretched out his arm, pressing the palm of his right hand against the top of the side table. "It might be possible if we have enough information, like his last known location, the businesses he worked with and for, any known companions, and that sort of thing. Oh, and of course, his name."

"It's Rafe," Lily said. "Rafe Glenn."

Initials R. G., I thought. *R . . .* I inhaled a sharp breath. The man who'd sent Patricia Clewe love letters, who was undoubtedly the father of her child, had signed all those letters with only the initial R. Unnerved, I looked at Cam to see if he'd had the same thought.

He obviously had, since his face had gone bone-white and his smattering of freckles gleamed against his nose and cheeks like spots of blood. "Rafe Glenn," he repeated in a hollow voice, the fingers of his right hand rhythmically drumming the table.

Lily leaned against the arm of her chair and reached across the side table to press her hand over Cam's restless fingers. "Yes, my dear. Rafe Glenn, who is your father."

Lauren gasped and slid off the desk to run to the left side of Cam's chair. She didn't say a word, simply laid one hand on his tensed shoulder.

"Which makes you my grandmother," Cam said, in a conversational tone that belied the shock haunting his eyes.

"Yes, and I'm extremely happy to see you again after all these years," Lily said, her fingers still entwined with Cam's. "So you see, Aircroft does belong in your hands, Cam. Not only because your stepfather bought the estate and willed it to you, but also because you are Calvin Airley's grandson."

Acknowledgments

It's not simply the author who brings a novel to life—it takes a team. My sincere thanks go out to all those individuals whose skills, talent, and support have helped *A Killer Clue* become a published book, and all who support my writing:

My agent, Frances Black of Literary Counsel.

My editor at Crooked Lane Books, Faith Black Ross.

The Crooked Lane Books team, especially Matt Martz, Dulce Botello, Rebecca Nelson, Stephanie Manova, Thaisheemarie Fantauzzi Pérez, and Madison Schultz.

Cover designer Alan Ayers.

My friends and family, especially my husband, Kevin, and my son, Thomas.

My fellow authors, many of whom have become friends as well as colleagues.

Bookstores and libraries—who not only support my work, but also provide me with wonderful reading materials.

The bloggers, podcasters, YouTubers, and other reviewers who have mentioned, reviewed, and promoted my books.

And, as always, my lovely readers!